BRIAN COX

The perfect Lover

(Part 1 - Second Edition)

This book was professionally typeset on Reedsy.
Find out more at reedsy.com

Preface

Many years ago as a photographer I was asked by a lady to do a portfolio shoot for her.

This year there was a lot of snow on the ground so instead of driving to London in a car I decided to take the train. Once in London, the snow had fallen very heavy, so I decided to take a cab to her house.

Upon knocking on her door I honestly thought I had been set up, and the person was a cross-dresser! But on completing the shoot for this lady and talking to her during the shoot, she actually has a heart of gold and was telling me she was an erotic author.

At the end of the shoot, she gave me a copy of her book, which was a collection of short erotic stories. I then thought I could write my own short erotic story and send it to her to have her opinion.

The reply I got from the lady was:

"Are you taking the Micky? Because if you are not already an erotic author you should be!"

And my story as an erotic author begins...

Chapter One

My name is Adam and I will tell you my amazing story. It all started when I was about 18 years old. I had come from London and was now living in the South West of the UK. I had attended my secondary school in that area and whilst at school; I kept myself to myself there was a girl called Donna who most of the boys at my school fancied, but no one really ever got to date. I too was infatuated with Donna. She was amazing, well to me. She had long blond hair and was beautiful, and so friendly, she would talk to anyone. The school years passed by, I became close to her and she spoke of her dreams for her future.

I listened, as to be honest, I really had not given much thought to what I wanted to do. Her dreams were to go on to further education, but not in the UK. She wanted to go to the USA, as that's where she thought her future was. The time came that we left school. I thought this was it I would never get to see her again, but how wrong I was? As the months passed, we left school and became very close. I said nothing. To me, it truly felt as though we were a partnership Boyfriend/Girlfriend, we used to hang about together quite a lot. It even got to the stage where I was staying the night at Donna's, more than my home. I can remember this one time, Donna inviting me back to her parent's house.

I had been there twice before, but this time something felt different.

I remember sitting there watching a film with Donna. It was a dark winter's night, and I realized that Donna's father was not there.

I asked Donna "where is your father?" She got a little upset and explained that her mother (Rosa) and her father (Paul) had split up, and Donna explained why. She said that her father had an affair, and had left the family home to be with his lover. Even at 18 years old, I found this well hard to believe that Paul could have left Rosa. Rosa was stunning, she could have been a top model. Even at 38, Rosa looked so much fitter than most ladies years younger than herself. I recalled that even when we were at school, the other boys used to say you should see Donna's mother, she is like every schoolboy's dream.

As the evening wore on, and the film had finished, I asked if I could use the toilet. I went upstairs, walked along the long landing towards the toilet. As I came out, I noticed that Rosa's bedroom door was slightly open. There was the most beautiful smell of lavender that drifted along the landing, it was a soft fragrant relaxing and felt inviting. I knew it was wrong, but by this time; It hypnotized me. I wanted to have a peek at Rosa's room. I crept slowly along the landing, pushing the door open very quietly just a little more, to get a better look. Oh my God, Rosa was in there. She had not heard from or seen me. Fear was the first reaction, but the beautiful smell of lavender and perfumes from her room had totally overcome my normal senses. I could not understand why Rosa's husband would want to leave such a perfect-looking woman. Rosa had the most perfect body, her breasts were not overly big but firm and full, I could see Rosa's erect nipples standing hard and erect, the whole of Rosa's body was in perfect shape, totally toned and tanned.

All this time I thought Rosa had not heard me push the bedroom door open that bit further, but she had. She did not flinch away in shock, not a jump saying to get out at the top of her voice, nothing. Still, I believed she had not heard me or seen me looking at her. She lay there on her bed in only her knickers. I could not help myself. I felt myself becoming aroused and became erect at seeing such a hot lady. This is the sort of thing that you only see in man's magazines. I could not believe my luck. Rosa was pleasuring herself intimately. Still thinking she had not noticed I was there, her hands were trembling over her body. Her fingers just barely touching one of her fantastic breasts, her hand was traveling the circumference of the fullness of her breast, the other hand now moving slowly up and down her body, just barely touching it. My breathing getting heavier and heavier at what I was seeing, Rosa let her head fall gently, slowly to the side (facing me).

I still in my ignorance still thought she had not seen me, there was no reaction from Rosa, not a flicker in her face, her hand was now grabbing harder at her own breast harder than before, as you could see the indentations her fingers were making in her beautiful breast. The other hand now had her fingers firmly under her knickers line. Her very soft gentle groans of pleasure were bringing me to exploding point. I'm sure my penis was trying to climb out of my trousers. I truly wanted to just walk in and join her in her bed. This was like a porn film that I used to watch with my mates from school. I really wanted to feel what Rosa felt like. Just then, I heard Donna coming up the stairs. I quickly shuffled as quietly as I could back along the landing and back into the toilet. I closed the door as if I were just coming out. Donna asked if I was OK, as I had been for a long time, and asked if I would like a drink. I answered with a really dry voice, as what I had just seen had sapped all the strength from me.

As we were going down the stairs, I heard Rosa close her bedroom door behind us.

Rosa too was now coming down the stairs, she was dressed in only a small silk black kimono despite that, Rosa said nothing. Donna was making the tea for us all. I was in the living room with Rosa. I was now feeling embarrassed and very shy. I looked up at Rosa and she was just sitting there and gave me what I thought was the naughtiest smile I had ever seen, which just made me feel more embarrassed. I felt like a naughty schoolboy.

Donna came in with the drinks and sat beside me. If she had known what I had just been doing, she would off thrown, the tea over me and kicked me out. It was all I could do to hold my cup. It felt as though my hands were trembling, one with fear, or was it excitement. I was sitting with Donna but in my mind; I wanted to be all over Rosa and ripping her clothes off. Well, it came to the end of the night. I was saying my goodbyes to Donna, standing at the front door. I gave Donna a kiss and told her I would see her in the morning. As this happened, Rosa walked to the bottom of the stairs. Before she went up the stairs, she turned her head, gave me another naughty-looking smile, and winked at me. Oh my God, did this mean she had seen me at her door the whole time?

As I was walking home that night, all I could think about was Rosa. I really liked Donna, but her mother had now got me in a hypnotic state. I eventually got home, went to bed that night, and all I could think about was Rosa and the events I had just seen. The thought that she might off seen, me looking just excited me all the more. *"All I could think was how wonderful Rosa was"* but in all honesty, I had nothing to compare her to as I was still a virgin.

The next morning came and I could not get round to Donna and Rosa's quick enough. Needless to say, I had a very sleepless night that night, but the thoughts, hopes, and wishes were far better than any sleep I could have had. The visits were pretty normal over the next few weeks, but; I was just happy to be in their company and that's just how it was for about 6 weeks. I and Donna became closer even inside if I wished it were her mother I was seeing. Donna and I became very close and on an odd night, I stayed over, even if it was just sleeping on the floor of Donna's bedroom.

Chapter Two

A few weeks had passed and again, could not wait to get around and see Donna. Or was it Rosa? When I got there, Donna was ecstatic with happiness. She was nearly bouncing off the walls. Donna had got a letter from the university in California that she wanted to go to, we spoke for what seemed to be a lifetime about her going to America and then it hit me like a brick if Donna went away that meant no more Donna, it also meant no more Rosa. I tried my best to be happy for her, which in a way I was, but inwardly I felt gutted that I would not be able to see Rosa, neither the less we had a nice day together. We did all the things Donna wanted to do, told all our friends about her going away it was an exhausting day.

The evening came, and I stayed that night like I had many nights by now. We watched a film together in between Donna, getting about a million texts on her cell phone. Eventually, Donna and I went to bed. We lay there cuddling each other so tight not even water could not have got between us. I was going to miss Donna, but hell, I was going to miss Rosa, her smiles and her smells, oh and of course my occasional peaks at Rosa.

We awoke the next morning, still in a firm embrace, before we got up and went downstairs. There was Rosa cooking us all a really nice breakfast. The smells coming from the kitchen were amazing, just like

Rosa's bedroom, but a different type of smell. As we walked into the kitchen, there stood Rosa again in her tiny black kimono, hardly even fastened. Donna had previously explained to her mother about the USA. Rosa turned to me and said "has she told you everything then," I said: "yes" in a sheepish schoolboy voice.

Rosa replied as quick as you like well I hope when Donna goes you are still going to come round and even stay the odd night. Rosa said I have a sort of got used to you being around, and as you well know, myself and Paul have parted so there are loads of jobs for you to do around here if you want to. I said of course Rosa, I would love to, then the stirring within me, I thought to myself, *"there is one job I would love to do for you"* or was that for my satisfaction.

Rosa said, good, there's one big job that now Paul's gone I am desperate to do, is the old outhouse it needs a total overhaul but a lick of paint would not go a miss, for now. But honestly, she said there are loads for you to do and keep you busy, with yet another cheeky smile. Was I misreading the signs here, was Rosa giving me the come on??? The weeks before Donna's departure flew by, so I spent as much time as I could with Donna and Rosa. Well, to be honest, I was almost living there nearly full time. The weeks flew by and before we knew where we were; it was time for Donna to leave. It was sad to see Donna go, but at the same time, I had become very close to Rosa, very close.

Well, it was Donna's last night we held each other tightly and said really nice things to each other. It was a very sad night because I was saying goodbye to my first love even though still nothing had happened and I was still a virgin. The love that had built was very strong, even though my mind wandered to sexual thoughts about her mother. They were only just boyish sexual thoughts; we lay they very tearful that night as we really knew we were saying goodbye, as a long-distance relationship like that was never going to work at our age.

The next morning came a very tearful morning for lots of different reasons, really. Happiness for Donna and what she had dreamed of, and the sadness that Rosa and I were about to lose someone very close.

We got to the airport and said our goodbyes Rosa left us alone for a while; we had a hug, then both Rosa and I watched as she went through the departure lounge. She turned and shouted:

"Hey mum, look after him,"

And was gone. Rosa gave me a cuddle and said:

"don't worry, I'm going to really look after you,"

Not quite knowing what she meant at the time. Early to bed that night in our own rooms. As the days went past and turned into weeks, Rosa and I became closer. Nothing sexual but a definite bond there that was clear for anyone to see.

Chapter Three

As the weeks went by, Rosa and I spoke very freely about everything she had got me. A place on a trade course covering Carpentry, Bricklaying, and Plastering. To be fair, it was a total builders course which I enjoyed and took to like a duck to water. As I said, we spoke freely and one night we were sitting around just Rosa and I having a bottle of wine or two, and I said "Rosa can I ask you something personal?" Her reply was: "you know you can" and smiled at me, so I asked Rosa: "why did you and Paul separate?" Not really expecting much of a reply.

She explained she said that she and Paul had got together at a fairly young age, not really knowing each other fully just being swept along with the situation. They were in at the time and shortly after being together she had fallen with Donna, and it was not in either of us to do an abortion. They decided to keep the baby and give it a go with each other. Back then she said Paul was a bit of a player but a damn merry laugh.

But as the months passed she could see that herself and Paul had some major differences, and she laughed, and said to be totally honest he was not that great in the bedroom department and laughed again. She said the principal thing was he could not come to terms with the sexual feelings that I had and have. I had to interrupt at that point and said, what's that then not really expecting an answer from Rosa.

But she was very open really, don't know if it was the drink that made her open up. From that night on, all I know is she was totally open with me about everything, and everything I asked, Rosa answered.

She said, "well Adam, I'm bisexual and always have been and that's what Paul could not come to terms with. He tried, but like all men, think it's for their benefit. But the truth is, Adam, I believe that only another woman can truly know how to love another woman. How a woman needs to be held, loved, and touched. Most men just think it's their god-given right to be sexually fulfilled, and they rush things and the woman is not completely satisfied." Well, with those comments I felt totally put in my place, and did not really know what to say to her. Again I felt like a schoolboy who had been put in his place.

But she saved me because she said she loves a man's body as much as a woman's and likes what a man has to offer. She then laughed and said if you know what I mean, I nodded in agreement but I really had not got a clue. Even though I had a relationship with Donna, I was, after all, still a virgin and nearly 19. I was thinking maybe I should start to worry about that.

She then said she wished a man was more in touch with what a woman wants and needs, and would take their time to understand the way a woman's mind and body works. This is where I wanted to jump up and say, teach me, Rosa, please teach me to be the perfect lover, but no my shyness got the better of me and I just sat there.

Chapter Four

One day Rosa said to me "so Adam, are you happy with the course I managed to get you on". I said yes as my dream job would be to be an all-around self-employed builder. There was just one thing in my way and that is I can't drive yet. Rosa said, well that's not really a problem, and told me to leave it with her.

Rosa said I looked like the sort of person who was good with his hands and smiled at me, God knows I wanted to show her how good I was with my hands, as I had never forgotten how good she looked that night when I peeked through her door. But I had to keep a firm grip on reality as I knew nothing, but in my mind, I was some kind of super stud. At this point, I wondered if life was just going to pass me by, regarding the sexual side of things, since Donna there was not anyone on the scene and I did not even do anything with her.

Later that evening, Rosa sat in the lounge with me and said that she could probably help me with the driving lessons side of things, as she had an excellent friend who was a driving instructor. Wow, when she said she would look after me, she was not kidding. I could not believe my luck. She had me up on a building course and was now about to sort out driving lessons for me.

A few days passed, and we were sitting together one evening, having our usual bottle of wine just relaxing, and there was a knock at the door. Rosa went and answered the door and in walked this stunning blonde lady, a little younger than Rosa. Rosa introduced me. Adam, this is my excellent friend Pippa, and Pippa, this is Adam, my student, and giggled to her friend. I said hello, and she walked over and gave me a kiss on the cheek. Pippa turned to Rosa and gave Rosa a kiss on the cheek and said, yes he looks like he would make a talented student. Not really understanding what they were on about student I had been leaving school a long time by now.

We all sat talking for ages. Although I had only just met Pippa, but it was as though I had known her for years, she was very easy to talk to the same sort of mannerisms as Rosa. We sat talking for hours about many things, but they seemed to want to chat about me more than anything else, which I found fantastic. Two beautiful women wanting to know all about me. I too wanted to know all about them. I asked Pippa "what do you do?" her reply was "I'm a driving instructor" Rosa piped up and said, "See I told you I was going to help you out".

I was so pleased. I jumped out of the chair and gave Rosa a big kiss on the cheek, Pippa said: "Hey Adam, where's my kiss? After all, I'm the one going to be teaching you". Who was I to refuse, so I jumped at the chance to kiss two beautiful women in the same room at the same time. Wow! I thought all my prayers had been answered, and I gave Pippa her kiss. She said, "See, now you're my student too" and laughed in a nice sort of way. Still not really understanding why I was Rosa's student.

But he would not rock the boat. Well, it was about 2 am by the time we all finished chatting and drinking. I said my goodbyes and took myself off up to bed. I could not think of anything else but the two ladies downstairs, and what I wished I could do to the pair of them. I lay in my bed, just constantly thinking about them. The thoughts I had were very sexual, but it was never going to happen but hell, what a wish.

What were they on about? OK, I could understand Pippa as I was soon going to be her student, but Rosa, how was I her student? Neither the less I lay there in my bed and could not help myself. I touched myself. My penis was very erect, and I found my hand slowly rubbing up and down, all the time thinking of the two ladies.

As I lay there, I heard the two ladies coming up the stairs. Pippa was staying the night. Oh, my God, was this Rosa's bisexual partner. I lay there still, listening as hard as I could. I heard the girls giggle a little, but trying to be quiet as they got into bed. I lay there as quiet as a mouse, trying hard to hear what I hoped was going to happen. All the time I was rubbing my penis. A couple of hours had passed, and I thought I had worn it out and would never manage another erection. I took myself off to the toilet. Again from Rosa's room, there was that beautiful scent of lavender and the smell of unique perfumes in the air as there was that time before, and again the door was open to her room.

I could not help myself I had to have another peek, and wow there they both were fast asleep on top of the bed, both girls totally naked, their arms wrapped around each other. I so so wanted to slide between them and hope they would both sort me out. Sexually, they looked so nice. I was only a young man, so you can imagine the thoughts that were going through my head. I took myself back to my bedroom, shut the door quietly, and at some point, fell to sleep with the thoughts of what a wonderful night I had with these two ladies.

The next morning came, and after breakfast, Pippa helped me fill out the forms for my driving license. She said she would sort it out for me. I thanked her, and shortly after Pippa left. The thought of me being Rosa's student was still going through my head, and I could not get it out. I felt I had to ask? I said, "Rosa, what did you mean when you introduced me to Pippa as your student?" I asked nicely and finished my question with a laugh.

She laughed and said don't worry then gave me a kiss and said that she had some things to do that day, but if I met her back at the house at 4 pm, she would explain.

The day unfolded and I could not, for the life of me, think what she was going to say or tell me, but sure of my word by 4 pm I was there, ready and waiting for what this lovely lady wanted to tell me. Rosa arrived home just after 4 pm I could not wait. I had made her a cup of tea and said, "Rosa, are you ready to speak to me?", you said you would explain the student thing to me.

Rosa laughed and said, "OK, come and sit in the lounge". I followed her into the lounge, she sat me on a chair and explained, she said now if I did not want this I was to stop her at any point while she was speaking. I sat there listening to her, and this is what she said. "OK, Adam, the reason I said you were my student is that I want to teach you to be the perfect lover. Are you OK with that?". I could not get the word yes out of my mouth quick enough. At long last, I was going to get to make love to this beautiful woman.

Rosa put her finger to my lips as to shush me and carried on. Rosa said, "well, I told you I am bisexual, but do like a man's body and what he has to offer". She also said that she had noticed that whilst I had been going to the gym, that I had toned my body up very nicely, I thanked her. I said, "well, how will you teach me that then, Rosa? How are you going to teach me to be the perfect lover?". I felt compelled to tell her I was still a virgin. As I did this, she just smiled.

She said Adam;, you have to trust me; I said yes, of course, Rosa. I would have agreed to anything at this point, as I thought we were heading straight upstairs to bed. Rosa then said she would try to teach me, but it would be over a long period. She was going to teach me how a woman wants and needs to be touched and loved, and not rushed and spoiled the way most men do. It's about mutual experience and pleasure, not just one-sided as most men believe. After our conversation, she asked again if this something I wanted to do, as she never wanted me to think she was taking advantage of me. My answer was quick yes, please Rosa, teach me. That conversation had come to an end, and I thought we would run upstairs and just start making love to each other straight away, but that was not the case. We went back out to the kitchen and Rosa and I prepared a meal together and just spoke of our days' activities and how each of our days had gone.

That evening came, and I was so full of excitement at what my future our future held in store for us both, we did what we normally did in the evening, drank a bottle of wine together but this time it was different we sat together on the same sofa and she seemed closer to me. I thought it was my call to touch, so this is what I did, first putting my arm around her, then when I felt she was OK with that which in my haste was only 2-3 minutes. I made a grab for her breasts. She gently took my hand and laughed and said "no not yet" laughed again and said, "you're very eager aren't you". She reminded me this was going to be a long lesson, and what I just did was typical of any man. I felt a little ashamed that I had rushed her, but hell the excitement was nearly exploding me I just wanted her so badly.

The evening was coming to an end, so Rosa got up off the sofa, went to the kitchen. As she came back in she reached out for my hand and lead me up the stairs. We got to the top of the stairs at the entrance to my bedroom she gave me a kiss. I thought OK now I'm being put to bed, and after the kiss went to walk into my room, she held my hand tighter as I went to walk into my room. I turned and looked at her. She winked at me and said come with me. At that, I could have run down the landing, stripped off, and been there waiting for her before she even took another step. I did not, and Rosa slowly led me to her bedroom. I was allowed to be there and standing freely in this beautiful fragrance room. Rosa asked if I knew what Tantric/

tantra sex was as it's better known, no I replied, but "in my head, I was thinking hell any sex is better than none".

Rosa explained what Tantra's sex was. She said Tantra is all about touch, getting to know each other's body's fully and completely. "Yes, it is intimate," she said, and touching is allowed but tantra is no actual penetration, it really is about the touch and feel of each other's bodies. It's a slow gentle caring process and you should learn from this, and know instinctively how to please each other, no words are spoken but this is the basis of a great love relationship and if done correctly can sometimes be more sexually satisfying than normal penetration sex. My immediate thoughts were oh no, what a tease, but hell, at least I was going to get to feel this lady's beautiful breasts.

Rosa sat me on the edge of the bed. I could feel that I was almost fully erect before she had even done anything to me or me to her. She was still fully clothed. As I sat there on the edge of the bed, Rosa began to slowly take my clothes off. First with my shoes gently easing them from my feet, then followed by my shirt. As she removed my shirt, I felt her hands well, her fingers gently trembling up the side of my torso. She gently eased the shirt over my neck and head. When my shirt was free from my body, she lowered herself to her knees in front of me. She traced the contours of the outline of my body with her hands, her fingers barely touching.

It was like I was being gently electrocuted her fingers felt so charged when her hands got to my trouser she gently pushed my body back onto the bed, I now could not see her but felt her hands fumbling with the buckle on my belt then the actual button on my trouser I felt it pop open. She so slowly unbuttoned each button until my trousers were free, Rosa then seductively removed my trousers from me. Rosa told me to move onto the bed I did as she requested, and watched this lady as she very slowly removed her clothes in front of me, like my very own personal striptease. And God, she was good at this.

I wanted to shut my eyes, as I never wanted this night to end, and I thought I would explode at any point. Then it's over before we start 5 minutes later this beautiful woman was standing before me totally naked and oh my god what a sight she looked and smelt amazing. Rosa was perfect in every way her body looked as though it had been photoshoot, not a blemish. Her pubic area was shaved and looked so smooth. The contours of the shape of her breasts were fantastic. I was truly in a hypnotic state, looking at this beautiful woman.

Then Rosa spoke, "OK Adam this is what I would like you do to, sit in a kneeling position on the bed". I followed her every command to the letter. There I was sitting on the bed totally naked, getting onto the bed to join me and adopted the same position, both of us just facing each other. I was so erect I thought if she just touches me, I will cum and the evening will be spoiled. Rosa then spoke, "OK Adam, so what would you like to do?". I said "I would love to feel you" she smiled and said OK have you listened to everything I have said to you? Yes, I replied instantly, without even thinking about what I was saying. She smiled at me, OK then darling feel me. I did not need to tell twice. My arms shot out in front of me like two racehorses to the finishing post before she could say another word. Both my hands were now holding and grabbing at these perfect breasts, even pulling at some point.

No, Rosa said, Adam if this is going to work please listen to what I say. I released my grip on her. She smiled at me and said, "look, sit back and relax, and take a few deep breaths, breath slowly in through your nose and slowly out through your mouth and asked me to close my eyes". I did as Rosa requested: my now full-blown erection was so hard as I breathed in and out, and finally relaxed, could feel my penis throb and no one was touching me or it.

She said in a real soft voice, "typical man, just out for what he can get, and not really taking the time to see and enjoy what's before him". Her voice was so soft it felt like an angel talking to me, which actually relaxed me even further. It was as though Rosa was massaging me with her voice.

Rosa said I should not open my eyes and to carry on with the breathing, Rosa started by gently running her fingers through my hair, she was so gently massaging my skull I was so relaxed I nearly forgot where I was or what I was doing. Her hand then went to the sides of my face, and it felt like her fingers were trickling down either side of my face, then her hands went to my neck surrounding my neck with her nimble fingers, her thumb tracing the contours of my Adam's apple. Her hands slowly slipped to my shoulders, her fingers even though barely touching, never leaving my body. It was so hard to keep my eyes shut and even harder to keep my own hands from reaching out for her.

I had tried to reach out twice but each time I did; she lent forward and whispered, no darling, relax. Her hands now tracing the contours of my pectoral muscles. Her hands gliding effortlessly across the top half of my body, occasionally her fingers would gently cross my nipples. Then both hands on my now erect nipples, *(was this even possible for a man's nipples to become erect?)* the answer was yes, as mine were so hard I could feel her pass over or flick, gentle squeeze then every so often.

When Rosa pulled or twisted my nipples, it was like I was being tortured just a little bit of nice pain, not hurtful just to bring you back from the trancelike state she had put me in. She eventually moved from my nipples to my abdominal muscle, her fingers trembling over each muscle individually. Then one of her hands moved down to my penis and testicles. I felt Rosa's fingers trembling up and down the length of my now very hard, throbbing penis at every touch I thought I would explode. Her touch was so soft and gentle.

I begged her Rosa please let me make love to you please let me feel you, again in her soft angelic voice she refused and whispered: "darling you have to learn from this you have to master control you have to learn the right way". She put her finger to my lips once again to make me be quiet. I was not about to stop her for what she was doing I did not even think was possible, she moved her face in front of mine and I could feel her hot breath on my face she barely touched my lips with hers, and somehow gave me the most erotic kiss ever.

She moved her face to the side and began flicking my earlobe with her boiling, moist tongue. Her kisses moved to my neck and then to my shoulders. She was kissing the top of my shoulders, the back of my neck, her hands still tumbling over my abdominal muscles. Her hands were slowly covering every part of my torso, one had still every now and again stroked my erect penis, her lips now cupping my nipples, not biting, just cupping my nipples between her lips.

Rosa lay me on my back, I so wanted her just to get on top of me I was not sure if I had already climaxed or was about to. I was in such a trance. As I lay there on my back Rosa's hand trembled over my torso not really touching but I felt every movement of her hands and finger, her lips now joining her hands this was too much I wanted it to stop but at the same time did not want it to end.

One of her hands was gently caressing and massaging my testicles. I could hold on no more please Rosa, make love to me I can't hold on anymore I said.

Rosa moved her head down to my penis, one hand still massaging the other, now holding my penis since Rosa had helped me out. Now I could feel her lips cupping the side of my penis, her mouth running slowly up and down the full length every so often she would whip the end of my penis with her tongue, but she was being so careful not to put my penis in her mouth it was only external play allowed. It was obvious that I had my eyes open for some time now, as I was not going to miss what this wonderful lady was doing to me. Just before she stopped, she held my penis in her hand and began slowly rub it, that was it. I could hold out no more, and with a deep breath, I felt my body tense, and I climaxed. This did not stop Rosa as she carried on licking and was licking my climax over the full length of my penis.

Rosa then brought her head next to mine she kissed me passionately on the cheek, and whispered, "now are you ready to try again, Adam?" I said yes, but to be honest, I thought we had finished as I had climaxed. She then said "it's your turn, but this time please do not rush at me like a bull in a china shop", listen to my words take your time this should be an enjoyable experience for the two of us. OK, I could hardly breathe I thought that was it and that was sex. How wrong was I because there was this beautiful lady before me and she was now wanting to be pleasured, she said this time I will instruct you what to do or maybe slow you down if I feel you are going wrong is that OK? To be totally honest I did not have a clue where to start, there was Rosa knelt on the bed in front of me, I made a slow move towards her not rushed as before in my mind I was thinking OK just copy what she had done to me in reality what I wanted to do was throw her on her back and put my now tingling penis between her legs.

But this is what then happened. I moved my hands slowly towards Rosa's head and began to massage her scalp, her hair slipping through my fingers as she had done to me. Rosa was giving out tiny little groans of pleasure as I did this. She felt soft and warm, and I could tell she was very relaxed. I then started to kiss her neck and suck on her ear lobes very gently. I could have just done that for hours as I was feeling relaxed at hearing her groans her fingers still trembling up and down the sides of my torso, as I kissed her neck it was as if my hands had been possessed. Where before I was rushing in and grabbing like a fool this time my hands found her full breasts, still sucking gently on her ear lobes my hands this time were gently squeezing and feeling the fullness and shape of these beautiful things. As I did this, my thumbs would occasionally flutter across her now hardened nipples.

She whispered to me there is so much more to a woman's breasts than what a man thinks. She said also pay attention to the complete area of the nipple, not just the erect part when I took my mouth down to her nipples yes they were erect, but the darkened part surrounding the nipple had like little goosebumps on.

So without hesitation my tongue was now circling and doing a figure of eight around her nipple, feeling the bumps on what I now know to be called the aureole, whilst licking and sucking ever so gently on her breasts. I could see Rosa pushing her head back onto the pillow and just ever so slightly groan with pleasure. Every now and again I would feel her fingers dig into my shoulders that little harder. As I was doing this, I slowly let one of my hands travel down to her amazing flat belly. She had what people call a washboard stomach as flat as you can imagine and so soft and smooth. There were no stretch marks. God, this lady looked as though she had been sculptured. Her hands moved my head towards her flat stomach and whispered, OK baby, kiss me there.

I did not need to tell twice, if this I what Rosa liked then this is what I would do. While we were doing this, I let one of my hands slowly go down the length of her leg, well as far as I could reach, then I worked for my hand slowly up and down the inside of her legs slowly stroking the inner thighs of her warm soft legs. My hand was drifting closer and closer to the moistness of her vagina. I was being directed not by voice but by her hands, which were now on my head. She had positioned my head to just above her vagina it was as though I could feel the warmth from there lashing against the side of my face. I could see that Rosa was moist and what a fantastic smell. It was like nothing I had ever smelt before. I so wanted to take her. My penis had sort of become erect again and could feel a gentle throbbing in my penis. I wanted to enter this beautiful woman this would have been hard to do as she had directed my head to her vaginal area. She had adjusted herself and one of her hands was now massaging my semi-erect penis, then Rosa spoke softly "OK now feel the outer edge of my pussy with your lips and tongue, but please do not go inside just the outer edges". With one of my hands massaging the cheek of her bum, and my tongue now feeling the moistness of her vagina, I heard her mutter under her breath, "oh God yes" but it was only just about bearable. With this, I felt Rosa cum. Her vagina shuddered, and my mouth was awash with her juices. Such a lovely warm feeling. One of her hands still on my head I felt her fingers stiffen, as this happened, the other hand still on my penis also grabbed a little tighter, my penis which was now fully erect. I could hold back no more. Rosa was massaging my penis so nicely and for the second time, I cum.

We lay together just cuddling for a while no word needed to have been spoken there was the occasional kiss her hands were playing with my hair. I thought we had had full-blown sex, or at least this is what it felt like. Rosa in a soft voice said, "there darling, that's tantric sex" and smiled. Well, tantric sex was the most explicit thing and most enjoyable thing I had ever done, and it was the most intense three hours of my life. We lay there together. Neither of us wanted to speak or move, and at some point, both fell asleep in one another's arms.

Chapter Five

WOW, what a night! The next morning I woke up and Rosa was not in bed. I could hear Rosa, she was already downstairs preparing our breakfast. I lay there for a short while. Oh, my god, how lucky was I to have been part of that, and there was no end to this woman's talents. Looking after me in every way she did and to top it all was there preparing our breakfast, I eventually pulled myself together got up showered and went downstairs to see Rosa, as I walked into the kitchen she turned smiled at me and said sit your food is ready. As she sat at the table with me, she said, "so Adam, how did you like tantric sex then?"

I just said it was amazing, hell you are amazing. She smiled, I then said "can't wait for that to happen again", Rosa smiled at me and said, "actually Adam you were very good" and if I continued to listen to what she said I was going to have no problem in becoming a great lover. Never the less I was not to get too carried away. She said there is a lot to be learned and Rosa said I'm looking forward to teaching you and gave me another kiss.

A few days had passed, and we went about our normal lives, just ordinary stuff, no more funny business or goings-on. Rosa did whatever she did, and I was coming to the end of my work well on the course. One evening we were sitting around the table in the kitchen and Rosa was looking through her paperwork of the villa/farm house she owned in France. She said there are loads of jobs that need doing over there too, and we should at some point go out there and spend some time in France. Rosa said would I like to do that obviously I said yes as I wanted to spend as much time in Rosa's company as possible. Yes, I had only had the one sexual encounter with Rosa, well in my life, but knew I was falling for her already.

A week or two went by and every now and again we would discuss our tantric adventure together. Over the previous two weeks, Rosa would laugh at the way I first launched myself at her and grabbed at her, but she said I hope that's all in the past now and you know to take your time and both enjoy what was happening. I assured her I would not grab at her like that again and explained it was just excitement. She nodded, smiled, and said I know.

One evening we were sitting in the lounge and out of the blue Rosa said, well young man, I think you're ready for your next lesson. I thought, yes, great at long last I'm going to get to make love to this amazing lady. Rosa said at the end of the evening, "so are you ready for bed then, Adam?" Once again, Rosa led me upstairs to her bedroom. We both stood at the end of the bed and very carefully watching each other, we slowly stripped each other, kissing as we did so. Every time I saw Rosa's body I could not help but stare she was amazing. I was about to get in bed and Rosa said no, took one of my hands, and led me to the bathroom.

Rosa said there is nothing nicer than a man who smells nice and that we should have a shower and assist each other. Was this to be my next lesson? Rosa ran the shower until the bathroom was totally full of steam from the hot water, I could hardly see Rosa for the steam and she said "OK in you go", I got in the shower expecting to lose a layer of skin the water looked that hot. As I got in, Rosa wasted no time and followed me in. Rosa had wet my body all over and was soaping my body in every nook and cranny. There was not one spot Rosa was missing. It was nice and slow and gentle. I could feel her hands everywhere, her hands gliding over me with ease. I felt like I had been given a soapy massage, and that's just what it was. She washed everywhere and paid special attention to the genital area. She was so gentle washing and soaping my testicles and penis, and was often asking if I was OK. As she washed my penis, she got to her knees and was so gentle her hand would rub back and forth. I could still not see Rosa because of the steam. So while she was down there, she was out of site. I swear it felt like I was getting a blow job from her. The soap made her hands glide across it and felt so soft. Out of the steam, Rosa rose to her feet, her body shining like a star, her hair and hands were covered in soap. She hugged me and said OK baby, your turn. I wasted no time at all. Her body was already soaked. I covered my hands in soap and started on her neck, then her shoulders. She was standing with her back to me, and as my hands soaped her back, I could feel every vertebra in her spine. She seemed to like this, so I took my time and basically massaged the whole of her back, each and every individual vertebra. My penis was standing proud and as I brushed against her, I felt my penis glide across the fullness of the cheek of her bum. When I was washing her vagina area, it was hard not to insert or want to insert my fingers into her warm, damp vagina. I could feel her labia lips fold through my fingers as I washed her I so, so wanted to make love to her here and now in the shower.

But this did not happen we both exited the shower at the same time. We both took big white fluffy towels and started to dry each other off even a shower seemed to be erotic with Rosa.

I was thinking Rosa had said that I was ready for my next lesson. Was this it to be clean?. We both stood there naked, me admiring her body and not saying a thing as we sprayed perfume and aftershave. We let the towels drop to the floor and Rosa again took my hand, we were both naked and she led me to the bedroom. As I climbed into bed, Rosa went to the sideboard where her sound system was and she put on some soft-sounding pipe music from the Andes I think. She was a very well-traveled lady. She got on the bed, pulled the sheets back, and lay there next to me, nothing was said for what seemed like an eternity but in reality was probably only two minutes. Then Rosa spoke OK Adam, you're ready for your next lesson, its oral sex. "I thought to myself, that's great but I'm already erect. I have had my shower when do I get to make love to you".

Rosa has always initiated the moves. She turned to her side, and I followed suit. We were laying there facing each other; she said are you ready for this then my darling, put her arm around me, pulled herself closer to me and we kissed. This time the kissing seemed a lot more intense, we did not speak much after that the word love was or had never been mentioned, she then whispered remember all I have said take your time don't rush and it's important for you to breathe it helps you to control yourself, with this Rosa started kissing on my neck I was all ready and still fully erect from the shower and there was no sign of that decreasing it started pretty much the same as the tantra sex we had. Rosa's hands were caressing my body I guess relaxing me which did work as a start all I wanted to do was fuck her , she muttered see foreplay is a form of tantra sex there all related Rosa, was now kissing my neck and her fingers gentle squeezing on my nipples hard so you knew she was there, I suppose a little bit of pain but not the hurtful sort the sort where you think ouch but hell don't stop.

Rosa was working her magic on me with her tongue, which you would have thought was electrically charged oh my god I did not think it was possible for a man to have these feelings, I was really enjoying her sucking and licking and flicking my nipples with her tongue; I told her how much I was enjoying what she was doing in between my gasps for breath I wanted her to stop and at the same time did not want it to end in fact I wanted her to bite and pull a little harder on my nipples, and without me saying anything as if I had actually asked her to do it as I thought it that's exactly what she was doing.

I asked her, was this normal for a man to enjoy his nipples being played with? As I really was enjoying it so much. She said yes; it was OK for a man to enjoy being touched like that in a sexually sensual way. If only more men relaxed and lost some of their inhibitions in the bedroom department, they would find they would have a lot better time and enjoy their self's so much more and that touch can be so for filling whether it hands, finger, lip or tongue.

Rosa removed her lips from my nipples and headed towards my now throbbing waiting penis, leaving one hand playing with my nipples because she knew how much I was enjoying it, I think. She continued to pull tweak and twist at both of them which I found amazing, Rosa set her warm soft mouth to work on my penis, my penis was standing so tall and proud like a soldier on parade, her mouth was working its magic, and her lips were cupping the outside edge of my penis, kissing and licking all the way up the full length of my now throbbing shaft her tongue licking around the bottom edge of my helmet occasionally her tongue would lick just inside the eye of my penis, her other hand would be around my back passage and she would rim my bum.

Suddenly Rosa opened her mouth fully as if she had dislocated her jaw and took the full length of my penis deep into her throat whilst she was doing this to me one of my hands had found one of her very hard erect nipples and as she was doing to me earlier I was pulling and tweaking hers the more I tweaked her nipple the harder she sucked on my penis. Whilst she was doing this, one of her fingers had entered my rear and at first, felt very strange, but she worked it very slowly, and I thought I would explode in my mouth. She must have sensed this, as my whole body tightened and she slowly removed her finger from my bum. Rosa was still sucking on my penis and her hand was now rubbing up and down and her hand was making a twisting motion. She removed her mouth from my penis and continued to rub in the fashion she was; I grabbed hold of her shoulder with my one spare hand, just had time to say oh sorry and I came like you would not believe her face was covered in my climax she was not phased by this at all and carried on sucking and milking every last drop from me. Rosa, I thought, would have stopped, but no she carried on sucking me, my climax dripping from her mouth and being smeared up and down the full length of my penis. Before she had finished my penis was worse than useless, I really wanted her to stop but again did not want it to end I was grabbing at the sheet of the bed the feelings this woman had given me were out of this world exciting, despite that, I had not made love to her. When Rosa had finished down there, I thought, god that has to be the end of that, but no, she had not finished yet as she came back up to the bed. She paused at my now very tender nipples, and dribbled some of my climax over my nipples, and began massaging my nipples with the sperm she had dribbled out of her mouth my nipples were as tender as you could think the slightest touch sent my whole body quivering she eventually stopped came up level with my face and we lay there kissing for a while. If I thought tantra was good, this just blew my mind as we lay there a little longer that had to be the most sensual erotic 30 minutes of my life. What was this lady, a sexual angel of some sort?

This lady was one hell of a tutor, and now it was my turn. How was I meant to beat that which she had just done, compete, or even come close to satisfying Rosa as she had just done to me? Surely she would realize that I could not even come close to her sexual perfection.

Well, I started as she had started with a little tantra gently touching I asked Rosa to do something for me; I said please lay very still, and this time closes your eyes at first I asked her to turn onto her front so her slender back was totally exposed as she did this I gentled massage her back, paying attention to her shoulders at first. I cheated, as I had put some baby oil on my hands so I could really work the muscles on her shoulders she seemed to like what I was doing as I was sitting astride her slender back. The thought of just sitting on Rosa like this was in some weird way, feeling very sexually pleasing as my hands worked from her shoulders. I very slowly started on her spine again, feeling every vertebra as my fingers were pushing and sliding between every one of her vertebra. I was doing this I lent down and was kissing the back of her neck all this time I could feel my limp penis rubbing against her buttocks her buttocks felt so warm and soft. I had to remind myself that this was her turn and what I was meant to be doing.

Rosa seemed to like me kissing the back of her neck, so I seemed to stay there for what seemed a long time, but I guess if I was too slow or something wrong, she would have told me. I heard Rosa groan a little when kissing her neck as my lips soon moved to her spine, and as I had been massaging with my hands before, I was now doing so with my lips. As my lips worked her spine, my hands were now slowly, gently caressing the side of Rosa's body when I had got to the bottom of her back. I could not help myself. I had to taste the fullness of her buttocks, so I kissed them alternately and gave the occasional tiny bite. I was not sure if this was something she would like, but she obviously did, as each time I took a little bite of her buttocks she would push them a little harder into my face. Although this seemed to be working well and seemed to be satisfying her, I carried on with the kissing. I kissed the entire length of her legs, slowly licking and kissing all the way down one leg and back up the other, paying special attention to her inner thighs. I asked Rosa too, slowly roll over so she would now be lying on her back as she rolled very slowly over my lips, never left her body.

Even though I personally had really enjoyed paying attention to Rosa's back, I loved it when she turned over, and I could see this woman's amazing body in all its glory. When she was comfortable laying on her back, I once again sat on top of her. I lent forward once again and kissed the sides of her neck. This she liked, as I was doing. This one of her hands was pulling my head closer into her neck, while her other hand was now moving ever so gently up and down my spine. This only continued for a few minutes as I was now sitting astride this beautiful woman, looking down at her fantastic body. I must have been doing something right as her nipples were so hard that it had pulled the dark surroundings around her nipple also tight. Seeing this not rushed as before, I moved my head closer and closer to her fantastically hard nipples. Not sucking straight away this time, but just gently circling them with my tongue. Every now and again I would let my tongue flick hard as to whip her hard erect nipples. This she too seemed to like, as she would pull my face hard onto those beautifully erect things.

As I was doing this my hand slowly caressed her abdominal, one hand playing with her nipples, my head now kissing and licking her flat stomach. It was not long before my face was right in front of this lady's perfectly neat vagina, I could see that Rosa was very moist and as she had instructed me to do before my mouth and tongue were playing with her labia lips still I had not entered this lady. And it took a lot of control not to do so, I would cup each side of her labia in turn gently sucking on each lip in turn I heard her groan "oh yes" and with this she gently pushed my head a little harder onto her vagina, OK it was time I very cautiously dipped my tongue in and out of her fantastically wet vagina, tasting her warm sticky love juice with each push my tongue went that little deeper until my tongue was lubricated by her climax. I found myself letting my tongue dart deep in and out of Rosa's wetness each time I would go deep with my tongue she would hold my head hard onto her wetness now. Both her hands working with my rhythm, her fingers digging deeper into my scalp the deeper my tongue went.

As I pulled out on one of the rhythms, my tongue came slightly out of her vagina, and I found her clitoris. This too was very erect, and I did not know this could happen for a lady, but this was an amazing feeling: each time I flicked her clitoris she would buck her pelvis towards me or wriggle her wetness hard into my mouth. Rosa was now really pushing my head hard into her vagina with one hand and the other was tugging and grabbing at the sheets of the bed as I found her wet clitoris. Once again I sucked on it, it was so hard it was like a tiny penis so I sucked on her as she was sucking on my penis just before, as I sucked she screamed 'Oh god and I felt Rosa explode she gushed climax from her vagina. I felt a sudden gush from her wetness. This time Rosa had exploded, both her hands now grabbing at the bedsheet, asking me to stop in a very quiet voice. I could not help myself I lowered my mouth fully onto her vagina and sipped and licked my way through her hot juices. She grabbed at the hair on my head and gently pulled me towards her, my tongue still never leaving her body up over her flat stomach then to her breasts, having a suck on each nipple. As I slowly was being pulled level with her face when at her face we just kissed for what seemed forever, neither of us wanting to stop or even breath. The sensual state between us was one of 100% of sexual satisfaction. My thought was of yes, I must have done this right as not only was Rosa satisfied I was too. Was this what Rosa meant by taking your time to appreciate what is in front of you? As we lay there kissing as if my hands were on automatic pilot, my fingers were still caressing her vagina, and my fingers were folding her labia lips, my fingers coated in this lady's juices. As we kissed, Rosa's hand had joined mine and was mimicking the movements of my hand as my fingers still slipping in and out of Rosa. Her fingers were too entering and leaving her own vagina shortly afterward. We just lay there kissing and cuddling, and at some point, we both drifted off to sleep together.

Chapter Six

The next morning came, Rosa took hold of my head and gave me a massive kiss.

Got up, had her shower and went downstairs, shortly after-wards I too got out of bed, had my shower dressed, and went downstairs. When I walked into the kitchen, both Rosa and I were sitting at the table and I said Rosa, you are so beautiful and a fantastic lover/tutor.

I laughed and said when you were cumming last night, as you cum, you held my head, pushed me hard and deep into your vagina and you called out Pip pa's name. She smiled at me and said, I know, and that's the only other person who has ever made me cum like that before. So Adam that should be an excellent indication of the lover you are slowly turning out to be.

That morning, the post arrived. There were two letters, and they were both from the USA: one was for Rosa, the other was for me.

My letter was obviously from Donna and my letter was just saying how she was and hoped everything was good for me, and she put a smiley face she went onto explain that we had done the right thing breaking up as at our age a long-distance relationship would never off worked. Neither of us knew or know what our future holds. She also said I know my mother would look after me with two smiley faces and said in brackets. Shush, I think she has a soft spot for you she then finished her letter by just saying, see ya mate, take care signed Donna.

Rosa's letter told her mother how she had fallen for one of her tutors at university and she did not want her mother to be ashamed of her, but she had fallen pregnant by him. No matter what anyone thought they were going to have, the child as abortion was not in either of them. She asked her mother not to be annoyed with her as she was about the same age when she fell pregnant with her. She also said she hoped she could understand their decision and would give them her blessing. She explained that the university had taken a dim view of what had gone on between the tutor and the student and had subsequently ended the tutor's contract. They were both going to live in Australia where the tutor was from once again she asked her mother not to prejudge this man and that she was welcome anytime she wanted to come over.

That morning Pippa came round as I heard Rosa explaining about Donna's letter and

Pippa just said do what the girl wants. She had done very similar at her age and that everything would turn out fine; she said.

Then I heard Rosa and Pippa laughing, not out loud, but it was more of a dirty laugh than anything. Rosa was explaining to Pippa what she had been teaching me to be the perfect lover, she explained I had made her cum, and whilst Rosa was cumming she said I called out your name. Then I heard both the ladies laugh, but that was it. They were just both so laid back. I did hear Pippa say "god he must be getting good then because you said I was the only one who ever made you cum like that before" and giggled.

Rosa replied, yes he is a superb student and is coming along nicely but still has a lot to learn and sometimes he is in too much of a rush like most men but he listens.

Pippa came into see me, I thought she was going to go mad at me but smiled, walked over to me, and gave me a kiss. She said I have something for you darling, put her hand inside her bag brought out a letter. She said there you go it's your provisional license, when would you like to start your lessons with me then smiled and winked at me.

Wow, I said thanks Pippa, thank you very much and yes I would love to start my lessons as soon as possible. Pippa then said OK darling we will start tomorrow is that OK with you, or do you and Rosa have anything planned?

My life was so good I was getting taught sex lessons by some sexual angel and now driving lessons from some equally hot blonde lady. I thought life could not get any better than this.

I took Rosa out for a meal that night if she would come. To my amazement she said yes and was not ashamed to be seen out with a younger man in public. We went out that evening as I had promised. Over dinner, I asked Rosa what she had said to Pippa. Rosa smiled and said all will become clear soon enough. What sort of answer was that I was thinking.

Pippa arrived the next day as promised. We all sat in the kitchen had a chat and a cuppa together. So Pippa said are you ready for your first lesson with me then Adam. Rosa giggled out loud as my mind froze for a minute. Wow, was Pippa about to teach me the same way as Rosa. I had to stop myself from thinking this way was. Every woman a sexual instructor. No, stop it, yes, I replied to Pippa.

So off we set, we sat in Rosa's driveway for a while. Pippa wanted to go through some basics with me. As I had never driven before, we had a drive around here, there, and everywhere for a couple of hours. Then Pippa said OK, take the next left please, and go down that little lane. I did as Pippa instructed. I thought we were going to talk about driving or at least the theory side of driving. Pippa said OK, pull in over there in that little lay-by please and turn the engine off. Again, I did as I was told. Pippa said "so how did I like living with Rosa then?", I said, "oh yeah, it's fantastic she is such a wonderful person, never been happier".

Pippa then said, "so is Rosa teaching you well then?" I said, "what do you mean?". Not knowing that Pippa knew everything that was going on there. She said "so you had a nice evening together then?", then Pippa just came out with it, she said "no I meant is Rosa teaching you the ways of sex?" the sex lessons how are they coming along. Not quite knowing what to say or where to put my face, I laughed and said, "well I guess you will have to ask Rosa that one, hey". Pippa smiled and said, OK, then I will.

She then just switched straight back to driving I think and said how did I enjoy my first lesson with her. I said, "it was great thanks" she then said the lessons with her were going to get a lot better and far more interesting. I asked in what way, she said you will see. I could never get a straight answer from Rosa or Pippa, so it would seem. Then Pippa said OK, nearly time to head back, but before we go she would like a kiss "was that OK?". She then said look at it as your payment for the lesson I have just given you. Well, I thought that seemed like a great deal a kiss for a lesson, so I went to kiss her on the cheek and she smiled and said no, no, no and she reclined the seats of the car. We lay there and Pippa initiated what was happening, we lay together just gentle cuddles and a soft kissing session. I was starting to feel terrible that I was being unfaithful to Rosa as we lay there kissing. I felt her hand move across my leg and then felt her hand on the buckle on my trouser belt.

She started to undo my trousers. I was miles away from home in the middle of nowhere and really did not know what to do for the best. Whilst still kissing me, Pippa had managed to release my trousers, and I felt her hand gently caressing my penis. She then pulled at my shorts and got my penis out. I felt so nervous, but at the same time could not help what was happening. Even though I knew this was wrong, my penis was responding to her touch and very slowly found that my now semi limp penis was becoming a little harder. Her hands, if I had not known, could have been Rosa's. Her hand movements were exactly the same, their touch was near identical. Then Pippa spoke, "oh Rosa was right, you have an amazing penis". After about ten minutes of kissing Pippa and her playing with my penis, she said OK and started to put the seats back where they should have been.

All along we straightened ourselves out, and we had a very slow drive back to Rosa's. I had this terrible feeling of guilt come over me at what we had just done, but deep inside I wanted to take it further. As after all, Pippa was an amazing-looking woman herself. We eventually got back to Rosa's house. Again that terrible feeling of guilt came over me as I pulled on to Rosa's drive, but the car came to a stop. Pippa said, "Adam please don't look so worried". We both went in at the same time and I felt as though I had been unfaithful to Rosa, but Pippa came right out with it. Well, Rosa, she said you were right he has an amazing penis and is a really lovely person. Rosa looked us both in the eyes and smiled "so have you two both just had sex then?" Pippa said, "no of course not, that's your job to train him is it not?"

Rosa then said "look Adam you know I have told you, I'm bisexual, and you have probably worked it out for yourself that Pippa is my bi partner and has been for several years. There are never any secrets in our relationship and never will be." So I have told Pippa all about our adventures together. Jealousy is a terrible thing and Pippa is as keen to get to know you as I want to. "Are you still OK with this situation?" I never want you to think I am taking advantage of you or using you in any way.

Of course, my answer was yes I am OK with this situation. The guilt immediately left my body, and now I wished I had taken it further with Pippa in that little lay-by.

Pippa suggested that we all go out for a meal together so the three of us can get to know each other properly and iron out any problems if there were going to be any.

By now, I was thinking inside how very lucky I was, and if I was reading the signals right. I was going to get to sleep with both girls, hell I had to be wrong, as I had not really even slept with Rosa yet. I just hoped I was thinking right.

Chapter Seven

Two or three days had passed. Not a lot had happened between Rosa and I, and Pippa was nowhere to be seen. Then out of the blue Pippa turned up one night "so shall we go out for that meal then?" Both Rosa and I agreed yes let's do it we went out had a fantastic time. We ate, we drank, we laughed, and it was like the three of us had known each other for years. Pippa fitted right in. Or should I say they accepted me into their relationship? Both girls made me feel very welcome. We got some looks from the other people in the bar as we were eating our meal, as it was quite obvious that all three of us were together.

We eventually left the restaurant where we had, Our meal. We arrived back at Rosa's house. We carried on chatting and another bottle of wine. Before I really knew what was happening, Rosa and Pippa were kissing and cuddling on the sofa. I, out of politeness, asked if they would like me to leave them alone to have some privacy, but inside I wanted to join in. They both said no, they wanted me there. Was this an invitation to join them? The two girls sat there just as open as you can imagine and carried on kissing each other. God, I wanted to join them. I just sat there watching. That in itself was an amazing turn on two see two hot ladies acting the way they were. Then they got up off their sofa and came and joined me on the sofa I was sitting on, one lady on either side of me how special and lucky did I feel. I felt like a king, to be honest in his harem. After a little while, Rosa said "shall we call it a night then and head to bed?"

We were all going up the stairs, and I was heading to my room thinking these two ladies would want to spend the night together, even though I wanted to join them. I thought I better not push it. As I went to go into my room they both stood there and said, "well where are you going?" Rosa grabbed my hand and the two girls led me to their room, wow was this really happening to me? Not really knowing what was about to happen or what was going to happen to me at the hands of these two stunning ladies. The two girls sat on the bed with me, and Pippa said well how are the lessons going then Rosa? Rosa replied, so far so good, but we have only covered two stages but he is very OK at what has been covered. Pippa asks "what stages have been covered?" then Rosa smiled at Pippa and said we have done tantric and oral and by god does he know oral and smiled.

While the two girls were chatting, they were also stripping. Pippa looked at me, still sitting on the bed. Come then, Adam, it's time for stage three. What's that I replied. Rosa then said it's time to sample us both and us to both sample you. But I have in the past asked you to keep your eyes shut, and I have noticed you broke the rules so we are going to blindfold you. Are you happy to continue, yes I was up for holding these two passionate women but blindfolded what sort of game was this they wanted to play?

Rosa said you will still not be getting any full penetration this is like a refresher on what we have already done with each other so far. But I will blindfold you just to make sure your eyes are closed this time, and you do what we are about to do purely by touch alone is this OK with you. Oh, my god yes, I was now going to get to hold touch and feel two hot ladies at the same time. I honestly thought I must have been in heaven. I had no problem agreeing to this. My only wish was

I would want to see who was pleasuring me or who I was pleasuring. I pleaded with Rosa "before you put the blindfold on me, please just let me have one last look at both of you two ladies together naked now". Rosa said, "I can do better than that if you sit in the chair and promise not to interfere, you can watch as Pippa and I make love to each other". Wow, I was going to see two beautiful women getting it on with each other. What a fantastic sight! I went straight to the chair and sat myself down in anticipation of what I was going to witness.

The two girls proceeded to get on the bed, totally naked. It was hard to choose between them. Both had bodies that most men would have loved to have had the chance to ravage. I sat there quietly as the two girls lay on the bed together. Pippa was straight on Rosa, not rushed as I had done, but in a very sensual way. Maybe this was also my lesson to watch and see how it should be done. Pippa was kissing Rosa's neck whilst she did this. Her hands were being restrained. Rosa's hands with some soft type of rope were tying Pippa's hands to the head of the bed. Then Pippa used her hands and covered them in a beautiful smelling lavender oil. Once her hands were covered and sliding with ease, Pippa then, while kissing Rosa's neck, massaged the top half of Rosa's body. The more Pippa kissed and nestled into Rosa's neck, the deeper Rosa's fingers pushed into Pippa's buttocks. Pippa then released Rosa's neck from her very sensual kissing action and moved to her breasts. Pippa circled Rosa's nipples with her tongue, Rosa's nipples seem to grow and harden with every touch of Pippa's tongue. Rosa was groaning with pleasure at every touch that Pippa did. I had not managed to make Rosa feel like this and knew that everything Pippa was doing to Rosa she was enjoying.

Pippa decided to get on top of Rosa, whilst on top, Pippa used her well-oiled fingers on Rosa's now rocket-like nipples. Rosa was biting her bottom lip in a sort of sexual frenzy at her lover's touch. Rosa's groans of pleasure got louder and louder with every touch. Pippa obviously knew her lover and her body well, as Rosa was nearly at the screaming point. Rosa's eyes were rolling about, not able to focus as Pippa was bringing her to an amazing climax. Rosa then said "please Pippa now" and with this Pippa moved down in between Rosa's waiting open legs. Rosa's groans now the loudest I had ever heard her. Pippa was where Rosa wanted her, with her head between her legs.

Pippa looked so in control of what she was doing to Rosa. Rosa was now bucking and pushing her pelvis hard onto Pippa's tongue. With one last shudder and a scream of ecstasy, Rosa came for her lover. Pippa, not wasting a single drop, Pippa was there to sample her lover's juice, and that's exactly what she did. Rosa wasted no time at all in returning the favor or sexual pleasure to Pippa. Pippa, still licking her lips, was now laid on the bed. There was no time-wasting. Rosa restrained Pippa's arms as hers had been, and Rosa went straight to Pippa's vagina, her hand tweaking and pulling on her nipples. Pippa obviously liked it rougher, as Rosa's fingers were pulling as hard as she could. Rosa now, with her head between Pippa's leg. I knew how her tongue worked. It was like it was electrically charged. Rosa was doing what I thought she did best and giving Pippa the most amazing oral sex ever. Pippa's head was being thrown from side to side at the lashings her vagina was getting from Rosa's mouth. Pippa's long blonde hair was now sticking to her sweat-covered face. There was an almighty shriek from Pippa as she climaxed. And did she climax. Rosa's face was soaked, but this did not phase her in any way. Rosa never wasted a droplet of her lover's climax. The two girls lay on the bed very still, not exhausted, in a state of pure sexual satisfaction.

Finally, now it was my turn even though I was myself sexually satisfied with what I had just seen. I would have been quite happy just to watch these two ladies make love to each other forever. Now I was worried about how was I meant to even compete with what I had just seen. My erection was the biggest and firmest I had ever seen it grow, too. I suppose in my mind I had actually been in that mix-up of love with them as the two girls lay there together. I strolled to the bed and in turn gave both girls a small kiss. As I was kissing Pippa, I was releasing her from her restraint, which Rosa had done at the start of their session.

Rosa smiled at me, and in a soft angelic voice said, "OK Adam, are you ready to join us". No one had even touched me, but that did not matter: I was so sexually aroused I could feel my penis throb with every breath I took. Rosa sat up on the bed and beckoned me to come to her. As I got close, she sat me on the bed next to her and the blindfold went on. Still not quite understanding how this game was going to work.

The girls gently lay me on the bed. As the two girls were both on either side of me, I could feel the heat generated from their bodies after what they had just done with each other. So there I was, and this was now going to be my turn blindfolded. The girls took an arm each and tied me to the bed in the same way that they had been. Tied, a girl on either side of me, my arms now firmly tied up. Both girls kissing each side of my neck, their hands caressing and moving all over my torso.

I was already in sexual heaven if you like. I did not know which girl was on what side of me, but one girl moved from my neck and began starting to flick my nipple with her tongue. One of them now had their hand on my throbbing penis. I thought it was Rosa on my nipples. As one she knew how much I enjoyed this, and two it was the touch. I felt no one can have another tongue like that. At some point, one girl had moved down. I could feel a set of lips and their hot breath on my penis, and a hand gently massaging my testicles. I was totally lost, not knowing who was doing what. All I can remember was it really was an amazing feeling. Now, with two hands on my nipples, it felt like two different hands from different people.

I felt one girl slowly hover, her mouth gently just barely touching the end of my penis as if she were going to catch my sperm or cum. Then there was some movement, and I felt the girls change their position. One was now sitting on me, rubbing their vagina against my penis, but not allowing me to enter whoever it was.

The other girl was sitting on my chest, facing the other girl. The two girls were now both sitting on me with all their weight just hovering over me. The two girls were facing each other. I could hear that the two girls were kissing each other. Their arms were also moving, so I guess they were also touching each other.

One girl cupped my testicles in her hand, the one who was sitting hovering above my chest pushing her rear towards me and slightly lifting up and was pushing her vagina closer to my face and mouth. I moved my tongue as far out of my mouth as I could. Then I could feel the dampness of one of these fantastic ladies. She moved a little closer to help me, I think, and I was just able to make my tongue pop in and out of her moistness. I could not tell which one it was as the sweet taste I was getting was so hypnotic I liked to think to myself it was Rosa, but could not be 100% sure.

I had no way of knowing who was who and who was doing what. Now I could see their reason for the blindfold, so I would have to try to work out who was who. From just one touch I was so sexually charged up I was not really able to think straight. Then Rosa spoke "OK Adam, we are going to release your hands, but only if you promise not to remove the blindfold?" do you agree with these terms? I agreed, and I was now free. They asked me to carefully get off the bed, which I did. There was a lot of movement and then Rosa spoke again "OK Adam you must keep the blindfold on OK I agreed". The two girls now laying side by side on their backs on the bed. It was my task to see if I could work out who was who just by touch. I carefully got back on the bed and moved between the two girls on all fours, like a dog. If you can imagine this, I started by kissing each of their necks in turn. Both necks felt warm and soft to my touch. This blindfold was starting to become a pain.

Their perfumes had mixed with each other so there was no way of telling by smell. Their skin felt the same, both girls had beads of sweat on their necks, both their hair on the head felt soft. By touch alone, I could not tell who was who. It was frustrating but also exciting at the same time. I could hear small, very quiet groans of pleasure as the two girls continued to touch each other while I was doing what I was doing. Even from their sexual groaning, I could not tell who was who. I thought I would move slightly lower down and surly by the size and texture of their nipples I would now be able to tell one from the other. Where they had been playing with each other and touching each other, they had covered their hands in that lavender oil. Yet again my mouth tried to work out whose nipples were whose, but both their nipples felt as hard as each others but just about the same size. One girl was very gently rubbing my penis, the other massaging my testicles. It was as if they were synchronized.

Just to confuse me all the more, I kissed my way down both their bodies over their navels across both their flat stomachs. Surely now I would be able to tell from the taste and texture of the moist vagina. In turn, my mouth moved from one to the other as I licked and set my tongue to work on their damp labia. Both girls would wriggle and buck in turn with every touch of my tongue. They moved a little faster. I was licking and sucking for ages, as they both tasted so sweet and perfect. By this stage, I really could not care who was who all I knew is I was getting to sample these two fantastic ladies. My mouth was awash with the mixture of these two girl's juices, it was the perfect warm sweet cocktail of love /lust.

I then heard the girls whispering to each other, not loud enough for me to make out which was which. Then Pippa spoke in a gentle voice, "OK Adam, move to the edge of the bed still keeping that blindfold on". This I did. I could feel the girls get off the bed. I was now sitting blindfolded on the edge of the bed with my penis throbbing away, wanting it to have a release from its torment. Was one or both of these ladies going to ease my suffering, my torment? Would one of them show me mercy and make me cum, I so wanted to feel what both women felt like. After all, you have to remember I'm still a virgin. Really never has my penis felt the inside of a woman's vagina, my penis throbbing with every breath I took. As I sat there, both girls took an arm each and tied it with some sort of soft rope. They tied each arm to the legs of the bed. What was now going to happen to me?

Then from the distance, I heard Rosa say, shall we? Then it went sort of quiet. Then I heard them move towards me. Was this it, were the two girls now going to take my virginity. I felt their hands touch my legs as they knelt on the floor in front of me. Then one girl lent forward, and I felt her mouth cover the top of my now aching penis, then another set of lips tracing the full length of my shaft. One girl was now bobbing up and down, licking and sucking at the end of my penis, the other sucking and licking the length of my penis. Occasionally their lips would meet and sort of kiss whilst doing what they were to me. My hands were now trying in desperation to free themselves from the restraints. Please, I said, "please release me, let me feel you". The action on my penis was at bursting point, then the one who had been sucking my penis. It was "Rosa remember breath darling relax and breath" now I knew who was who. So it was Rosa giving me the most amazing blow job and performing the most fantastic oral sex. It was Pippa who was now sucking and massaging my testicles, now knowing for the first time who was who and doing what.

Rosa went back to doing what she was doing. Although I tried to do what she said with the breathing thing, it was too late I could hold out no more and I exploded into Rosa's waiting mouth. She did not stop and carried on gently sucking my penis. I could feel my sperm dribble from her mouth down the length of my now satisfied penis. As the sperm dribbled down my penis, there was Pippa, not letting a drop go to waste. Still tied I was allowed to lay back on the bed, my hands still tied. These two ladies had made me climax in such a fantastic way. As I lay there, I could hear the two girls kissing each other. Eventually, they released my restraints. We all lay on the bed together, kissing and cuddling. Totally naked and everyone totally satisfied, and that's how we eventually all fell asleep in a naked twist of sexual satisfaction. I remember as I fell asleep how, after all, I had done or had done to me, how was I still a virgin. Rosa was right. This was going to be a long lesson and in my eyes also very frustrating, as I still needed and wanted to feel my penis inside one or both of their vaginas. Was this a lesson or just sexual torture?

We awoke the next morning. Rosa was already downstairs. Pippa, still lying next to me, was naked and just coming round from her deep sleep. Her first reaction was a smile then she said: "oh you are getting good and not a lot of men could have done as Rosa and I asked of you last night". I said to her I thought last night was fantastic but finished it by saying I still think I am a virgin. She gave me a kiss and went to the shower, not even bothering to cover herself up. Again, I felt like a king. Even though as I just said I was a virgin, I felt sure that there were not a lot of men that had experienced what I just did.

When Pippa came back from the shower room, she said, 'I've been thinking about what you said about the virgin thing and it will happen all in good time. Rosa obviously has her reasons for doing things the way she is. I'm sure Rosa will let you know when you are ready or she is ready and smiled. We both got up and went downstairs to join Rosa, who was in the kitchen. This lady always seemed to be the first person up in the mornings. As we walked into the kitchen there she was in all her stunning glory, "morning she said my lovely's how are you both today?" Smiled and said "I thought you were both going to spend the whole day in bed", I walked over to Rosa and gave her the most loving kiss I thought I could ever give anyone and whispered in her ear thanks for last night and gently kissed her earlobe.

Chapter Eight

We were all sitting around the table just chatting about normal everyday stuff, and the post arrived. Whilst still sitting at the table, Rosa had read a letter she had received from Philip. This was the man who looked after the farmhouse in France that she owned. He mentioned to her that there were a few things that needed to be sorted out with the farmhouse. Not terribly urgent, but advised that it would be best to sort them out before the winter set in.

Rosa said that we should all go out there and sort of make a long holiday off it, and asked me "Adam you would not mind going over there with us? Would you mind, it would sort of be like a working holiday for you". Obviously, I agreed I wanted to do all I could to please Rosa and now Pippa, as there seemed to be three of us in this wonderful relationship.

It was a fantastic relationship I now had two beautiful women who wanted to teach me the ways of sex the right way from a woman's point of view. Rosa had put me on a type of building course and Pippa, who was teaching me to drive. I had to be the luckiest man alive. With this Pippa got up and said, OK Adam you must soon be ready for your next driving lesson, then said we will have you passed your test by the end of August then you can drive Rosa and me to France.

Wow, yeah that would be nice I replied shall we go now. She laughed and said, "OK let's have another cuppa and then we will go". I have got some things to do. You could take me there and that can be your lesson if you like. I hastily agreed wow I was going to be passed my test real soon, then my business can really take off, I was thinking to myself. Thirty minutes later, we set off on a driving lesson. Rosa said she had something to arrange so did not come with us. We were driving down this A road somewhere it was quite busy. It was not like a normal driving instructor/pupil relationship we were relaxed and had many laughs during our driving lessons together.

Pippa piped up and said, "Hey Adam, you up for a laugh this morning?". Well, I was always up for a laugh, especially with my two gorgeous girls. As we were driving along, she started to unbutton her thin, pure white blouse. I could see that she had no bra on, and I thought, oh god yes, I'm going to get to have her. I so wanted, was so desperate to have full-blown sex. I thought Pippa was going to start giving me another private lesson, but Pippa said to me "drive alongside this lorry which was in front of us". So I drove alongside the lorry and drew level with the cab. She said, "give a little beep on the horn Adam". Whilst I did this, Pippa had totally unbuttoned her blouse, her fantastic-shaped breasts now fully on show. She was playing with her breasts as we were alongside this lorry, playing with her nipples, twisting and tweaking them. It was a show for the lucky lorry driver, but hell, I was getting the best view sitting right next to her. The lorry driver must have seen what she was doing, because he was blowing the horn on his truck, shouting out of the window, "go on girl, get those tits out".

I was driving along laughing, she then said "OK Adam drive on", as I carried on she sort of re-dressed herself and made herself look respectable. I don't know about the lorry driver but she sure did it for me, because as we were driving along I felt my penis becoming a little hard, not a full erection but hey definitely bigger than normal. She had not had a laugh like that before. She said she knew of a cafe down this little lane, a country park cafe and we should stop there for some lunch. We had our lunch and made our way back to Rosa's this time she was well behaved and did not excite any other road users well apart from me. Being with Rosa and Pippa it felt as though my penis was always semi erect. The girls excited me in every way. The mannerisms, their sexual behavior, their looks, everything. I truly felt I was the luckiest man alive.

As we were driving back, she asked me not to tell anyone what she had done, as she would be in a lot of trouble if that ever got in the wrong hands. I said "no worries what happens with us stays with us" and she smiled and leaned across and gave me a kiss.

We got back to Rosa's and Rosa was still not back, so Pippa said it was time for some theory work. She said your actual driving is very good but the theory side of things was down to me, and that was something she could not help with. She stayed with me and together she helped me out where she could with the theory. We did about an hour or so.

Rosa came home and asked how I was getting on? Pippa said "yeah his driving is coming along nicely", and Rosa said "yes he is coming along nicely with our private lessons too" and laughed. We asked how Rosa's day had gone and she said fine. She had sort of booked the tickets for the channel but could not be totally sure of the dates. So the rest of my day was down to business. Rosa had previously asked me to board out the inside of the outhouse, which was actually on the edge of her property. She said the boards had arrived and would I mind starting on it or at least get them inside so the weather did not destroy them. I agreed and took myself down to the outhouse, and that's where I spent the rest of my day. Later we were all sitting around chatting with a bottle of wine or two, and I asked Rosa what she had in mind for the old outhouse. Once again the answer I got was all will come clear in the end, again another not really answered question.

It seemed as though I was in the mood to ask questions that night, as we were all relaxing. I asked Rosa, "why have I not been allowed to have penetration sex yet?" She said I would be when I felt she was ready for it, she said "you are nearly there darling" and just asked me to be patient. Then she asked how did I feel about the age gap between us. I said it was only about 20 years. I did not find it a problem and had not really even thought about it before. In fact, now thinking about it, I said I actually liked the age gap, and it really did not bother me. And I also felt so proud to be with her and Pippa.

I also said that I liked the fact that she was bisexual. I also thought Pippa was amazing, too. I went on to say that I would be happy to spend the rest of my life living with her and Pippa. Rosa said it was a lovely thing to say, but I should not make any heavy decisions like that not yet not at my age. I asked why she asked that and said was she OK with our age differences. She said she thought my age was great and even though I was still only very young; I was a lot more mature than my actual age. With the way that I thought, she said I hope that you do understand the way that she was teaching me and that it would mean I would be the perfect lover. She also said that there was lots more for me to learn but so far I had been great she just wanted me to learn it right (from a woman's point of view).

She then put it bluntly she said "anyone can shag, anyone can fuck but to do it right" and it not come across as I have just said it. You have to be patient it has to be nice and mean something. It has to be something that's very loving and caring. Not something just to be done and mean nothing or for just one person's own sexual satisfaction.

And that's what she and Pippa were trying to teach me. She loved the fact that the three of us got on so well, and it made the relationship so special. She also said "that making love, having sex, fucking, whatever way you want to put it, however, it's done has to be a very sensual erotic thing for all included. Whether it's two people, three, or multiple people it has to be erotic and everyone needs to feel that special something or it's just not worth doing."

I just said I so wanted to feel her and Pippa in every way. She said I was so nearly there and not to give up just yet. I sighed and said "OK Rosa", I would never give up on her or Pippa as the two of them meant so much to me. Pippa walked in and joined in the conversation and we got off that subject and got onto the subject of likes and dislikes.

Pippa said one of her loves and passions was horse riding. My first thought was "yeah I bet she looked good in jodhpurs". I would love to see her canter around on the back of some horse, or even better, sitting astride me, cantering away. She had a fantastic figure I bet she looked wonderful, girting her buttocks on the back of some horse.

Rosa said she enjoyed sailing, traveling across the water just under the power of the wind. No noise from a smelly old engine. She said that when we go to France, she would take both Pippa and I out on her boat, which she had moored near the banks of the old farmhouse in France. Then Pippa announced she had to go away for about three days, something to do with her driving instructor's course. Rosa said OK baby, and that she was going to miss her and that she was to keep in touch. Pippa said of course and smiled at Rosa. I explained that my hobby or like was photography. Both girls looked at each other and smiled, and I heard Rosa say that's handy to know.

Chapter Nine

Well, we all went off to bed that night. Rosa asked if just Rosa and Pippa could have some time together on their own because of Pippa going away for a few days. I lay there in my bed that night on my own, which had not seemed to happen for some time. I sort of got used to sleeping in the same bed as my two beautiful girls, but hey I realized and understood that they wanted to spend some time alone together, much to my regret.

I laid there listening to their conversation. I heard Pippa say to Rosa, "hey do you know how much Adam wants to make love to you?" I heard Rosa reply it's not just me but yes, I have a good idea. I then heard Pippa say, go on, teach him he is crazy about you. Rosa said look, Pippa, to be honest, Adam is crazy about the two of us, which is just the way I want it said, Rosa. He has to learn there are three of us in this relationship, and yes, you might well at some point have great sex with him alone, as I will, but he needs to learn a little more. Rosa said he is crazy about the two of us I have spoken to him, Pippa said "what has he said?" Rosa explained that he said I would be quite happy to settle down with the two of us for the rest of his life. Pippa then said wow what a really nice thing to say and how nice it is that a man who knows us intimately understands how we feel about each other and wants the three of us to be together. Someone who wants to be with us equally that's what we were hoping for, is it not?

Rosa said, yeah that would be nice, but it is still early days. We will just have to see how things go. I want it to happen but only time will tell. He may have to learn t nothing and still go on like a typical man, just out for what he can get. Pippa said well unless you/we try Rosa we will never know. Rosa said I know and so far he has hit all the right buttons, Rosa said I just don't want to lose him. He could be our answer to what we always wanted. A man who excepts us for who we are and what we want. I heard Pippa agree. I don't really remember much more, as I was feeling exhausted and must have drifted off to sleep. As I was falling asleep, maybe in a state-like coma, Rosa had come into my room. She had very quietly got on her knees, placed her head next to mine and she whispers soon Adam, soon my perfect lover, please be patient that little longer, and gave me a kiss on the side of my face. It felt as though I had been stroked by an angel and I was sure I put my hand on the kiss so it did not fall off.

Chapter Ten

The next morning when I woke up, the house seemed very quiet. I got up, showered, went downstairs, but there was no one about. There was a note on the kitchen table for me. The two girls had shot off to town to do some stuff. I had a quick cuppa and took myself off down to the outhouse and continued with my work down there. Working down there on my own gave me lots of time to think. Rosa and Pippa were so special to me. I cherished everything Rosa and Pippa were doing for me and too me. My first love was Donna, but I seemed to have come a long way since then in what really was a brief space of time. I felt like a different person now. It felt like I had left that life behind me. It seemed such a long time ago. I thought I had now turned into a man, but saying that I was still a virgin. I felt sure you could still class yourself as a man, even if you were a virgin. I had experienced some fantastic things and was so happy and proud of what had happened to me so far.

But inside, the yearning to enter Rosa and Pippa sexually was driving me crazy. I wanted to make love to the two girls I was living with so much, wanted to feel what they felt like, what it felt like. I so wanted to feel what it was like to have actual sex and penetrate, and always wondered if sex was everything I thought it was. What Rosa and Pippa had already shown me was fantastic maybe I was expecting too much.

And what I had already sampled was actually better than full-blown sex, but I felt in my heart that was just a sample of what was to come. While I was working away down in the outhouse and my mind was playing tricks on me and I was having these weird and wonderful thoughts, my cell phone went off. It was a text from Rosa saying she and Pippa would not be coming back that night. She hoped I was OK and said she would see me in the morning.

I worked till late that night and when I went up to the house and the day came to an end, I decided to go and sleep in Rosa's room. If I could not spend the night with her at least I could go to sleep with the fragrance of Rosa and Pippa surrounding me. I slept like a log that night, such a peaceful night's sleep. When I woke up, I woke to the sight of Rosa just sitting in the chair, looking at me. She said "I did not like or want to wake you up you looked so peaceful" we had a quick kiss then I went to the shower and got ready for work. I went down the stairs and into the kitchen Rosa had made me a wonderful breakfast. As I was eating, she said "OK I'm going up for a bath", I had just finished eating and I heard Rosa shout from upstairs, "Adam please come and wash my back". I could not get up the stairs quick enough. I had had a night away or without my Rosa and missed her so much.

When I got to the top of the stairs, I casually walked in. I wanted to run in and jump in with her "maybe she was right, maybe I did still have a lot to learn as the rush thing was still in me evidently."

There was my Rosa as breathtaking as beautiful as ever, the water and soap shinning on her body. It happened again as it always did (like clockwork)

Every time I saw this lady naked, I had a string in my trouser and began to feel myself get aroused. I tried not to show it; I tried to act casual. I walked towards her. There was that beautiful smell of lavender again. She must have been using lavender bubble bath or something. Her body glowed under the bathroom lights. If her breasts were fruit, her breasts looked so ripe and in such a perfect shape, ready for picking and eating. I soaped my hands and slowly began washing her shoulders and back. My hands glided effortlessly over her smooth skin. Occasionally my hands would work my way round to her beautiful breasts as I did this I cupped her breasts, gentle on both hands and would give a gentle squeeze. I could see Rosa's eyes were firmly shut and she would give out the tiniest of pleasurable groans. Rosa then said, eyes still shut, "oh God Adam you are so good with your hands" I leaned forward, lowered my face to hers, and gave her a tiny little kiss. I went to give another kiss and as our lips met, this time they did not part. We were in a full-blown, heavy kiss, and it was one of the nicest kisses I had ever had that day. I went downstairs and made Rosa one of her favorite drinks, a mixture of exotic juices with a couple of ice cubes.

While she was finishing of her bath, I went quickly to the outhouse and did a little more work which ended up turning into about 4 hours. It was about tea time when I got back to the house. She smiled and said "what happened to you" and smiled at me. I said "sorry I got stuck on a job in your outhouse, she said no our outhouse".

Whilst I had been at work she had prepared the most fantastic dinner for us. We sat alone and ate our dinner and we just chatted for hours about anything that popped into our heads. She asked how I was getting on with the jobs down at the outhouse, and I was so pleased with myself I told her how I had got all the wall boarded out, and painted she was impressed. She said we would have a walk down there together later that night and have a look. We were finishing our meal chatting as we did, and as we did so Rosa was stroking my leg with her foot.

Oh god, how nice it felt just to have her touch me like this. I knew I was falling for this lady, the lady of my dreams who I first peeked at when I was with Donna. Was now wanting to touch me with no prompting had we turned a corner had we now moved on to another level. Without even noticing the plates were empty, we were still sitting chatting with the occasional cuddle and kiss. Rosa said "OK my man, let's go and have a look at your handy work" then wow, she had never called me her man before this was real. We had turned a corner. I felt sure, and somehow I felt even closer to her.

We put our coats on as the sun had long gone down and there was a definite chill in the air. Even when this lady put her fur coat on, she looked like something out of the movies, totally stunning and good enough to eat. I had, had my steak, my red meat, so again was now starting to feel horny as hell. God, I wanted this lady and all her trimmings.

We walked down the pathway together through the small wooded area that separated the outhouse from her house. We walked hand in hand I kept thinking; I wish you knew how I felt, Rosa. We got to the outhouse, and I opened the door for her. She walked in and said "oh you clever man", you have done such a great job. She was overjoyed with the work I had carried out she said no one has ever worked this hard for her before, no one has ever wanted to. Again, she gave me a cuddle and a kiss. Our mouths met and our tongues entwined with each other, as they were earlier that day when she was having her bath. I wanted to melt into this lady so we could be as one and never parted again. I wanted my Rosa in so many ways we had a slow walk back to the house, stopping every now and again for a kiss and a cuddle. We got back to the house, off with the coats, and we sat together talking about the old farmhouse, but I noticed something was different this night, or at least the way Rosa was looking at me. She kept looking at me in a strange way, hard to describe, a sort of glazed look but warm and wanting look. I asked if she was OK Rosa replied, "oh yes, I am very OK and very happy". I'm looking at you in a new light, darling, and it's all good. I actually now believe you when you say you want to be with Pippa and I.

I interrupted and said yes Rosa I will never lie to you I really do want you and Pippa. I would love to have you both as my permanent partners, Rosa said yes Adam at long last I think I can actually see this and I have never seen this before. Adam, you're so special, so lovely. We sat there gazing at each other, the TV on in the background, that's all it was: background noise. Rosa said I hope I'm right I really do, Adam. She took me from the sofa and we went upstairs. She took me to her bedroom and lie me on the bed on my back. Rosa then said, now don't be nervous don't rush at me breathe and relax. Remember all we have spoken about and all we have done.

Rosa slowly seductively removed my clothes, Rosa started by kissing my neck and massaging my shoulders. I was responding by kissing her neck and running my hand down her back. Rosa moved from my neck to my pectoral muscles and gently nibbling at my pecs. I held her tight as she did this. She then slowly sat up, her hands not leaving my body. She was sitting bolt upright on me, naked as the day that she was born. I could feel her freshly shaved vagina pushed hard against my again hardened throbbing penis. Her hands now just rubbing, flicking, sliding over my nipples. She would occasionally squeeze, pull, or tweak them in a nice, sensual sort of way. One of her hands was hovering over her own perfect breasts, her fingers pulling on her own erect nipple, my hand on the other breast copying what she was doing to her own.

Rosa paused for a moment, so darling, are you ready, "oh God, yes!" I replied. Rosa, I have wanted this for so long she lent over to a set of drawers beside her bed and as she did this, one of her hardened nipples pressed against my lips. I trembled, my lips parted, and I took this fantastic dark hard nipple in my mouth. I licked and sucked I felt her aura full of bumps too, her nipples were like she had goose bumps and I tried to feel every one of them. I licked and sucked her fantastic nipple, nearly sucking to trying to suck it as far into my mouth as it would allow. Rosa slowly sat upright again and produced some warm lubricant gel. She took my hands and generously poured the gel over my hands, she then poured some over her chest, I watched her hands as the oil ran down this perfectly formed body. The oil covering her full breasts, the oil was dripping from the end of each erect nipple. I covered her shoulders in oil too as I watched the oil drip and cover her perfect breasts. I then massaged the oil into her long slender back her tiny framed shoulders where shining with the amount of oil massaged onto them.

I went to speak; her oil-drenched finger came to my mouth as to shush me. I was not allowed to speak. She spoke in a very soft voice and muttered, no darling no words need be spoken, just soft gentle erotic movements. She moved her head back down towards my body and went straight for my nipples "she knew I liked this" and took my nipples alternately into her mouth. She was sucking so hard, harder than she had previously done. I could feel my own nipples becoming erect in her mouth whilst she was doing this. She was holding my arms firmly down, her long dark hair was flicking my face. I could hear her groaning as she sucked away on my chest. She was now enjoying my body like never. Her head moved slightly down my body, her hands still holding my arms down. She was sucking and licking every one of my abdominal muscles. Suddenly, she released my arms and slowly sat up.

Rosa was now sliding and gyrating her very moist vagina, trying to cover every abdominal muscle. My hands now free, I was running my hands from her shoulders down the length of her back and right onto her buttocks. She was sitting on me and now leaning backward. Her well-oiled hands were now running up and down the length of my legs. As she lent back, I could see the moistness of her freshly shaven, very neat vagina. Her hand massaging my legs were diving into my inner thigh. Rosa lifted her fantastic body, turned, and pushed her buttocks and hot pussy close to my face. Her head now lowered, and I felt her electrically charged tongue and mouth run up and down the full length of my throbbing penis. Rosa had now positioned her damp moist wanting vagina over my eagerly waiting wanting mouth.

I held her well-oiled buttock and pushed them apart and lifted up my head. I slowly but surely pushed my tongue as deep as I could into her oil and juice-soaked vagina. Rosa at the same time was now taking my throbbing, aching penis deep into her throat. I felt Rosa's juices completely soak my wanting tongue. I pushed Rosa up just a little by the buttock, just enough to operate my tongue. That little better I was licking just inside Rosa's labia lips, and she was wriggling and squirming about. So much with each wriggle, she seemed to climax again. The more I would do this, the further she seemed to take my penis into her throat. I was sure I was fully in, and now well inside her throat, but still she rose and sank, sucking harder each time she went down on me. Whilst she was doing this and with her slight body movement, I was able to find her clitoris. I licked and sucked it for as long as I could, every now and then my face would receive a gush from this lady's hot vagina. She was climaxing over and over again. Every time her body shuddered, there was another delivery of this perfect sweet juice.

Rosa was so in control of what she and I were doing. My whole body felt like someone had electrocuted it. I thought I could feel every nerve ending in my body as if they were on the outside. Rosa started to speed up now, going further and further, harder and harder onto my thumping penis. All of a sudden she stopped quickly, moved her body around so she was now sitting on me. Her hand stretched back and took my now at bursting penis in her hand, she rose a little from my body and slowly, cleverly, and gently placed my penis at the entrance to her vagina. Slowly, she lowered onto my penis. When she had all of me inside her, she spoke again. "Close your eyes, breath in very slowly and very deeply", I did exactly as they commanded me to do.

I felt I was going to explode for sure. Rosa was very careful not to go too fast. She watched my facial expressions and would just sit still every so often. The more I got used to being where I was, she could sense. And after a while, Rosa began to move her perfect vagina up and down the full length of my penis. Sometimes thinking she was getting off then sink hard again onto my penis. After a while, she spoke again, "keep your eyes shut, breathe, and as I push down you push up". OK, I just nodded. I was actually biting my bottom lip, as the excitement was just too much as she rose and sank. I pushed as she had asked. My legs tensed the whole of my body. Tensed, I held her legs, and she rose up and down really fast that it was as if for the first time in my life I had cum inside this wonderful creature. Rosa just carried on rising and falling till my penis just fell from that very hot, moist love box of hers.

We lay there together, me unable to think really. I was in some sort of trance, both our bodies covered in a mixture of our sweat. Her breathing was deep, as was mine. I thought I would never get another erection. I truly thought it had been destroyed. In its first time, we lay there cuddling, our hands moving over each other. The stillness of the air in the bedroom drying and cooling our juices, evaporating it from us. We cuddled and kissed and at some point drifted off to sleep.

Chapter Eleven

Neither of us woke the next day until midway through the morning. Once we were awake properly, we headed to the shower together. The water was just right and seemed to caress both our bodies; we washed each other as we had once before. My nerve endings still feeling as though they were on the outside of my body, still tingling from the previous night. Rosa held me tight in the shower that day, the warm water bouncing off both our bodies. Our kisses seemed more intense. It all felt so right we spent the rest of that day just chilling about the house. Rosa said, well I guess that's you in my bed every night from now on then, I felt like the cat that had got the cream. I had done it I was no longer a virgin, Rosa said, "well I have to ask, how do you feel now? It was such a big thing for you to lose your virginity". I said I felt fantastic, but also hoped she felt OK about what we had done. She then said that she enjoyed what we did and felt great about it. She said, "Adam you were very good actually and lasted longer than most men she had known".

But with a smile on her face, she said you do still have a lot to learn, I could not wait. I would do anything too and for this angel of sex asked of me. I said, "what else do I have to learn then, Rosa," she just said, "just because you have made love once does not make you an expert lover, although you felt very nice inside me. But Adam, you have to remember there are three of us in this relationship if that's what you feel you still want?" I said, "yes of course Rosa that's what I still want, I would not want to leave Pippa out, but Rosa I was glad it was just you who took my virginity." I then said "I was looking forward to Pippa coming back" as much as she was I knew it had only been a couple of days but I too was missing her. Rosa said to me "Adam you once said that you wanted to live with me and Pippa permanently as a threesome." I said "yes, and that's still the case," she replied, "well then, you have got a monumental task in front of you. You will have to learn to sexually please the two of us. No, the three of us, as your enjoyment is of equal importance. And we must learn to please you this has to be a very equal and fair thing we are trying to do."

We must never forget our sexual roots and always try to include tantric, or tantra, as most people call it. It is very spiritual and allows you to control yourself better. Pippa comes home tomorrow and will be very excited about our news. The day just seemed to slip away from us. We stayed on the sofa just lazing around watching films having the odd cuddle.

The end of the day just vanished; the evening went just as fast, so we took ourselves off to bed. It felt a little strange walking past my bedroom door, as that was no longer my room. I had graduated to Rosa and Pippa's room, both Rosa and I went to bed. We stripped, got under the covers, and just lay there, gently touching each other. Nothing too heavy, just very gentle caresses, the odd kiss, and plenty of cuddles. And just general chit-chat. It was as if we were both worn out, as it was not long before we were drifting off to sleep. Rosa smelt totally fantastic, as she always did, and I fell asleep just watching her.

We woke up bright and early the next morning. We showered, had a quick bite to eat, Rosa said she was off to get some things for the outhouse. While she did this, I said I would go down there and continue working. I still had a floor to lay. Rosa and Pippa were so relaxed one day seemed to roll into the other. Life was so happy and peaceful. I was happy. Pippa was coming back. She had only been away a few days, but did not feel right without her being around. Whilst working in the outhouse, I secretly felt very pleased with myself about what I and Rosa had done. Rosa was never out of my mind for long. Putting the floor down seemed to take all day. As I was walking back to the house, I noticed both girl's cars on the drive, then suddenly I came across feeling very awkward. Do I rush up to her like a schoolchild, had Rosa already mentioned what we had done.

No one had seen me coming. I thumbed about, not quite knowing what to say. I sat on the chair outside the kitchen window; the window was half open, and I heard Rosa say to Pippa well the deed is done. And she explained about our activity together. Pippa seemed pleased and, oh yes, very interested. She asked Rosa loads of questions. Well, how was he? First Rosa paused for a while then said: "Pippa he is bloody fantastic you would not have thought that it was his first time of real intercourse, his stamina was great he lasted much, much longer than I ever expected". She even thought at one point I was not really interested as he just lay there biting his bottom lip. Rosa explained in great detail about everything we did that night. I thought more to the point of how well Rosa controlled the situation perfectly.

She said to Pippa; I was surprised he lasted as long as he did. I was trying every trick in the book to make him cum. But somehow he kept his composure and held on for ages. And that she had climaxed several times. I don't think he noticed; It surprised me that he was holding it back; he was doing amazing things with his mouth and tongue and it was as if I were the student and giggled. Pippa then said, why were you trying to make him cum so quickly. Rosa said well it was his first time, and I thought he would have climaxed more or less straight away, and once he had the initial explosion out of the way, I would then have made him hard again. I thought it would have lasted longer for me whilst we were having sex, and he would have had a better time as would I have had, well so I thought, laughed and said maybe I don't know everything the two girls giggled again.

Pippa said, "oh yes I can now see your reasoning behind your actions now, but Rosa, you had him wrong and he lasted well. Anyway, yes Rosa said he lasted better than well, Pippa then said fantastic Rosa so how does he feel now does he still want the three of us". Hope you have not turned into just your lover, Rosa. Oh no, don't worry there. We had that conversation. He still wants us both a three-way relationship. He can't wait for you to come home, yes she said where is he now. Rosa said I don't know, he should have finished ages ago, since he was working on the outhouse.

It was great to hear Rosa singing my praises like that. I was sitting there and my head was getting bigger and bigger. It was also great that Rosa had broken the ice if you like by telling Pippa. I made some noise as if I were approaching from the distance, walked straight in through the door, and said "hi girls" as if I had heard nothing. Walking up to Rosa, gave her a kiss, then turned walked towards Pippa. "Hello Pippa" and gave her a big squeeze and cuddle, "told her I had missed her" and also gave her a nice big kiss. Sitting down with the two girls and listened to what Pippa had been doing while she was away. The girls laughed in the middle of our conversation and said "oh yes we have been talking about you too, Adam". Little did they know I had heard everything and was feeling very proud of myself?

Nothing really happened that night we spent the evening chatting about the work I had done for the girls on the outhouse. We also spoke again about Rosa's farmhouse in France and, of course, we spoke of the course that Pippa had just been on. Nearing the end of the evening, Pippa said "oh God nearly forgot" and smiled and winked at Rosa. I have had a special word with an old friend of mine, and she had got my driving test brought forward and my test was going to be within the week. I said, "Christ I had done no revision while she had been away, on the theory side of things" the girls giggled and said, "well that's something we can't help you with". This is something I would have to do for myself. I said I would stay up late that night and study the book from one cover to the other. Shortly afterward the girls took themselves off to bed and left me to study as I had promised.

I actually fell asleep downstairs that night. I studied for as long as my brain could concentrate. I woke up to the sound of Pippa rattling her car keys on me. Come on, Adam, you can catch up on your driving lesson. She said how much sleep had I had; I said about 4 hours; she said, that's OK then, a young man like you does not need that much sleep. Within 30 minutes of being awake, I had some food and a couple of teas, and then Pippa and I were off in her car. Before we left, Rosa gave us both a kiss, and said have a nice day, and gave me one of her what I thought naughty smiles, and winked at Pippa.

She then whispered in her ear to be gentle with him. This time we drove around in an area that Pippa had never taken me to before. Pippa was talking to me as I drove, and she said that she and Rosa spoke for a while about me last night before they went to sleep. My first thoughts were I would have loved to have been a fly on the wall and heard that conversation. She said, don't be nervous, Adam, it was all very good, and smiled at me. We carried on driving for about another hour or so, then Pippa said to take the next left. We went down this little country lane. I would not have actually classed it as a road it was full of potholes, after about 10 minutes we arrived at some stables. We got out of the car and headed to this rough-looking little building at the side of the stables. Where was Pippa taking me now, I thought? It was her tack room where Pippa kept all her riding stuff, old horse blankets, bridles, saddles, everything you would need. Pippa then said OK, darling, put the kettle on, and pointed in the direction she wanted me to go. I was thinking great I have driven half the day to come to a shed and make tea. It smelt of horses. There were bridles and reins hanging from the rafters, horse blankets drying on a 2 ft wall. As I was making the tea, I turned to Pippa.

Pippa was changing out of her neat black skirt and the thin white blouse that she wore. There stood a beautiful sight, her piercing blue eyes looking me up and down, my half-tired eyes trying to register as much of this lady as I could. She had the most beautiful lingerie that I had ever seen. Her wearing, God, she looked good in the tiny white lace bra that held her also perfect breasts so nicely. She wore a pair of lacy white knickers and a delicate lace suspender belt. She was unrolling her lace stockings from her long, slender legs. The sunlight coming through the tack room window she looked amazing I thought yes I was now going to get to make love to this stunning lady. She slowly peeled each stocking off each leg, very slowly, as though it were my own personal striptease. By now my thoughts were totally on her, and it did not matter where we were. As she took them off, she would push her perfect-shaped buttocks towards me. I took off my jacket and sat on a pile of old horse blankets, but hold on this was not a striptease. For she kept the bra on. She stood up, thinking this was it. Was she now going to teach me as Rosa had?

Was I now because of another private lesson in the ways of sex? But she walked to a rusty old set of lockers, opened it, and pulled out this pair of jodhpurs. She put them on, still with her back to me. She bent over and that jodhpur left nothing to the imagination as she bent down. She pulled out a pair of shiny black knee-length boots which fit her calf muscles like a glove. She then turned and walked towards me. Sitting on the wall next to me, she gave me a pleasant kiss, different from how she had ever kissed me before, and drank the tea I had made. She looked like a million dollars sitting there in what she was wearing.

The weather outside seemed to become really overcast. Cloudy and Grey, typical English weather. She then said "so do you like horses then Adam", I said "yes but I had never ridden one before, or not really been close to one but I did not have a problem with them". Pippa then said that's why they were here. I have been away for a couple of days and I never usually miss a day. One of her friends had been doing the necessary with them, but her horses needed to be hacked out, "ridden" she explained.

I said how many do you have she said three. She smiled and said she needed a pleasant ride and felt sure that was something I could help her with, and smiled at me. I wanted to say hey Pippa; I give you a pleasant ride, but the shy young man was still in me. She said she would take out the big filly and that I could ride her old cob. I nearly choked, thinking she had said something else. But as hard as I tried, my thoughts kept straying from the horses and my thoughts would be of her. I said, "Pippa, I have never ridden before and if that horse ran for it, it would probably kill me". She laughed and said it's called, bolting off not to run for it. And that's why I was on the old cob, as he was bombproof, apparently. That just meant he plodded along. That was fine with me. As to be honest, the thought of being on this thing actually scared the life out of me. Pippa laughed aloud "well she said you say you can't ride", well that's not what I hear, and actually you are a wonderful ride. I felt embarrassed, as I knew what she meant. She and Rosa had been talking about our sexual encounter.

We were both laughing as we walked out to the horses in the stables. First Pippa did her horse and left me to do mine I was just trying to copy what she was doing she called it tacking up mine looked like I had messed up. She looked at what I had done or attempted to do, giggled, and said you poor thing. Patted her horse or the one I was meant to be going on gave the horse a kiss and re did my horse for me. Just before we set off she put her riding jacket on and said "OK the last thing", hell I did not know there was so much involved with riding a horse. She grabbed this metal hook-type thing, lifted the horse's feet, and picked out any stones or grit from the horse's feet. As she did this, I had the most amazing view as she bent over her jodhpurs stretched over her tight bum. I just wanted to run up behind her and have sex with her. She looked so nice. Well, her bum did. It was so provocative to watch her do what she was doing but saying that anything Pippa looked provocative if she put her mind to it.

It was not long before we were off. Thank god all Pippa decided to do was just walk. Whilst we were sitting on these things, we walked around the outer edge of a couple of fields. Pippa was saying what Rosa had been saying about me and my bedroom behavior. I'm sure my head was getting bigger and bigger listening to the praise or compliments I was hearing, from what Rosa had been saying about me/us.

Pippa said she was gutted that she was not there for my first time. She too would have liked to have been part of that, and in taking my virginity. Just as we neared this wooded area, it started to spit with rain. Neither of us really dressed for the rain. As we set off the weather was fine, Pippa said she thought we better shelter in the woods for a while. We took our horses into the wooded area, and Pippa dismounted, tied her horse's reins to a tree. I followed suit as we stood there in the thickness of the trees. We both just stood there with our arms around each other, watching the rain get heavier and heavier. Suddenly Pippa stretched across and grabbed my hand, "oh Adam I can't wait I really want to see if you are as good as Rosa said you were", and before I could say anything to Pippa she was kissing me full on the lips. Well, not just her, as I was responding and kissing back with the same intensity. No, it did not feel wrong I was not cheating on Rosa there were three of us in this wonderful relationship. It was not long before Pippa had slowly moved to her knees.

The sky had come over as black as black, the rain now pouring down on both of us. Holding onto my waist with one hand, her other now thumbing about with my belt. The rain was freezing cold, but this did not seem to matter or bother either of us. In no time at all, Pippa had now released my semi-hard penis from my trousers. Both her hands now squeezing my buttocks, she slowly and carefully took my now very interested penis deep into her mouth. Oh, how nice she felt, slowly moving up and down the length of my penis. Every time she pulled away from my body, I felt droplets of freezing rain hit my now rock-hard penis. I was standing with my back to a tree, holding her head, running my hands through her soaked, wet hair. I could feel the warmth of her scalp on my hands as this petite blonde was bobbing back and forth on my shinning shaft.

She must have felt my body tense and jerk after 10 minutes of this fantastic woodland oral experience. Pippa then said "no Adam not yet please", as she said this she slowly stood upright to her feet. My penis was now fully erect and open to the elements. Rain hitting my erect penis, she then placed herself with her back to the tree. She then unbuttoned her tight black jacket to reveal her soaked, now see-through bra. Her dark soaked wet nipples showing through her soaked see-through bra, her gorgeous blonde hair stuck firmly to her scalp, and water now dripping from her long locks down her pink glowing skin. She pulled me close to her soaked body. With her other hand, she had slipped her jodhpurs down. Her buttocks were now resting against the rough bark of the tree and revealed her perfectly shaved vagina. As she pulled me gently towards her, she made sure I stayed hard by rubbing my penis in her hand, which was being naturally lubricated by the droplets of rain.

My hands now feeling Pippa's smoothness and how warm and damp she was, she moved herself just slightly to make herself more comfortably against the tree. And with one final pull, she had cleverly put my damp but hard penis in the warmth of her moist vagina. She felt truly amazing I felt the walls of her vagina hugging the length of my penis. Her labia just cupping the end of my penis, which was deep inside her. We stood there against the tree, making slow but very passionate love. Just then we heard a noise from the distance there were two people, an old couple walking their dogs, they were walking along the outer edge of the woods and we were only about 25ft in. We were in a little clearing. They were only about 15 feet away. Pippa was in control. She did not want this to finish, not yet, as I did not. She whispered in my ear, "stay inside me, stand very close, no movement and just kiss my neck" I did exactly as she requested. As the people walking their dogs passed us, she said morning gave them a wave, and went back to kissing me. The people passed us not suspecting a thing, waved back and carried on walking their dogs, and had not seemed to have seen anything.

When they had passed and were out of earshot she whispered again, now fuck me, Adam, fuck me hard. I was still inside this lovely lady and still very hard, as I actually found the thought of being caught by strangers a real turn-on. So I penetrated Pippa hard. With every forward movement I made, I felt myself sink deeper into her moistness. With every forward movement, I heard her groan yes, yes, yes, do it, Adam, do it. As I pulled my chest away from hers to look at her face, I could see she was now biting her lip, her eyes sort of rolling in their sockets. She pulled me close once again and girted her pelvis. I sank deep into Pippa and felt my body tense once more. I climaxed, as I did this, until Pippa had climaxed at the same time. We stood there holding each other in the rain, now just kissing. As we separated from our embrace, we kissed again. The rain was now stopping. We sorted our dampened clothes and bodies out, straightened ourselves up, returned to our waiting horses, and made our way back to the tack room.

Once back at the tack room, we found a couple of old towels and dried ourselves off the best we could. I was again at the table and was making us both a hot drink. As I turned around, there was Pippa, fully naked, laying on that little wall. Pippa then said, "OK Adam, one good turn deserves another". She lay there as if it were a hotel bedroom, not a care in the world who might walk by or in. She laid there and very slowly parted her legs. She beckoned me over to her, which I did. She stretched out her hand and pulled me closer to her. As I neared her, she said, your turn, baby. Asking me to drop to my knees, I knew exactly what she meant, and what she wanted me to do. I willingly put my head to her soft pink vagina, and I slowly started to lick the outside edge of her sweet vagina, starting gently licking the outside edge of her labia. Then slowly but surely my tongue soon managed to find its way inside this beautiful woman.

Pippa was groaning with pleasure as I tried my best to satisfy and please this wanting lady. Her hand was now inside my shirt, pulling and tweaking my nipples. My tongue, concentrating on what I was doing, had now found her semi swollen clitoris. Pippa was groaning with pleasure the whole time. I would every now and again use my tongue and lick from the lower edge of her vagina slowly up to the top, and gently circle her clitoris or suck, maybe. Even the tiniest of nibbles my tongue was now soaked in the ladies' warm juices. As I sucked on her clitoris, she pushed my head hard into her wetness, and with a muffled scream, she cried. God, yes, she had climaxed, and this time she was fully satisfied. We lay there together, barely able to balance on the wall; we laid as still as we could, letting the cold air from outside cool us down. We eventually started to move. We got up and every now and again would steal a kiss from each other as we managed to dress ourselves.

We had a slow drive back to Rosa. We spoke very freely of our day together. On the way back we were so both relaxed and chilled out, it was the most peaceful feeling ever. On the drive back, Pippa had moved her hand across and placed it on my leg every now and then she would either squeeze or rub my leg up and down.

We got back to Rosa's house about 8.30 pm that night, we walked in together and Rosa with a smile on her face said: "have you both had a nice day my darlings". Then looked at us and said "oh my God you look soaked" gave us both a peck on the cheek, and said, "up the pair of you go have a shower and get changed and I will have your dinner waiting for you when you come down". As we left the room, she laughed and said no more frolicking around up there.

I want to hear all about your day together. Just as I was leaving to go upstairs I heard Pippa say, "oh Rosa you were so right he is fantastic". Rosa just smiled at her go on Pip, she said: "up you go get out of those wet things you look frozen". I heard Pippa say ouch and laugh. I guess Rosa gave her perk bum a little pinch or something.

I was under the shower first, ran the water until it was just at the right heat. The shower room had totally filled with steam again, just as it did when Rosa and I had had our first shower together. I was washing the soap from my face and opened my eyes and there, to my amazement, was Pippa, totally naked in front of me. I never heard a thing, Pippa said seductively, "help remove the remaining soap from my body". She gently pushed my body to the back wall of the shower, nestled her body against mine, kissed my chest, and said, "oh Adam", I hoped I had enjoyed their day together as much as she had. She said thank you because I had fulfilled one of her sexual fantasies that was making love outside in the rain. And that I had made great love to her and so nicely. I was still standing there against the wall. One of her hands slowly traveled to my limp penis. She took it in her hand, pulled it gently, and said "out you get it's my turn to warm up". And with a wet slap smacked my buttocks, and I left her to have her shower.

I turned to have one more glance at this beauty, but she had vanished into the steam of the shower. Getting changed, I could think of nothing else. But what a perfect day I had with Pippa. As I left the bedroom and headed towards the stairs, Pippa came from the shower room, still naked, the water shining on her skin. We kissed briefly, and I headed down the stairs, when downstairs I was greeted with a loving kiss and a huge cuddle from Rosa. I could not wait and started to tell of how my day had unfolded, but Rosa raised her fingers to my lips shush she said "I'm sure Pippa wants to be part of this too". I smiled at Rosa and she gave me a large glass of wine it was not long before Pippa had come downstairs, she also got a nice kiss from Rosa, we all sat at the table eating our meal and drinking our wine.

Whilst eating the meal, we all took part in the conversation of the day's activities. Once Pippa started talking, neither Rosa nor I could stop her. Was it the excitement of what had happened that day, all I could see was she had such a perfect pink glow about her body, her complexion? About her body, her blonde hair shining like silk.

Pippa was singing my praises so much, and it was great to hear all that Pippa was saying. As I had to remind myself, it was only my second time of full intercourse. Eventually, Pippa got onto the part where the dog walkers were walking past. But up to that point had not left a solitary thing out. I could see how engrossed Rosa was in the story she was hearing, as was I, even though I had very much been a part of it. The dog walkers she continued as she laughed. She said she could sense how frightened I was and explained to Rosa what she had asked me to do. She said, which he did with perfection.

She said how she just waved at the dog walkers and said morning. Rosa smiled mischievously. Then Pippa went on to explain how 90% of people do not actually see what is in front of them. Throughout the course of a day, people misread or not even notice lots of things in life. So she knew that if we just acted normal, the people who were also in a hurry to get out of the bad weather would not off even noticed. Pippa went on to say to Rosa that I deserved a medal for lots of different reasons.

As the evening went on, we spoke about lots of different things.

Rosa said to me, "so Adam, is there anything you would like to know?" Questions for either Pippa or me. I said, "yes there is something I would love to know, but it's a real personal question is that OK?" Rosa said you should know by now there is nothing kept secret from you, and if there was anything at any time I wanted to know all I had to do was just ask and never be worried about the reply. I said yes, I know, but it's personal about your life. She smiled and just said ask away darling. I said, "Rosa, how did you make your money? How are you so rich and well off?". She looked at Pippa and said I will explain she did something years ago that went against all the rules at the time, I just sat there listening to what Rosa was about to say.

Chapter Twelve

She said that when she was younger she and her family never had much money and life was very hard in France. When she got to the age of about thirteen, she noticed that her body had developed far quicker than any of her friend's bodies. She had a body far in advance of her actual age, and at fifteen she was a fully developed woman, and shortly after her 15th birthday her father had been killed in a road traffic accident. They were living not too far out of Paris, and she used to go there to find work of any sort

There was this time that she saw all these half-drunken men going into these burlesque clubs. And as a child, well fifteen years old, I used to wonder what went on inside these clubs. One night I sneaked around to the back entrance to this club when peeking through a window. That was it. I was hooked. She saw all these beautiful women dressed in the most glamorous clothes and fantastic lingerie. She said I so wanted to dress like these ladies. They were beautiful and the smell of perfume escaping from the window she was looking through was amazing, and to top it all off the men inside these clubs were half if not fully drunk, were throwing money or giving money to these fantastically dressed ladies. She said to us, after a few more visits, I was convinced that this is what I wanted to do and that it was a way out of poverty for her and her mother. On one of her many visits to the club, she saw a lady standing outside the back door of this club and they got talking. Rosa said that she was a grand lady and had turned out to become a wonderful, lifelong friend.

The lady's name was Elisa, Elisa told Rosa, as a young girl, how the men would finish work, and with their wages go drinking and end up in these clubs for whatever reason. To see a lady dance for them, though the ladies never actually gave anything more than that, just a dance. For them, even if it may look like they were going to give more. And if the ladies looked like they were going to give more than just a dance, the drunken men would part with even more of their money. Elisa gave Rosa some friendly advice, she said Elisa's words were, it's not the perfect job by any means and not a long-term option. Whilst your looks lasted and you could dance and entice the men to part with their money, you also would earn very good money from these drunken hopeful men.

Rosa said she was spellbound by what Elisa had told her. Elisa said to Rosa is this something that she thought she would want to do? Rosa said she would jump at the chance if given it, but would only be a temporary thing. Although so I thought at the time just to sort out, her's and her mother's financial situation. Elisa asked how old Rosa was, then Rosa said she lied to Elisa and said she was sixteen and a half. That's all Elisa needed to hear that Rosa was old enough legally to work in these clubs.

Within a week Elisa was showing Rosa how to dance to entice the men to part with their money. Elisa taught Rosa, and it was not long before she had become a very well-known dancer locally. The better known she became, the more men would come to watch her, and people would throw money at her. Soon word got around, and men were coming from all over Paris to watch this young Rosa dance. Rosa, not being silly, learned quickly that the men obviously wanted more than just a dance. Then Rosa said the better known I became, the more upmarket the clubs I danced in became.

Rosa said that she seemed to move on from the small clubs where she started and was soon dancing in the top burlesque clubs in Paris. Staying excellent friends with Elisa, Rosa then said that's when I broke the cardinal rule. There was this rich man called Marcus. Marcus would pay her well, well, over the top. Private dances were not heard of back then. When I started she said but I did this for Marcus. Rosa said I had been dancing for about three years and her mother had passed away unexpectedly. It was as if her body just gave up. One minute she was fine, the next she just died. She said I think it was the heartbreak of losing my father. She said her mother just went to sleep one night and never woke up. Rosa said I took a couple of weeks off work as there were no financial problems. Whilst she was taking time off, Marcus came around to see her. She was first confused about how did he know where she lived.

Rosa confided in Marcus. Rosa said she had explained about the death of her mother. Marcus was in his mid-sixties. Rosa then said that Marcus pleaded with her to move in with him, so she was not there alone. He tried to explain to her he only had her interest at heart. He said that he wanted nothing more from her than just her companionship and maybe the occasional dance apart from that your life is your own. For this Marcus said that he would pay Rosa to double what she was earning as a burlesque dancer, and if she agreed, she would live with him in the farmhouse. Marcus's offer took aback Rosa, and in her mind rang the words of Elisa. Was this it, was this the way out of her dancing career?

Rosa said that she asked Marcus for a little time to think about his offer, but said it was a magnificent offer and did not want to look ungrateful. Rosa then said she explained to Marcus that this was a major step in her life. A few weeks had passed she put the idea to her good friend Elisa. Elisa said this is what most girls hoped for, a safe financial way out of the career. Rosa contacted Marcus and asked if his offer was still available. Marcus was so pleased that Rosa had decided to take him up on his offer. Marcus had moved Rosa into the farmhouse within the week.

Chapter Thirteen

Rosa said I stayed with Marcus for about 4 years and he was true to his word. The old man never tried anything on and they too had become great friends. If anything, she was more like a daughter to him and a father figure to her. Marcus had nearly reached his seventieth birthday, and Rosa told us he was struck down with a massive heart attack, and his body was too frail, and he passed away.

Rosa then said I felt lost as I had given up my dancing and now her beneficiary had died. I had lived alongside this great man for nearly four years. Rosa then said to us but I was so scared, where was I going to end up now the old house that she had lived in with her parents was sold. That really had no monetary value, so received nothing from that. After the death of Marcus, where was I now meant to go. What was she going to do as the ways of burlesque dancing had changed in the 4 years she was living with Marcus? These girls had become no more than strippers and private dancers. They were now part of normal activity, and she had been out of the public sector. Rosa said I contacted her old friend Elisa, and she took me straight into her house. I rented a small room from her,

I was only there about a week, and I had received a letter from a solicitor's company. The letter was asking me to meet them, not really knowing what to expect I went to this meeting, so I took my good friend Elisa with me. She said it was nothing to worry about and she would bet that Marcus had somehow taken care of her in his will and maybe left me something. A little keepsake of their time together.

When we arrived at the solicitors, which was a massive grand old building, they refused to let Elisa in. They said they would only let me in. It was like going to a parliamentary office the security was very strict. When inside the building, they asked me to sit in this grand office. A short while later, three solicitors came in. It truly felt more like a criminal court, she said and laughed.

They asked me my name yet again and asked to see some proof of identification. One of these very important men then began to read Marcus's will. And to my astonishment, Marcus had made me the sole beneficiary of his estate. I inherited the old farmhouse and all the cottages on the land, loads of land, and there was also a very substantial amount of money.

Pippa and I were just gob smacked at the detail she went into. Rosa then said you asked Adam. Now I have told you everything, and that is how I am financially self-sufficient

So Adam, now you know of my past and the way I have seen men behave around women. Maybe you can see why I am looking and hoping you are going to become that perfect lover who treats women with equal respect. I am trying to teach you how to love a woman, how a woman wants to be loved, and if I continued the way I was going in return, I would be the best-treated man that there could be.

As always, when Rosa started talking of an evening the hours just seemed to drift away. Before the three of us knew what time it was, it was again the early hours of the morning. We were all exhausted that night, Rosa's story as interesting as it was had sapped all of our strength. We made our way to the bedroom. We all stripped naked, as that was the way Rosa liked us to sleep.

It was good sleeping that way. It seemed to bring us all closer together. We all got into bed that night, me in between the two girls, as always, as I lay there with an arm around each of my beautiful ladies. To feel the warmth and softness of their skin next to mine was the best way to fall asleep, and the mixture of their unique perfumes was enough to send anyone into a night of fantastically deep sleep. Our bodies entwined as though the three of us were one.

Rosa enjoyed sleeping with her head nestled into my neck, and Pippa liked to lie with her head on my chest. I truly believed I was the luckiest man alive. We all eventually fell asleep. This way no funny or sexual business that night, just a beautiful, relaxed sleep.

Chapter Fourteen

We awoke the next morning. This time for a change it was me who was awake first. So I thought I would surprise everyone by getting up and making them breakfast for a change. So I carefully got up, trying my hardest not to wake either of them. I went down to the kitchen and made them breakfast. Still no disturbances from upstairs. I took the breakfasts up to them. As I walked into the room, they were still fast asleep. I put the breakfast on the side cabinet, walked over, and gave them both a gentle kiss. Said morning ladies as they sat up. They both smiled at me and were very grateful for what I had done as they came around from their sleep. At that time of the morning, Pippa always seemed full of life. Rosa, on the other hand, seemed very reserved, maybe a little down, I asked are you OK Rosa. Pippa now up and in the shower, I lay next to Rosa and said "what's wrong? You seem a little low". Nothing really, just a little low. I gave her a kiss and said, why both Pippa and I are so happy to be with you. Rosa said that she hoped she was not being left out of the relationship. As she said this, Pippa walked back into the room. Pippa lay the other side of Rosa and we both reassured her that there was no way she would ever be left out, she smiled and said she was a little concerned because of the age gap differences between us all. Pippa being ten years older than me and Rosa being twenty years older. Both

Pippa and I said at exactly the same time, as if it were rehearsed.

Rosa, you will not ever be left out or behind in this relationship, and that she was the one who made all of this possible and held us together. I got up from the bed when Rosa seemed a little more like her old self. I took the breakfast things downstairs. Twenty minutes had passed and there was no sign of the girls. I made my way to the bedroom to see what was holding them up. As I walked into the room, the top sheet had been peeled back. There was Rosa laying on the bed looking as good as she always did, laying there naked on the bed, Pippa kneeling by the side of her, she too was still naked.

The morning sun burst through the blinds of the windows as the sun hit the two girls' bodies it was as if the two girls were under a soft spotlight, the sun catching every contort of their perfect bodies. Both lady's breasts shinning as though they had just been molded, Pippa lent forward, her long blond hair settling on Rosa's tanned skin. Pippa's hands gently trembling over Rosa's body, Rosa's hands were gently stroking Pippa's arms. Pippa was now kissing Rosa gently on her neck and one of her hands gently stroking Rosa's legs. Pippa then moved her head to Rosa's shoulders. I was now sitting on the old rocking chair in the room's corner. I kept silent and just watched what the two girls were doing, what seemed to come so naturally to them. I could hear Rosa saying to Pippa that she had missed her touch. Pippa was being so soft and gentle with Rosa, her lips barely touching Rosa's. She kissed the top half of Rosa's body, Pippa now moving her soft lips to Rosa's breasts, circling Rosa's nipples. I could hear Rosa. Not very loud, but definite groans of pleasure were coming from Rosa as Pippa worked her magic on her.

I saw that every time Pippa's lips moved closer or passed over Rosa's nipples, her mouth would envelop her dark, hardened nipples and Pippa would give a prolonged suck on these things. I could now clearly hear Rosa groaning with pleasure as Pippa was doing what she did. I was still sitting there quiet as a mouse, looking and listening; I did not realize that someone could be kissed so sensually, just hardly touching Rosa's body and the other person enjoy it so much.

Pippa, without lifting her head from Rosa's chest, looked across at me, and with the other hand that was caressing Rosa's leg, she beckoned me to come to them. I slowly stood up and placed my dressing gown on the back of the chair. I silently made my way to the bed. I could see Rosa was enjoying Pippa's every touch, Rosa's hands now massaging Pippa's head, playing and running her fingers through this lady's blonde hair. I knelt at the end of the bed. Rosa's feet were right in front of my face, Pippa now enjoying Rosa's breasts and her shoulders. I moved my hands to Rosa's feet, gently massaging them with my hands. When I first touched them, she jumped a little. As I was massaging one of them, I could not help myself. She had fantastic feet and perfect toes. As I held her feet in my hand, I began to lick the outer edge of her feet. Every now and again, my mouth was finding its way around Rosa's feet. I would suck on one of her beautiful toes.

In turn, I took every one of her toes into my mouth. Rosa was now enjoying what both Pippa, and I were doing to her. I then licked the top side of Rosa's feet and my tongue soon found her ankle bones, which I kissed and sucked on them in turn. My tongue was eager to experience this lady's body, my tongue now tracing the contours of every bone in her foot. Then, with one hand, I was massaging one of Rosa's legs as I licked my way slowly up to the knee, then back down. The back of her leg tracing the outline of her calf muscle to her ankle. I had been trying to mimic how I had seen Pippa kissing and nibbling at Rosa previously. It seemed to take forever I spent a long time kissing and circling her calf muscle. I then slowly licked the full length of her leg going above her knees, as one hand was kissing and now nibbling at Rosa's thigh. My other hand was now massaging her other leg, just gently touching and massaging, as I did this with Pippa.

Had now positioned herself on top of Rosa. She was now facing Rosa and was now covering her hands in this warm lavender oil that Rosa kept just to the side of her bed.

Pippa was now massaging oil into her shoulders, neck, and breasts. While Pippa was working her nimble fingers on Rosa, I too was doing my best to please Rosa in every way. I could see that Pippa was gliding back and forth on Rosa, my tongue now licking and sucking on her inner thigh. While doing this, I saw one of Pippa's hands come back while massaging Rosa with one hand. Her other pushing my head towards Rosa's warm moist vagina I did not put up any struggle and pretty soon my tongue was licking and sucking at this lady's warm moist vagina. Rosa's hands, which were also covered in this oil, were now massaging, tweaking, and pulling at Pippa's breasts. I could hear from Pippa's reaction that Rosa was now also satisfying Pippa.

Pippa was now gliding back and forth on Rosa's body with more speed. The lavender oil that Pippa has used had now managed to get under the softness of Pippa. Pippa was using this to her advantage, rubbing her smooth vagina against her lover Rosa, just as if Pippa was moving back and forth on a penis. The faster that Pippa rode Rosa, the wetter Rosa became. Rosa then opened her legs wide apart. I repositioned myself so I could take full advantage of her warm, moist vagina.

I too was just barely touching Rosa with my tongue. I moved my head up to Rosa's clitoris and was circling this erect part of her. As I had moved up, I had slowly inserted just one of my fingers inside her moistness, first gentle circular movements, then after a while I moved my finger as though it were a small penis. I kept feeling Rosa wriggle to the movements of my finger, which was now well lubricated by her warm juices, my tongue still licking and flicking her now erect clitoris. I kept feeling Rosa still continue to wriggle and shudder occasionally, while Pippa and I were doing what we doing. Pippa lent forward and was now kissing Rosa's neck as she did this. She exposed her pink oil-drenched, equally wet vagina.

While I was playing with Rosa, with my fingers and tongue, my mouth moved from Rosa's wetness just up to Pippa. As my fingers continued to please Rosa, my mouth was sampling Pippa's warm moist vagina, both my tongue and mouth working in unison with each other. I had my mouth firmly over Pippa's moistness, sampling as much of her as I was able to. I could hear both girls still moaning and groaning as we were all pleasing each other in what we were doing. Rosa massaging Pippa's back and shoulders. The girls were now laying belly to belly and both moist vaginas were in front of me. I was now standing upright behind them, my hand intermingling with Rosa's on Pippa's back.

Both Rosa and my hands were covered in oil as we rubbed and massaged Pippa's back. Every now and again Rosa and my own fingers would lock together and our fingers tied in a knot and we would squeeze each other's hands gently together. Whilst doing this with our hands, Pippa was now sandwiched between us. I slowly re-positioned myself again and moved my now throbbing penis towards Rosa's soaked vagina. As we squeezed each other's hands once again, I held her hands longer. I pulled on her hands and slowly but surely I entered Rosa's wet vagina and continued to push until the full length of my penis was deep inside this lovely lady. As I did this Rosa shifted just a little to accommodate my penis, as I did this her mouth was now firmly sucking and kissing Pippa's neck. I could hear how both girls were enjoying the closeness of each other. I somehow managed to get a little more depth inside Rosa. I felt the walls, the muscles in her vagina, hold my penis tight.

Slowly I moved back and forth inside this lady, her fingers now digging into my buttocks. I could feel her fingernails nearly pierce my skin, and all the time Pippa sandwiched between us. I slowly removed my penis from Rosa, massaging Pippa's back using my hands, which were still entwined with Rosa's. My one freehand now, firmly gripping the long soft blonde hair of Pippa. I tugged on Pippa's hair as I had done with Rosa's hands. With a gentle but steady motion, I was now deep inside Pippa, who was equally as wet as Rosa. My penis went in so smoothly and soon was deep inside Pippa, I felt her fantastic vaginal muscles clamp around my struggling penis. How tight she felt and her vaginal muscles clamped around my penis, but also how very well lubricated she was. Pippa then arched her back and began to suck on Rosa's very hard, erect nipples. As they did this, I leaned forward, and Rosa and I began to kiss. We both felt Pippa stiffen, one hand on my buttock, the other holding Rosa's breast in place as she sucked on it, Rosa and I now biting on each other's lips as we kissed. First Pippa, then me, then Rosa: it was a massive three-way climax, and somehow we had all cum within one minute of each other. We lay there in a twisted human flesh lump, our bodies not wanting or not able to move, and for 20 minutes that's just how it was, as we untangled ourselves.

Chapter Fifteen

When we had overcome what we had just done, I took myself off downstairs and made us all a cuppa. I left the house shortly afterward and took myself off to the outhouse to continue with some work. I was really enjoying working on this old outhouse, as it really looked quite good. I worked hard that day or at least what was remaining of it, putting the finishing touches on my handy work. The wooden floors looked amazing. About three hours had passed. Rosa walked in and smiled, and said "oh you are working really hard here my darling" and gave me a quick kiss. She had some paperwork under her arms and asked me to come over to the table she was sitting. As I walked over to her, she unrolled this massive sheet of paper. She then said, look this is what I have an idea for this old place. The plans looked great, they were plans for a bar area and a stage at the back of the outhouse behind the stage was just a big void area of nothing.

Rosa asked if this was something I could manage, or was she expecting too much? My reply was "well Rosa, I think I am OK with it and would give it my best shot". Rosa said she had every faith in me and my abilities, and smiled. With this, she left me looking over the plans and I seemed to look at them for ages. I worked well into the night that night, doing what I could.

When I got back to the house late that evening, everyone was just relaxing, doing their own thing. Rosa reading her book, and Pippa checking her lesson schedule out for the week. I suppose what you would call a normal evening in any normal house if you could call our situation normal. The day had ended, and we all headed upstairs to bed, me in the middle again. As always, nothing happened that night apart from we all seemed to sleep like logs.

The next morning came, and we were all up very early. We did what we had to do and got ourselves ready for what each of us had in store for that day. I as usual went to work on the outhouse, which actually felt like becoming a bit of an obsession to getting this looking just right. How Rosa had imagined the next couple of weeks just seemed to be filled with all of us doing our work and relaxing of an evening. It was like the sexual encounter had never happened, but it did, they just were not spoken off. But at least I was getting to feel the warmth of these two ladies lying next to me every night, and I was sure few men had the luxury that I had like that.

One night the girls said OK Adam upstairs and get showered it's your birthday tomorrow. We are taking you out somewhere to celebrate, somewhere very special to us. I loved it when the girls surprised me like this, which they did every now and again. The two girls had done themselves up and looked like a couple of princesses, Pippa was in this long red silk dress which went to the floor, it had a very low cut V, which showed off the contours of the shape of her breasts amazingly. The V cut was deep as it reached her naval. She gave me a twirl and the back of the dress was as equally revealing. She had this fantastic pearl necklace, which dangled perfectly between her breasts. She smelt like and looked like an angel. Rosa was dressed just as well. She had a long black dress that was dotted with diamante. Rosa just sparkled in the jeweled dress. Her dress was a different fitting to Pippa's. Rosa's went completely over one shoulder, the other side was cut sloping from the top of the other arm across her firm breasts and cut very low to her hips, Rosa also smelt fantastic.

I was dressed in a black suit which had been laid out on the bed for me. It fit perfectly, a black suit with an electric blue lining a new crisp white shirt. I left the tie on the bed, as I hated wearing ties. I left my shirt unbuttoned. Well, four buttons and a brand new pair of shiny black shoes.

My thoughts were of where we are going. Really, the way we were all dressed, you would think we were going to meet royalty. We all stood talking and admiring each other's outfits and passing compliments to each other. Just then, there was a knock at the door. Was this our taxi? No, Rosa and Pippa had arranged a chauffeur, and this fantastic limousine was sparkling white with blacked-out windows. The chauffeur opened the doors for us. We were being treated as though we were royalty. We all got inside. There were drinks laid on for us and we set off. The car drove around for about an hour, then we pulled up outside this theater. We went inside and we were ushered to our own private box very high in the stalls of the theater. We were very secluded in our box, not overlooked by a soul. The stage looked tiny, as we were so high. Rosa and Pippa had taken me to an opera house. As the hall filled with people way down below us, the hall was at its maximum capacity.

As the show was about to start, the lights dimmed, and it was as if we were the only people there. You could have heard a pin drop. It was amazing. The sounds coming from the opera singers. Their voice seemed to take over your body, mind, and soul. The voices were captivating. As they sang, it was as though they were hypnotizing you with their voices and sort of lead you into the story. The sounds of their voices moved you it somehow made your blood feel cold even though we were warm, we all had goosebumps. I looked across at the two beautiful ladies that I was with. Rosa seemed to be hypnotized by their voices, her glorious dark red lipstick applied perfectly to her lips, sparkling as some light seemed to hit the moistness of her lips.

Pippa was on the other side of me, laid back in her chair, her head also tilted back and she too was captivated by the sound of the singers. You could see the tightness of the skin on her neck as she tilted her head back. Her chest moving up and down, her breathing was so deep. The sight of those two ladies in their entire splendor totally relaxed and overcome by the sounds we were hearing. I too as I was listening to the voices and watching Pippa's chest rise and fall was to becoming hypnotized. I saw Rosa looking at me as she whispered, "so Adam, are you enjoying the show?" As she said this, Rosa had licked her lips. Her lips shone like a juicy ripe apple, so perfectly ripe you wanted to eat them. She very quietly stood up, crept quietly around the back of Pippa.

Pippa replied in just barely a whisper, "hello baby!". As Pippa said this, Rosa knelt behind Pippa and gave her neck a kiss. As Rosa did this, she used one of her hands and very slowly unzipped the back of Pippa's dress, and slowly lowered her shoulder strap to her dress. This exposed Pippa's breasts, rising and falling as she was breathing, still so deep.

The singing was still as powerful as ever. I moved to the edge of my seat. I knelt in front of Pippa. I began to run my hands very lightly over Pippa's breasts as they still continued to rise and fall with her breathing. Very gently flicking her nipples as my hands passed over her goose-bumped erect nipples, I heard in such a quiet voice Pippa say to Rosa "oh yes". Rosa now kissing and nibbling at Pippa's neck. I moved my hands closer to Pippa's waist. I then moved my tongue to her breasts that were still rising and falling with every breath she took. My mouth had soon covered the erect pink nipples of Pippa's breasts. Pippa's hand had now gently clasped my head, and it felt as though each time she breathed, her hand would push my head firmly onto her breast that little harder. Pippa's other hand now stretching back and had found Rosa inside her dress. Pippa was now also stroking the inner thigh of Rosa's legs. It was strange as not a word was spoken, not even the tiniest of sounds made apart from the occasional groan of pleasure from Pippa. I was moving slowly from one breast to the other, my saliva now glistening at the hint of any light that hit her breasts. Rosa was now kneeling at the other side of Pippa. We both now had one of her little pink rockets in each of our mouths. Pippa now silently massaging both of our heads. As we did this, Rosa had moved across to my shirt and had put one of her hands inside. She was now flicking and tweaking my nipples. Was I going to be able to keep as quiet as Pippa had been? Rosa's touch was so special and every time Rosa touched me, without fail, I would achieve a perfect erection. It only seemed fair that Pippa and I returned the favor we had received from Rosa.

My hand now had found a way inside Rosa's dress. Rosa had not worn any knickers that night, and straight away I could feel the heat and moistness from her vagina. As all this was going on, my hand had found this angel's opening very slowly and delicately. I inserted just one finger as I entered Rosa. I heard her gasp and take a deep breath. From there I did not have to do a lot. Rosa treated my finger as though it were a small penis, and she slowly gyrated and pushed on my finger. Rosa had now taken full charge of Pippa's breasts and her erect nipples, which freed my head. It just seemed the next natural move, and I moved my head to Pippa's moist vagina. I began just as I had before, my tongue now with the tiniest of licks licking the labia of Pippa's very moist vagina. I worked my tongue up this lady's little channel of love. Rosa now had her hand clasped gently around my penis softly but firm enough so she did not lose grip of it. She was giving me the most sensual masturbation ever, bringing me to bursting point. It was about thirty minutes of total pleasure, the three of us enjoying each other as we had always done, no matter where we were.

We reluctantly stopped what we were doing, we all very quietly straightened ourselves and without a sound returned to our own chairs. While sitting there, we were rubbing our hands over each other and watched the remainder of the show. It had certainly warmed up in that little box high in the stools. The remainder of the show was fantastic, as was what we had just experienced with each other. We were getting our stuff together. I could hardly believe what had happened in that box, the excitement and sexual fulfillment and not even actually having intercourse.

We made our way to our awaiting car. We had a lovely trip home again I felt like a king sat between these two ladies. The journey home had not seemed to have taken long at all. I was being cuddled and kissed the entire way home. Every so often, I would feel one of the girls just gently stroke my penis. I could not say which one it was, as I had my eyes closed and was in heaven. Rosa then spoke, "so then, my beautiful Adam, how is your birthday going so far?" I went to speak and just could not find the words. I was so relaxed and managed to stutter, then pulled myself together. I had so much to say. Eventually, all I could manage was "fantastic you and Pippa are so good to me you are just the best".

When we got back to Rosa's, we more or less went straight up to the bedroom. They told me to lay there, and that's what I did. I watched as these two beautiful ladies gave me a very erotic striptease, the two girls slowly stripping each other. First, Pippa, she stripped Rosa, slowly unbuttoning her dress and letting her dress fall to the floor. There she stood, a perfectly shaped woman tanned from head to toe. You could not fault this woman she was flawless.

Pippa was standing behind her, kissing the back of her neck. One hand on her shoulder, the other hand gently tracing the line of her spine. Then, Rosa, it was her turn to strip Pippa. Rosa was facing

Pippa, Rosa put her arms around Pippa, unzipping her dress, revealing her naked shoulders. Then letting Pippa's dress fall to the floor as she had just done to her. As Pippa's dress fell to the floor, Rosa moved her hands to Pippa's shoulders. Lowering her head slightly, and began kissing Pippa's perfect-shaped bosom. The two girls kissed, standing there in front of me for a while. It was a wonderful sight to see these two girls acting so naturally in front of me, not a care in the world.

I kicked off my shoes and unbuttoned the rest of my shirt. The two ladies saw what I had done and made their way to join me on the bed. The two girls just laying either side of me, rubbing my head or shoulders, Pippa was lying on her back. Our heads turned to face each other just, and only just close enough to kiss. Every so often our tongues entwined with each other, and one of Pippa's hands now traveled the length of my torso. Rosa in the meantime had lowered her head to Poppa's vagina before she had settled in properly with Pippa. She had removed the bottom half of my clothing.

There was Rosa now, settled at both Pippa's vagina and my penis area. Rosa was playing with my rock-hard penis with one hand while her other hand was satisfying Pippa with her tongue. I could see in Pippa's eyes how much she was enjoying what Rosa was doing to her. All three of us had our hands moving across each other. It was hard to tell who was touching who.

I heard Pippa groan with pleasure as Rosa had worked her tongue deep into her vagina, Rosa still gently rubbing my throbbing penis. Rosa lifted her mouth from Pippa's vagina. Rosa did not hesitate and moved her warm mouth over the top of my penis and enveloped the entire length of my penis with her mouth. I could feel the dampness of Pippa's vagina now being smoothed over the full length of my penis via Rosa's mouth. Rosa's hand was now playing a big part in Pippa's enjoyment. Pippa was riding Rosa's fingers, bucking and squirming to Rosa's every move. After a while, Rosa moved up and was now joining us, kissing. When we were kissing, it was hard to tell whose tongue was whose. As the kissing became more frantic, Pippa moved away from the three of us. She went down to my penis area, with her back to us she straddled me and took my penis in her hand, moving back a little more. Inserting my wanting, throbbing penis inside her. Rosa saw what was happening and without saying a word she knew exactly what to do, as if a script had been written.

Pippa was now in reverse cowgirl position, riding my penis hard and deep, pulling herself forward to get the maximum effect from my stretched, throbbing penis. Rosa positioned herself behind Pippa, kissing her neck and spine, and as she did this, her kisses traveled down the length of Pippa's spine. Rosa pushed her vagina closer to my face. I so wanted to taste this lady again. With a slight push from Rosa, I had her vagina level with my mouth. As Rosa moved up and down Pippa's back I would have Rosa's vagina in my mouth one second, then the next would be faced with her bum. Every time her bum was in front of my face, I would lick the entrance. I could feel the smooth, tight skin touch my tongue and could not help but lick, as I had been doing to her vagina. Rosa seemed to really like this as she would push towards my tongue, and I very slightly entered her bum with my tongue. Each time I did this, she would give a small shudder. Rosa's hands clasped around the front of Pippa, holding her breasts as she frantically rode my penis, rising and falling harder and faster with every stride. It was as if she were in full canter as she was riding one of her horses as she rode me. Her hands had cupped my very tender testicles.

I moved my tongue from Rosa's bum and slowly moved it down along her septum. Rosa liked this. I could hear her groaning with pleasure. I eventually found her now very moist vagina. My tongue was at this lady, trying in desperation to sample every drop of juice this lady had to offer. Pippa was so good at what she was doing I felt every movement from her damp but firm vagina as she rubbed the full length of my now about to burst penis. Somehow the two girls climaxed at the same time, as if they could sense I was about to burst myself. Both girls had now moved and were both between my legs, Pippa said "any time you're ready Adam so are we". We want to feel you climax for a change and wanted me to explode and climax in front of them as they massaged the testicles, gently rubbing on my penis. I could hold back no longer, my whole body tensed and I climaxed it was huge. I was sure it was two, maybe three climaxes in one go, the two girls were there and licking and smearing my sperm over my now going soft penis. I pulled the two girls up to my head gently by their hair and we lay together. Just kissing and as we were going to sleep both Rosa and Pippa said "Happy Birthday darling" then we all fell to sleep.

Chapter Sixteen

The morning came and as I come round from my sleep, there was no one to be seen. I just lay there in bed, just thinking about how lucky I was. I got up, showered, and went downstairs. There were my two ladies sitting at the kitchen table waiting for me. "Good Morning Adam," they both said, and both gave me a kiss and wished me a Happy Birthday. The two girls each gave me a card. Rosa's card read Happy Birthday, my perfect lover, and thanks for all you have done for me in the past year.

Pippa's card read; Happy Birthday lover, have a great day. She had drawn a big smiley face. We all sat together having our breakfast. It was the best breakfast ever. Everything you could wish for. The girls had left the table and when I finished, I too walked into the living room. Rosa said, "OK Adam, sit down, it's present time". Pippa gave me a massive box, very nicely wrapped up. As I opened the box, there was a picture of the latest camera. With a top-of-the-range professional camera a tripod and loads of extras, I could not believe how lucky I was. I jumped out of my seat and walked over to her, and held her for what seemed to be an eternity. Giving her a kiss, I could not thank her enough for what she had got me.

Rosa just looked at me and smiled, and she gave me what looked like a bar of chocolate. I unwrapped it and it was a bar of well-known chocolate. I smiled at her and said "thanks darling" she said, "well don't be greedy share it then". Who was I to say a thing, for what the previous evening had cost the girls was far more than I expected for my birthday. But I did as Rosa instructed and was about to unwrap the chocolate. I noticed there was a key sell taped to the back of the chocolate. I looked at the two girls, and Rosa and Pippa were just smiling, trying to hold back a laugh.

Rosa said Adam I have to put you out of your misery. Look out the window. As I pulled back the curtains there stood a brand new warrior pickup truck, black and shining like a pearl. The truck was facing the house, and I noticed it had a private number plate that read 4D4M. It overwhelmed me with excitement I just walked to Rosa and said, "why so much?" Rosa just replied, "you worth every penny, Adam, and it is not about the money". I gave her as equally long a kiss as I had given to Pippa, but just could not let go of Rosa and repeatedly was saying thank you.

I spent most of that day just sitting in the new truck, and going through the different modes on my camera, and all the time thinking just how lucky I was.

About halfway through the day, Pippa came out with a tea in her hand and gave me a kiss and cuddled me. She said some more good news Adam I have got your driving test date through I could not be happier my life was so perfect.

Pippa produced some L plates and said come on then stick them on the truck. Then I went back into the house and spent the rest of the day with the two girls. It was great spending my birthday with these two ladies well in my life. We spent the day relaxing around the house, watching films, just chilling out with each other. Me playing about with my new camera and getting up every five minutes just to look at the truck, just to make sure this was not a dream.

The day seemed to drift away at a very nice pace. The evening came, and I was still up and down at the window every so often. We had drunk about three or four bottles of wine that day. Bedtime came, and we all went off to bed together. Nothing like the previous night, but we were all still as relaxed and comfortable as the previous night.

We all fell asleep just holding each other in a nice, caring embrace. As we were drifting off, Rosa said she hoped I had had a nice day and a great birthday. I replied, "yes, of course, Rosa you and Pippa are and have been so great to me". Pippa just kissed me on the cheek and we all fell into a really heavy, deep sleep, more like a beautiful, peaceful coma.

Chapter Seventeen

When we woke the next morning, I went straight down to the outhouse. Well, after looking at my truck and still going through the different modes on my camera. After working in the outhouse for a few hours, Rosa came in with this other lady that I had not seen before. Rosa introduced me to this lady her name was Victoria. Rosa said this is the young man that I have told you about. I pushed out my hand as if to shake her hand but she lent forward and gave a small kiss on the cheek.

Rosa then said to Victoria that I had converted the old outhouse into this what she now saw. Both women were equally impressed with the work carried out. Victoria then said, well I would like to have my entire house renovated at some point in the near future, and would I be able to fit her into my work schedule. Rosa standing behind her winked at me, smiled, and nodded her head as if to say yes. I said yes, I would love to, and with this, both ladies left the outhouse and I returned to my work installing the stage.

The work on the stage was very near completion, so I took myself back up to the house. As we were eating our meal and yet another bottle of wine, Pippa came out with "Oh Adam you have your driving test next Monday". Wow, I was going to be able to drive my new truck alone, without supervision. The theory test I had somehow managed to pass, so this was the only thing stopping me. A few more evenings passed, and it was just normal everyday life, if you could call what the three of us had normal. I like to think it was very normal and loving.

Chapter Eighteen

The day of my test came round swiftly. As I left with Pippa that morning, Rosa was at the door and just gave me a kiss and said good luck. Pippa said he will be fine. So this time Pippa drove us to the test center, and she said just relax and you will pass with flying colors. When we got there, this really old-looking guy came out of the center, not a very chatty type of person, even a little cold in his mannerisms. We went through the normal stuff a few questions and he then asked me to read this number plate.

Pretty soon we were off, Pippa just said relax and concentrate. I drove around with this man for about twenty minutes, but God. It truly felt like hours. There were no signs in his face to as how I was doing. We got back to the test center and with the same emotionless face said "well done I'm happy to say you have passed" and for the first time managed what looked like half a smile. He gave a nod to Pippa. She came running over well done, well done, she repeated. We phoned Rosa, who would by now be wondering how I had got on, and gave her the good news. Pippa said, "OK let's go!" I said "where were we going?" and she said "back to the house, we have to change cars. You can take Rosa and I out in your truck", so that's what we did, and I drove as though I was still on my test only one thing different I had a happy Pippa next to me and not that sour-faced old man.

As we pulled into the driveway, Rosa was waiting at the door. Not a lot was said. I jumped out of Pippa's car and into my truck, quickly followed by the two girls. Pippa gave me the directions to drive, and it was not long before I knew exactly where we were going. It was Pippa's stables. When there we got out of the car and walked across the stable yard to that little old tack room, as soon as all three of us were in there Pippa just said OK Adam do your stuff.

I nearly choked they laughed at me and said with a smile on their faces put the kettle on. I thought oh OK but really was up for a repeat performance of what happened the last time I was in this tack room. As I set about making us all a drink, Pippa walked across the room and locked the door. I turned to look at Rosa and there was this angel sitting there on that 2ft wall with her skirt hitched halfway up her thigh. Pippa joined her on the wall and both my girls were now sitting there on those old, hairy horse blankets.

Pippa slowly pulled her own skirt off, easing it gently over her thighs. Rosa now unbuttoned her thin white blouse, nearly completely undone. Rosa was sitting there, just looking at me. Her eyes saying everything that she needed to. With just one of her fingers gently touching the exterior of her mouth, her own finger barely caressed her own lip. The look she was giving me was one-off I am going to eat you, or at least that's the way I liked to think she was looking. While now sucking on her own finger, the other hand was now inside her own blouse and her hand circling her own nipple.

Pippa was now naked apart from a small black thong she was wearing. Pippa was sorting out some old horse reins that were hanging from the rafters of this tack room. There seemed to be horse reins hanging from every rafter so low they were nearly touching the small wall.

Rosa still had not said a word. She just sat there sucking on one of her fingers erotically whilst her other hand still gliding over her own nipple. With her back to the wall of the tack room, Pippa was now tying each of Rosa's ankles to the reins that she had strategically placed over the rafters. Still, Rosa said nothing, just a glazed look in her eyes as if she were really not there or not thinking about what Pippa was now doing to her ankles.

Soon Rosa's feet, ankles, and legs were securely fastened. Pippa gave a slight tug and pull on the reins and began to lift Rosa's legs very slowly. Very gently Pippa then got this saddle and placed it over the wall just in front of Rosa, and a stirrup hung down each side of the wall. As she did this, all Rosa did was smile. Pippa came walking over to me she kissed me on the neck and whispered, OK, Adam, you have passed your driving test now is your first riding lesson so just watch.

She went over to the old locker in the tack room and fiddled about in there for a while. As she left the locker she had a plastic/rubber penis and it had straps attached to it. It really looked realistic apart from the rings that went around it from top to bottom. Rosa had now adjusted herself and was now laying on her back with her legs held securely in place by the reins. Pippa standing there, looking fantastic as the sun shone through the tack room window. Now totally naked, she turned and smiled at me. As she did this, I could see she had attached the strap-on penis to herself this looked weird, to see such a beautiful woman as she was but with a penis, it looked so realistic it was scary. Rosa still lying on the wall, her blouse totally unbuttoned and her own hands caressing her own nipples. Pippa was standing in front of Rosa, applying some lubricant gel to her fake penis.

Pippa then said watch Adam, this is how you ride and smiled at Rosa. She mounted the saddle as though it were on a horse and not the little wall. Pippa held Rosa's legs, giving them a kiss. As she did this, she pulled Rosa's legs slightly towards her. Whilst kissing and pulling at Rosa's legs, she inch by inch slowly inserted her realistic penis into Rosa's wanting, damp vagina. Pippa said just watch and listen to Adam.

Pippa gave me a blow-by-blow account of what was happening and what she was doing with this penis she had inserted into herself and fully entered Rosa, who seemed to really be enjoying what Pippa was doing to her. She was grinding her pelvis in a circular motion onto Pippa and that penis. Both Pippa and I could hear now much Rosa was enjoying herself from the groans of pleasure coming from Rosa.

Then Pippa started speaking to me. That in itself was weird, but she said first get yourself comfortable on the saddle. Pippa rocked from side to side still inside Rosa, adjusting her stirrups, Pippa's leg now bent right uptight and looked something like a race jockey. She pushed her pelvis forward just to make sure they were both comfortable. Pippa began to push down in the stirrups and lifted her tiny, cute buttocks from the saddle. As she lifted and settled back down to the saddle, her plastic friend was pushing in and out of Rosa's wetness.

Pippa continued to ride Rosa and the saddle for a few minutes longer. Nothing further was said to me as both the girls seemed to be locked onto each other and their eye contact was never broken. There were plenty of pleasant sounds coming from both ladies, so I guess they were enjoying themselves, and they looked like they had done this many times before.

Rosa appeared she could not get enough of what Pippa was now doing to her. As Pippa was moving her buttocks up and down in the saddle, Rosa would push herself onto Pippa, watching this as it was like Rosa and Pippa were actually having full sex. Pippa spoke to me again she said the next move is the most comfortable for both, it's called canter. Rosa's arms now desperately tried to hold Pippa's legs as she moved about. Pippa then sat firmly in the saddle and just rocked her pelvis back and forth. Rosa still seemed to be enjoying whatever Pippa wanted to do to her. It was weird but very erotic to see these two girls making love to each other.

Rosa was in a state of ecstasy as the two girls made love. She was biting her bottom lip. Pippa began to move faster and faster as Rosa's groans of pleasure became louder, Pippa placing one of her hands gently over Rosa's mouth to muffle the loudness of her groans. As she did this, Rosa began sucking on one of Pippa's fingers, and I saw Rosa shudder and stiffen and her eyes close. That was it Pippa had made Rosa climax, as Rosa lay there Pippa untied Rosa's leg and the two girls just lay balancing together on the little wall.

Shortly afterward Rosa said are you OK with what you have just seen. Adam, this is the sort of thing that Pippa and I did before you came along and we thought you would like to see what we used to do. She said she hoped I was not offended, and it was meant to be a surprise for me. It blew my mind away I could not believe what I had just witnessed. I could not believe that two women could enjoy each other so completely and fully sexually and not even a real penis in sight. In truth, I could not wait for me to start riding these two girls as they had just done. Although it was enjoyable to watch, I felt a bit like a privileged, stable boy.

They both smiled at me and giggled and said "we are glad and hoped you enjoyed that Adam?" Rosa then said, "so do you think you are up for riding now then, Adam?" I could not get my words out fast enough and started to stutter, but eventually managed a yes at the top of my voice. Once again, both girls giggled and smiled at me.

On hearing this, Rosa wasted no time at all. She gave Pippa another kiss, then slowly laid Pippa down on the wall. This time Pippa's hands were tied with the reins to the wall behind her and also had her legs tied as Rosa's were. Rosa was being ever so gentle with Pippa as she restrained her ankles and legs. Rosa helped Pippa move into a comfortable position on the wall. This time the saddle was removed, and Rosa said that I was just to sit on the wall. I had the real thing: a real penis, and was becoming more aroused with every word from Rosa. This time Rosa produced a blindfold and proceeded to place this over Pippa's eyes. I think Rosa had a liking for blindfolds, as she had done this to me once or twice before.

Pippa wondered what was going on and Rosa said don't worry and was just to think of it as blinkers. Both girls again giggled. I moved closer to Pippa, looking at her as the sun hit her body, as if to highlight every glistening part of her.

Rosa said she would help me as this was my first riding lesson and smiled at me. Pippa was not able to do anything as her hands were fastened behind her.

Rosa stood there naked, holding a horse riding whip in one hand. Even though I was very sexually excited, the sight of the whip did worry me as to who was going to feel this whip and how hard were they going to feel it. Rosa with a cheeky smile looked at me and said OK Adam, mount your filly, but remember she is a lady and remember everything I have shown and said to you.

I began by gently caressing Pippa's flat stomach, just barely touching her. My hands soon moved to this lady's perfectly shaped breasts. Feeling the roundness of her beautiful, firm breasts, my fingers occasionally passed over her nipples. I leaned forward as far as I could and started to kiss Pippa's neck, still teasing her beautiful breasts. As I leaned forward, I felt my throbbing penis gently stoke against the entrance of her wet vagina. I so wanted to push straight inside this lady. Pippa was moaning and groaning to my kisses and hopefully my touch. I heard Rosa say to me "no Adam wait", I dare not overstep the mark or do as I had wished to do. As Rosa was still standing there whip in hand and was not relishing the thought of her whipping my back.

I slowly worked my tongue down the front of Pippa's body. Just gentle, nibbling kisses. As I kissed Pippa, I felt the coldness of Rosa's whip trace along the line of my spine. It made me feel so goosebumpy, but at the same time seemed to increase the size of my erection. I found it a bit of a turn-on, but my mind was a whirl and I was fearful of Rosa's whip or what she may do with it. I still continued to work my mouth over Pippa's body, trying to sample every inch of flesh she had, my fingers tweaking at this lady's nipples. One of my hands had worked its way down to Pippa's wanting, damp vagina, my tongue now fully involved with the folds of Pippa's dampened labia. Pippa was grinding as much as she could onto my head as I did what I was doing with my tongue. Pippa was trying to push the fullness of her vagina on to my face with each movement of my tongue. Rosa had been on her knees by the side of us, and while I was doing to Pippa what I was. Rosa had been masturbating my penis very slowly, and I myself was at a bursting point.

As I continued to work my mouth on Pippa's moistness, I felt her stiffen and my tongue become wetter. Pippa had climaxed but hoped that no one had noticed, as did not want what was ending. If Rosa did not stop what she was doing, I too would have climaxed and it would off all been over.

As if Rosa could sense this in my body, she slowly stopped what she was doing and removed her mouth and the grip of her hand. This time it was different, as she never removed the saliva from my penis, but left it wet from the actions of her mouth. Then Rosa gave her commands as she said, "OK Adam, move closer to Pippa." I was moving closer as she was speaking, as I really wanted to sample Pippa. Rosa had seen that the restraints holding Pippa's hands were becoming loose and with this dealt with it. Rosa retied the restraints around Pippa's wrists. This time Rosa was taking no chances and tied the restraints very hard. As she pulled on the last rein to secure Pippa, Pippa let out a yelp as Rosa must have got carried away. As Rosa was tying Pippa, I moved even closer to her. I pushed with a gentle but continuous motion until my penis had now entered Pippa's moistness. Pippa gasped as I entered her. Oh, God, she said in a pleasurable voice, Rosa watching our every move and standing there with the whip in hand. "OK, Adam", she said standing there like a dominatrix madam, "I would like you to try rising trot as Pippa had shown me earlier." As I rose and lowered, I could feel Pippa's legs trying to clasp my body and pull me deeper into her moistness.

I held Pippa's legs, as she was slightly shorter than Rosa. The restraints had not been adjusted, so this made Pippa's body rise slightly from the wall. As I held Pippa's leg and was pulling on them, I felt her buttocks gently slap my legs. Pippa was biting her lips, her groans of pleasure increasing with every movement. She was pulling like crazy at the restraints that held her hands away from me. You could hear the wooden walls of the tack room creak as she was pulling so hard. Rosa and I heard I say under her breath oh god this is nice, and that she needed to touch me as this was torture. Rosa was relentless in her dominatrix role holding the whip to Pippa's lips and said shush, then ordered me to go straight to the canter position I had witnessed earlier with Pippa and herself.

Rosa straddled the wall and was now facing me, standing above Pippa as I make love to her. Rosa lowered her own soft vagina to Pippa's eager mouth now, wanting to have an active part in what was happening. As Rosa lowered her moist vagina to Pippa's mouth, I heard and saw Rosa stiffen. Pippa was now darting her little tongue hard inside Rosa's moist vagina. Rosa lowered even more so her lover Pippa could take full advantage of her.

Still making love to Pippa and somehow managing to hold off from climaxing myself, I pushed deep inside Pippa. I lent slightly forward and cupped Rosa's head in one of my hands; I directed her head to mine and our mouths met. We were kissing very heavily, our tongues entwined. Pippa was still frantically swinging her own pelvis as hard onto my penis as she could, her tongue still deep inside her lover. My other hand now tweaking and twisting gently at Rosa's very erect nipples. Rosa, still holding the whip, had stretched her arm back and was running the whip across Pippa's torso. We were all in a massive sexual knot, for a choice of better words I could hold on no more. I held Rosa's head hard onto my face. As we kissed, I pushed as deep inside Pippa as I could and just froze. I felt my own body shudder, and that was it until I climaxed inside Pippa. As I did this I also felt her body tense as she climaxed again, with all this going on Rosa had sunk hard onto Pippa's mouth and to was climaxing. Pippa, not wasting a droplet of her lover's juice, as this happened we heard some car pull up in the yard car park. So as quietly and quickly as we could straighten ourselves out, the restraints that held Pippa's hand had been pulled very tight, and the knots were hard to untie. Maybe just because we were in a hurry and did not want to get caught in the situation we were all in.

As we straightened ourselves out, we touched each other lovingly and grabbed the occasional kiss. We tidied up the tack room. We were all exhausted after our tack room adventure. We then made our way back to Rosa's. We got back to Rosa's, and we all headed upstairs for a shower. Even though the experience was beautiful, the smells from the tack room were not quite so alluring.

Rosa was the first in the sower, closely followed by Pippa. The two girls were in there for ages and not a sound could be heard. I got fed up with waiting my turn so went and see what the holdup was. When I opened the door, I could not see a thing as the steam from the shower had filled the room yet again the only thing I could hear from the depths of the mist was the two girls giggling again.

Quietly and slowly, I walked through the mist-filled room. There was Pippa she had totally covered Rosa in soap, she looked like some sort of sexy snow woman. As I got closer, a hand grabbed at mine and I was pulled to the floor and before I knew what was happening, I was lying on the floor of the shower room. Both these beautiful women were washing and soaping my body and washing every part of me. Again there was this beautiful smell of lavender. I still lay on the floor and was rinsed off, all the soap washed away. I lay on the floor for a while like a fish out of water, not knowing what to expect next. The shower had been turned off. As the mist cleared, I saw Rosa and Pippa just standing there. Their skin all shining, the light making their skin glow even more. From where I was laying the girls looked like a couple of angels.

Rosa stretched out her hand and helped me from the floor. We all very slowly dried each other. When all of us were dry, Rosa and Pippa led me to the bedroom, all of us still naked, sat on the edge of the bed. Rosa said to me, "well Adam, my lover, you really are not a virgin anymore". She smiled then said, "so Adam, tell me what have you learned?" I thought for a while, being hypnotized by the fragrance from the room. I began to talk. I said, "I think I have learned to make love and sort of thing, I'm OK at it!", as I found myself speaking to my Rosa, I found myself wanting her again.

Rosa said I still have a bit to learn, she said "yes you are very good but remember Adam you're going to be the perfect lover, not just someone who knows how to make love!". I replied, "yes Rosa, that's the person I want to be." Rosa said, "yes so far we have had some amazing sex and fantastic experiences and been very fulfilling."

There is so much more, she explained. When she and Pippa make love and there are no adult accessories or a man. She smiled, then continued our lovemaking is all about touch and sensitivity. I listened to every word Rosa was saying, trying to let all she was saying sink in. Rosa said, "do you remember how this all started, Adam?" I just thought to myself, yes I like to think so, but remained quiet. Rosa said it all started with tantric sex, the touching, and only touch, I said yes of course I remember Rosa.

Rosa said she did not want me to be like 95% of men who just think a woman is there for their needs and amusement. She said again, there is so much more to lovemaking. Rosa said you have to smell the air, feel the atmosphere when a man finishes his lovemaking. He believes that's it, but men are so wrong. That is not the case at all. When you make love to a woman and you climax first, it's not over, not at all. You should still continue to hold, touch, and caress the lady. Kissing is important and never leaves a woman unsatisfied. She has just as much right to be satisfied, Rosa said both Pippa and I love touching you and get a lot of satisfaction from just touching. She felt we should go back to the basics and do a trio tantric session. Rosa said penetration is very good with you, but feel you can be even better if you know instinctively how a woman needs and wants to be touched. Rosa said, "Adam, are you OK with this?" my reply was yes, how could it be anything but that answer?!

I really could not wait. I said to Rosa and Pippa that I wanted to learn everything I could from them and that I wanted them both to teach me everything they knew. I said to Rosa that I hoped I would never let her or Pippa down. Rosa then said, "Adam, do you know why I am teaching you to be the perfect lover?" I said I did not know why she had chosen to teach me but was glad that she and Pippa had.

Pippa was just lying there listening to the entire conversation and did not put any input into the conversation. Rosa said, "do you remember when I told you of how it was for me when I was a young girl?, and the men that I told you of and how they used to throw money at us when we danced?. Well, that's exactly how I do not want you to turn out like." She then went on to say, "if I was to show a woman true love and never take her for granted or just your object for sexual pleasure, you would never have to look for any kind of affection anywhere else. As the woman you were with would show you equal affection and care so there would be no need for you to stray as the men hoped to do in the clubs that I worked."

Rosa said if you treat your lady right and look after her, you would get every wish you could think of as if everything is 100% right. There is nothing either partner would not do for the other. I said yes to Rosa and told her I understood what she was saying and trying to teach me.

Again it seemed to be one of those nights where we just sat and spoke for eternity, none of us clothed just sitting there on Rosa's bed. Rosa seemed to make a lot of sense in what she was saying. We never even bothered that night with our evening meal. I was sort of hoping that the three-way tantric thing was going to happen that night, but it was not meant to be. We just seem to lie there together in a relaxed state with just general conversation. We were at this stage, all in bed together. The night just drifted from us, and at some point, we all falling to sleep, holding each other in a warm embrace as we always did.

As I lay there falling asleep I could not help myself, and my thoughts were soon on the tack room adventure that we had had that day. But as hard as I tried to remember every minor detail, I just could not, and the harder I tried, the vaguer it became in my head. That's how I drifted off to sleep that night with the smell of these two lady's fragrances on either side of me.

Chapter Nineteen

W e woke up the next morning we all seemed to have overslept a little, so there was a bit of a rush while having our breakfasts. I had arranged to go off and do some work for one of Rosa's friends, Victoria. Pippa seemed to have a heavy day, booked solid till late that evening with driving lessons. Rosa was again sorting out paperwork for the farmhouse in France and allowing funds for Philip to get some materials needed on the farmhouse. So after a rushed breakfast, we all seemed to leave the house at the same time.

I went round Victoria's and as soon as I was there; she offered me a cup of tea. Victoria showed me the work that she wanted me to do: it was, as she had said in the outhouse, a total renovation well on the upper floor. She smiled at me and said that I came with good recommendations, and gave me her credit card. Victoria said anything you need just get it on this card, so there is no need for you to ask if anything is OK. If you feel you need it, just get it and she would trust my judgment.

Just as Victoria was leaving she said oh I nearly forgot my daughter Rebecca is upstairs, but she should not get in my way and I should not be worried about making a noise. She is home from university as Victoria was leaving. She came back in and gave me a kiss on the cheek.

Victoria reminded me so much of Rosa, in her mannerisms and the smell of perfume, as she walked by. Of course, I had noticed her figure, and it was hard to tell Rosa from Victoria apart from the head. What the hell was I thinking eyeing this lady up, I had two beautiful women back at the house. Why would I even think this way? I would never risk losing what I had at home.

I started by stripping the wallpaper from the upstairs hallway and ripping up the old carpets, which I thought were actually in excellent condition. I seemed to be making a fair bit of noise, not on purpose, it just could not be helped. I heard some movement from Rebecca's room; I thought, Oh what a brilliant start, annoying her by waking her up.

I carried on the best I could, trying to be quiet all of a sudden Rebecca's door flew wide open. There was this girl, maybe a couple of years older than me. Half asleep she walked out of her room, nothing on apart from a little black thong. She had died her hair to fire engine red, her skin was of a pale complexion. The firmest pert breasts I had ever seen, both nipples pierced with tiny bars through them. This was something that I had not seen before, she just casually walked from her room to the bathroom having not a care in the world who was looking at her or who I was. She just said "Hi!" as if she had met me on the street. How open-minded was this girl?! If someone I had never seen before had seen me naked, I would have been embarrassed and tried to cover up.

I tried to carry on a conversation with her the best I could, but my eyes were now firmly fixed on this girl's nipples. As the piercing seemed to keep her nipples in a permanently erect state, she went into the bathroom and did not even bother to close the door. And still continued to try to have a conversation with me. I could hear her showering herself and I so wanted to go and look, but until this point,

I had been faithful to my two girls and that's the way I wanted it to remain. After all, no matter who or what any other girl looked like, they would never be able to replace my two girls at home.

Twenty minutes had passed, and I heard the shower switch off, just as brazen as before Rebecca walked from the bathroom straight into the hallway. "So!" said Rebecca "you're Adam" I did not know where to put my face. There was this naked girl standing before me, trying to hold a conversation. With her in front of me, all I could manage was her yeah hi. She introduced herself and lent forward and gave me a kiss on the cheek. I could not help myself and my eyes wandered. I had never seen pierced nipples before, and I thought they looked amazing. She saw me staring and laughed "oh do you like it?" she said as she pushed out her chest towards me. I said yes, not taking my eyes from her breasts. I might as well been having a conversation with her breasts as I did not look at her face.

I asked "do they hurt?" she laughed again and said, "no, don't be silly! If they hurt, I would not have them in" I asked again, "why have you had them done?". She said, "for sensitivity", I said, "oh! I see" and made my excuses and went back to work. With this, she went to her room. I carried on with my work and saw nothing of Rebecca for the rest of the day.

It was about 4 pm and I packed my work stuff up and cleaned the best I could. I knocked on Rebecca's bedroom door; she said come in, I just opened the door enough. Poking my head around the corner of the door, and said I was going now, and just to let her know, she said OK nice to meet you and said she would see me in the morning.

As I was leaving the house Victoria pulled into the driveway she asked how I had got on. I told her what I had done, and she seemed thrilled with that. I went back to Rosa's. I could not wait to see Rosa and Pippa and tell them about my day. Rosa was there looking as beautiful as ever: Pippa looked good enough to eat. We all sat down to dinner and spoke of our day's activities. When it was my turn, I could not wait to tell the girls what I had seen, meaning Rebecca and her pierced nipples. The two girls just looked at each other after I had finished my story. Pippa was the first to speak. "So, did you make any advances to her?" Rosa was just looking smiling at me. My reply was swift. "No, No Pippa, I could not be unfaithful to either you or Rosa, followed by what man on earth would risk losing what I have with you two."

The conversation just seemed to fizzle out about Rebecca, and as we went on to speak of normal conversations, we all headed upstairs to bed. I was first in bed in my normal place. Rosa came into the room next. Rosa said "Adam please come and sit with me," I thought I was in some sort of trouble. Maybe I went on a bit too much about Rebecca and her piercings.

But that was not the case I was sitting on top of the bed with Rosa as normal. We were both naked, as we always were. In walked Pippa she had her hands behind her back as she approached the bed I could see she had three blindfolds in her hands my thought were, what is going to happen now? Pippa said OK, let's all put a blindfold on. From past experience, I knew something good or exciting was about to happen so did not need to tell twice or question the girls so on went my blindfold.

All three of us were now sitting on the bed, as naked as the day we were born, all but these blindfolds. I then heard Rosa speak OK, she said this is going to be a very special night for us all, there will be no penetration, no matter how tempted we get.

Tonight is all about touch, feel and smell and feeling the tenderness between us. I sat there, not quite knowing what to do or how to start this. But I did not need to. The first thing I felt was a set of nimble fingers very gently run across my pectoral muscles. Then another hand started caressing my shoulders, then another hand gently squeezed one of my nipples.

Then another hand stroked the inside of my thigh, gently running, barely touching from my knee to my testicles. Not knowing who was who or who was touching what. I slowly stretched out one of my arms and found a calf muscle of one of the girls. They were we all were totally silent there was no way of knowing who was who. As I did this, a hand gently ran through my hair. I stretched out my other hand a little higher than the other and came into contact with a perfect-shaped breast.

I was tingling all over. I could feel my penis becoming aroused and slowly increase in size. One of the girls moved, and I could feel she was lying on her back. I stayed where I was, kneeling upright on the bed. I felt the movement of the other girl and she had moved around to the side of the one lying on her back. So I and one girl now had a naked body lying between us like a sacrificial lamb. I felt the hair of the naked body that lay between us; I felt sure it was Rosa, as I did this I felt what I thought to be Pippa. Starting at Rosa's feet, it was as if she wanted us to start at opposite ends of Rosa's body?

As my hand ran down through Rosa's hair, my other hand was trembling over her face. I felt the softness of her temples, which led my hand to her very neatly trimmed eyebrows, my fingers barely touching her. Trembling over her shut eyes, my hand carried on to the bridge of her little nose, both hands now caressing her face. My fingers running up and down the sides of her nose, feeling the redness of her cheeks. My fingers followed the contours of her nose until my fingers found the fullness of her lips, my hands now both exploring Rosa's face. I felt one of Rosa's hands stretch behind me and her finger tracing the line of my spine, feeling every one of my vertebra. It was as though her fingers had been electrically charged and made the whole of my body tingle with excitement.

My fingers were reluctant to leave Rosa's face and the warmth of her lips as she breathed in and out deeply. One of my hands had gone back to her hair and was now massaging the warm scalp of her head. My fingers entwined with her hair, my other hand now tracing the circumference of her lower jaw, feeling the softness of the skin under her chin. My hand moved to her neck, Rosa moved her head to one side to expose more of her neck for me to massage. She tilted her head slightly as my finger trembled across the side of her neck, as if I were touching them with a feather.

I could feel her pulse in her neck, feel the warmth of the blood pumping around this lady's body. I then felt the fullness of her stretched neck and the windpipe that gave this woman air her hand still tracing the line of my spine. Undoing every knot I had ever had in my back with her electrical fingers, she was able to relax me with one hand so much that I thought my body would turn to gelatin. My hands now working their way to her shoulders and were feeling her small but firm muscles. My hand then followed down to her chest plate until I felt the fullness of her perfect breasts. It seemed to take forever to trace the outline of her perfect breasts. I worked my finger very slowly in a circular movement from the outer edge to the Aureola. With rock-hard nipples, my hands were now trembling over her abdominal muscles, feeling every curve of every muscle.

Just under the surface of her skin, my tongue and mouth now enjoying her aureola and hardened nipples, easy but hard enough so she knew I was there and what I was doing. As my hand was feeling every muscle in her abdominal wall, my fingers moved to her pubic area. That's where I felt Pippa's head. She had been taking her time as equally as slow as I had, paying every attention to Rosa's feet and legs. Pippa's head had found Rosa's warm, soft vagina, and Pippa being ever so careful not to break the rules and enter her lover. With her tongue Pippa was massaging Rosa's labia lips with her tongue, her tongue found the folds of her warm labia and was teasing the hell out of Rosa.

Pippa lifted her head and saw me watching. As she lifted her head, one of her hands made a movement for my head and guided me into the area that she had been paying attention to. As Pippa's head passed over mine, Pippa gave me a slow, beautiful kiss, her lips shining with the climax that Rosa had given. Her lips were now being transferred to my own lips with a gentle push I was there now it was my turn to let my tongue play with the folds of this wonderful lady's labia. I felt a handhold in my head in place, not knowing whether it was Rosa herself holding me in place or Pippa making sure I stayed there. I knew the rules and there was to be no penetration, but it was so hard I wanted so much to feel the warmth of this lady's vagina wrapped around my tongue, but I somehow managed to compose myself and stuck to the rules.

Pippa's hands were very busy. I could feel her fingers gently touching, moving up and down the length of my penis. Rosa was also getting some play from Pippa's other hand, Pippa not even fully holding my penis, it was just her fingers stepping up and down the length of my delicate penis. It felt as though she had a full grip of it how could this be feeling so good. How did this feel as though I was having sex and making love to these beautiful women? Rosa and I parted from our kiss, our lips separated, and we both moved to Pippa's face.

Both of us were at either side of her neck, working in unison together, both now kissing the sides of her neck. It was as if there was a script written somewhere. As I moved down Pippa's body, so did Rosa, mirroring each other's movements. My hands now feeling every muscle in Pippa's trim, firm body. She felt as though she had the most perfect pack of abdominal muscles. As my hands were feeling Pippa's body, so were Rosa's and although our hands were barely touching Pippa, Rosa's fingers would entwine with mine.

I moved my tongue down to Pippa's perfectly shaped and formed breasts. Her little but firm pert nipples standing to attention. I could feel Rosa's hand next to mine the entire time, one of her hands still tumbling over her abdominal muscles, as were mine. Her other hand now passing, gliding over the other erect nipple, teasing and tweaking Pippa every so often. I moved my mouth just hovering over her erect nipple until I was blowing cold air over her breast and nipple; I heard Pippa moan (oh God Yeah) followed by you are both amazing.

Pippa's hand the whole time slowly, frantically feeling anything she could of mine and Rosa's bodies. I then seemed to be repeating the process of what I had done to Rosa previously, my tongue flicking and circling Pippa's little pink rockets. All of a sudden both Rosa and I began to feel our heads being massaged, Pippa was now holding both our heads her fingers running through Rosa's hair, whilst her other hand had a firm grip on my hair even as far as to say pulling or pushing at my head, as if to push my mouth heard onto her excited nipples and body. Every so often both Rosa and I would feel a tug at our hair and Pippa would lift our heads and guide them towards each other and push our faces together as if to force us to kiss. There was no need to be forced each time our faces met, Rosa and I were in a deep passionate kiss, only to be separated by the pull on our heads.

Rosa now breaking formation she moved her face to Pippa's nipples and took control of both of them. As I moved my head down to Pippa's abdominal muscles, I felt her hand, which still had a firm clasp on my hair, push as I glided across her muscles as she continued to push until my face was level with her moist vagina. As my tongue once again found her labia, I tried my hardest not to break the penetration rule and found my lips sucking the edge of her labials. Her hand still pushing harder at my head as if she wanted me to enter her. I felt my tongue go deeper inside her vagina folds, further than it should have, but stopped myself from full penetration.

As I was doing this, I felt Rosa move her hands across Pippa's body and her hand had found my hard but fragile penis. As she started just stroking my penis, I felt myself climax until there was no stiffness in my body as I came, this time my climax just seemed to flow from me her hand still slowly rubbing my penis and my climax being used as a lubricant.

The two girls were now in a heavy embrace and with such a deep kiss I lay there totally relaxed, not really being able to move as if I had been partially paralyzed. I just lay there watching as the two girls continued to please and pleasure each other in whatever way they sort and all this with no penetration.

I moved into a better position and just continued to watch as these two beautiful ladies satisfy each other. As I lay on the bed, the two girls separated and again laid on either side of me. I was thinking, OK it's now time for sleep as this is how we laid every night. The two girls started to kiss each side of my neck and to be honest, I did not remember anything else that night and slowly drifted off to sleep. I remembered us talking about our blindfolds and the three of us just lying there. I remember thinking about what had just happened. My mind a blur. Had we actually made love had the three of us had sexual intercourse.

I had to remind myself that no we had not I did not enter either of the girls that night, neither had either girl taken my penis into their mouths. How could I feel the way I was feeling from what we had done, it felt like I had had the most intense intercourse I had ever had or even heard of how was this possible? There was the most beautiful smell in the room, yes the lavender but something else, not the girl's perfumes. I could not place the smell in any way. There was also the feeling of pure bliss and relaxation. In the night's silence as we fell asleep together, the air in the bedroom seemed to relax and massage our minds that night as I fell asleep there were so many unanswered questions but I just drifted away.

Chapter Twenty

I woke up first in the morning and the two girls lay there fast asleep as soon as I had moved from between them. They automatically moved closer together. Even though they were still fast asleep, it was as if there was a magnetic force pulling them slowly together. I stood there for a little while just watching these two perfect women; it looked so natural for them to be lying there together as they were.

I took myself off downstairs, had a quick cup of tea and sorted myself out, and got my stuff ready for work. So off I set going to work at Victoria's place I arrived at 8.30. Victoria had given me a key the previous day so I could let myself in, just in case she had to go out on business early. As I walked through the hallway, I felt sure Rosa was there I could smell the perfume that she wore most of the time. But that was not possible, as I had left the two girls fast asleep in bed. I walked through into the kitchen and there sat Victoria in just her dressing gown. I thought she looked a million dollars sitting there in her silk dressing gown that hugged every contour of her very attractive body.

I said morning Victoria, oh Adam that sounds so formal just call me Vicki, I smiled at her and said OK. She asked if I would like a drink before I started work I said yes, please. We just sat there chatting for a while just general chit-chat really but seemed to keep going back to the subject of Rosa, Pippa and I. She said that she had another look at my work and was very impressed, and asked if I would do the whole house not just the upstairs. She also said she had recommended me to a couple of her friends. She went on to say that she also had a place in Cornwall, a sort of rest haven, and when I could would I please fit her place down there in for a total overhaul too. Obviously, I said yes.

My life was so perfect I had work coming from left, right, and center. Victoria was just as chilled as Rosa and Pippa and as equally as beautiful. Whilst I sat there drinking my tea she stood up and said, OK darling you start when you're ready I'm now going up to get ready, as unfortunately, I will be out all day again today. As she walked past me, she slowly ran her hands across my shoulders and said very nice. It was amazing how her and Rosa's touch were so similar. If I had my eyes shut and that had happened I would off swear it was Rosa that passed by me. Victoria's touch was the same as Rosa's they smelt the same it was a little spooky. It felt as though they could have been twins.

I finished my tea and took myself off upstairs to start work just as I had set my stuff up I could hear Vicki on the phone in her room. It sounded as though she were speaking to Rosa I heard her say, oh he is such a lovely man, and looks like his body had been photo-shopped. I then heard Vicki laugh and say no, no he has his clothes on, unfortunately, and laughed again then I knew for sure it was Rosa on the other end of the line.

Oh, I thought to myself, so Rosa is testing me out and using Vicki to do this. I just found it funny and went about my work. There were no signs of Rebecca so far, so I guessed she was still fast asleep, as she seemed to be a late riser. About 10 to 15 minutes later, Vicki emerged from her room I was gob smacked at how stunning this lady looked. Rosa had chosen someone very good-looking to test me against so I thought.

Vicki looked great her hair had been straightened, it was so silky it looked like it had just been ironed and the shine was amazing. As the light coming through the window only enhanced its beauty, her makeup was immaculate. Her lips a beautiful red gloss and shone as if wet, and as she closed the bedroom door behind her a great smell of lavender filled the hallway. She was wearing a white blouse and a knee-length black skirt which showed off her very nicely shaped legs and very toned calf muscles with a pair of black shoes that shined like diamonds.

She smiled at me and said had I heard her on the phone I said yes was Rosa checking me out then to make sure I was behaving myself. Vicki said no, we were just openly discussing you. She knows you would remain faithful to her and Pippa.

I was a little shocked and said, oh you know about the three of us then, Vicki replied yes and the three of you were so very lucky to have something so special. Vicki said if I were being truthful, Adam I am a little jealous of what the three of us had. This put my mind at rest that Rosa was not checking me out. I went back to work and as I turned around to pick up my brushes, Vicki pinched my bum and said yeah, very jealous. She laughed and walked off towards the stairs as she left there was that great smell of lavender that trailed along behind her body. I never saw Rebecca that day and Vicki was out all day as she said she was going to be. Just as I was leaving, the phone rang it was Vicki. She just reminded me that if I needed to buy some materials for the job, I was just to use the credit card that she had left for me on the kitchen table. I thanked her and said I would see her in the morning.

Before we ended the call, she explained she was going away on business and would not be back until the end of the week. We said our goodbyes and ended the call. Driving home that night I thought it was great that Vicki was going to be away, as this would enable me to nearly complete the job.

I went home that night and everything was great we had our meal together we just had a laugh about all our day's activities. After our meal, Pippa sat with me and taught me how to set out my books for work. We had many nice evenings together that week. It was nice just cuddling up on the sofa with the girls as we watched films together. Oh, and Pippa constantly helped me with my books, with Vicki away I had nearly completed the work in her house. There was only one room left to do. The room I had left till last was Vicki's room.

I set off for work early that morning, leaving the two girls asleep. I got to Vicki's

House at about 7.30 am. I was having a quick look around the work I had already completed just to make sure I had not overlooked anything, as I so wanted Vicki to be happy with what I had done. It all looked good, so I went upstairs and was sorting my stuff out and I heard crying coming from Vicki's room I gingerly opened the door and saw Vicki sitting on the edge of her bed. She had obviously come home early, but why?

She seemed really upset, and I did not know what to do or say as I had only ever known happiness and had never experienced this before. Sadness was a thing that just did not exist in Rosa's house. I asked Vicky what as the matter was there, anything I could do? She just stretched out her arm, grabbed my hand, and said please Adam, just sit with me for a while.

I did as Vicki requested. She was still crying and put her arms around me and placed her head on my shoulder. Still crying, I was confused I was in way over my depth here. I said shall I call Rosa still not knowing what the problem was. She lifted her head, her eyes all glazed from her tears, and said OK to me for phoning Rosa. As she said this, she leaned forward as if to kiss me. I just froze and got up, went to the phone, and called Rosa.

Rosa answered the phone and in a panicked voice, I said "Rosa I need you I need your help" I was really nervous and said that Vicki needed her help, I explained Vicki was crying and could she come over to her. Rosa was knocking on the door of Vicki's house within 15 minutes. Rosa went straight upstairs to Vicki's room. They were in there for a good couple of hours, which sort of left me standing around doing nothing as I had left her room till last. I found some minor jobs to do while Rosa and Vicki were speaking.

After a couple of hours had passed, the two ladies emerged. Rosa just smiled at me but did not speak the two ladies passed me and went down to the kitchen. 5 minutes later I heard Rosa calling up the stairs at me. I went to see what she wanted, and she whispered to me I will tell you later what the problem is at home I said OK and said my goodbyes to her and continued with my work.

With the two girls downstairs, I finished Vicki's room. Rosa had long gone by now. When I was finished, I asked Vicki if she wanted to check what I had done. She walked around with me, as we were walking around she said that she really did not need to check my work as she was very pleased with what I had done. We got to her room, and she just said its lovely Adam. In a quiet sort of voice, she said Rosa and Pippa were lucky to have me and began to explain why she was upset earlier.

It was to do with her daughter Rebecca. She seemed to just want to talk, and I thought this was a lot better than crying. She said that her daughter was dating this older man which she said I did not mind as you cannot help who you fall in love with. There was something about him she did not like personally, and Rebecca had fallen behind with her university work to such a stage that it was going to be nearly impossible for her to catch up. All she seemed to want to do was hang around with this man and she had just found out that Rebecca was now doing drugs and they had had a big row the evening before.

Vicki was getting upset again and started becoming tearful, so I suggested she grab some fresh clothes and come back to Rosa's with me and spend the evening with us. Vicki agreed and got some clothes and came back to Rosa's with me. When we got to Rosa's, she did not bat an eyelid that Vicki was with me. She welcomed Vicki in with no questions. Rosa greeted Vicki with a kiss on the cheek and a huge cuddle. Pippa kissed her on the cheek and held her close and said, "Sorry to hear about your troubles Vicki".

We sat in the living room most of that evening and Vicki explained what had actually happened. She told the complete story and explained that the older man Rebecca was seeing was a bad influence on Rebecca. Without Vicki noticing the partner of Rebecca had encouraged her drug-taking, and that Rebecca was now addicted to drugs, and the last that Vicki heard from Rebecca after their row. Rebecca was going off to Europe with this man. Vicki said she handled the situation badly and instead of trying to help Rebecca out and sort through her problems they just had a massive argument. Vicki said she felt helpless as she did not know where she was only, that she was with this man somewhere in Europe. And even if she wanted to, she was now unable to help her. I just sat there listening to Vicki's story as I felt there was nothing I could say or do which would help the situation out. Anyway, the minutes turned into hours and it really was late. I said to the girls I was going up to the bed and did not want to seem rude or uninterested in what was going on.

I gave all three girls a kiss as I went upstairs to bed. As I was going up the stairs I heard Vicki say to Rosa and Pippa, well lady's you definitely seem to have found a lovely man. She was really pleased with them and they explained they were teaching me to be the perfect lover. I thought, oh my god how much does this lady actually know? Vicki said you are teaching him so well, I was now sitting on the stairs listening to their conversation. How would Vicki know how good I was nothing had happened there while I was working at her house with either her or her daughter so how would she know if I was perfect in any way.

Then Vicki went on to explain that earlier when she had been upset I had found Vicki sitting on the edge of her bed crying. "Bless him," she said he came into the room and tried to comfort me and was really concerned at the state I was in. She then said please forgive me girls I know what you are doing with Adam. But in my grief, I tried to kiss him and he showed no signs of any sort in any way of wanting to kiss me back. He did not try to take advantage, as most men would have. He just phoned for you, Rosa, so I guess in that respect he already is the perfect lover.

I felt relieved and very pleased with myself with what Vicki had said to the two girls, as I did not want to lose them at all. But strangely, I was also very pleased. As if you remember I thought Rosa was trying me out with Vicki earlier in the week, but I was wrong and that was not the case whatsoever. I would never risk losing what I had with Rosa and Pippa.

I then heard Rosa say to Vicki, yes he is very good and well above his actual age and he acts far more sensitive than most men. With regard to how a woman wants and needs to be treated. Pippa then piped up and said, yes but Rosa and I have spoken and sometimes we feel we are holding him back, although they try to treat me right were we keeping him as our very own sex slave. Vicki said, no Adam is just so happy and content to be with you both you are all he talked of when he was working on my house. There is so much admiration in him for the two of you.

Rosa then said to Vicki that she would love for him to stay with us both for as long as he wanted to and was happy. Both Pippa and I hoped this would be a permanent thing, basically forever. Even though he is a young man and Vicki was promised secrecy. Rosa said 'he is by far the best lover that either Pippa or herself had ever met'.

With this, I heard some movement from the living room, so I quickly took myself off upstairs. About 5 minutes had passed, and I was in bed. I heard the bedroom door slowly open it was Rosa. Rosa said are you awake Adam, I said yes darling just waiting for you and Pippa. Rosa came in first and said "I promise you Adam we Pippa and I, both want you" I thought oh no it's going to be a Dear John speech and I was about to be told it was over as I had not heard the conclusion to the conversation downstairs.

I held Rosa close, not wanting to hear what I thought she was going to say but to my amazement, she said, look we have a guest tonight and you know what has happened. So she is going to stay the night and Rosa asked would I mind if Vicki stayed the night in our bed with us. I thought I was being told I would have to stay in my old room that night. So without any question went to get up out of the bed. Rosa smiled at me and gently pushed me back onto the bed. Rosa said, no Adam I meant she is really staying with us, all four of us were to sleep in the same bed. Again, being a little naïve, I just thought it meant no sexual stuff was going to happen. With this, Rosa took off her clothes, and in walked Pippa and Vicki. Rosa was now lying next to me on the bed, naked as she always had done. She was just cuddling me. As we lay there together, Pippa and Vicki both tripped. I hoped above all hopes that this meant I was about to get all three girls as I secretly really fancied Vicki. But in reality, I thought no, nothing would happen but hell; it was exciting to have my Rosa next to me and see the other two ladies slowly stripping in front of me. The moonlight coming in through the window was catching the contours of their bodies, their bodies not totally visible to me, just silhouettes, really.

Rosa's hands were moving up and down my torso, then Rosa spoke to Vicki, her hands not leaving my body. Her words to Vicki were well Vicki I see you have kept yourself in good shape. Rosa continued to say, "it's been a long time since Pippa and I have seen you naked". Pippa agreed with Rosa and commented on Vicki's body, Pippa now slowly feeling Vicki's body. Starting with her shoulders as they stood before us, Pippa wasting no time. Soon had both Vicki's breasts cupped in her hands. Pippa then said, as firm as ever, Rosa. All three girls giggled a little I could see Vicki looking at me to see my reaction. Listening to their conversation, there had obviously been something there between the three girls in the past. Pippa and Vicki then climbed onto the bed with Rosa and me.

Rosa whispered in my ear, "just relax remember everything we have spoken about and breathe deeply". Did this mean I was now going to be in a foursome, God this was the stuff dreams were made of? It did not take very long before I knew what was about to happen. I had Rosa to my left, and I had Vicki lying to my right, and Pippa was on the other side of Vicki.

It was like a giant human sandwich. Rosa's hands were still trembling over my body, my body feeling a little cold and even goosebumpy at the thoughts of what was about to happen. My penis was already as hard as it could be. How was I meant to be able to satisfy three women at the same time? The thought became a bit daunting, where was I meant to start and how was I meant to start.

This is where I was going to fail for sure, I thought, don't let Rosa down. I thought to myself that Rosa was expecting a little too much from me at this point. Pippa had turned to her side to face Vicki. Vicki turned her head towards me, but her body remained with her back on the bed. Vicki spoke to me as she was looking at me "Adam are you OK with this?" and kissed me gently on the cheek I said in a very nervous voice "yeah I think so". I felt Rosa's head come close to mine, and she said, just relax darling you will be fine. As she said this, I felt a hand just barely touch my erect penis. It was Vicki's hand as she turned to face Pippa. Pippa and Vicki were in a very passionate embrace, kissing as one of Vicki's hands was slowly, gently touching my erection.

Vicki's other hand wrapped around Pippa's neck, pulling Pippa's face closer to her own. Vicki sure looked like she knew what she was doing, the hand that Vicki had wrapped around my penis was now joined by one of Rosa's hands. I now had both Rosa and Vicki gently rubbing my erection with their hands. I could feel their fingers intermingle with each other as they did so. Rosa was now kissing the back of my neck. There was a fair bit of movement from Rosa. She was still doing what she was doing, but was now lying on her back.

Pippa was now sitting astride Vicki's body. I too moved and was now sitting astride Rosa's body. Pippa produced some of that warm lavender oil from a bedside cabinet' she poured loads onto my hands and lots onto her own hands. This much I had learned t and how to massage which is exactly what I did. I let my oil-drenched hands cover Rosa's body until my hands were gliding effortlessly across Rosa's body, as were Pippa on Vicki. The aroma in the air was amazing, so sensual, but at the same time so relaxing. As my hands moved over Rosa's body, my hands were only slowed by the hardness and erectness of Rosa's nipples. I could see that Pippa was doing the same to Vicki's body as I was to Rosa's. Vicki's groans of pleasure were not harnessed in any way, and Vicki's body wriggled and bucked beneath Pippa's.

Rosa was very willing to help me out here and took some of the oil from her own very oiled body into her own hands. One of her hands was massaging my chest and her other hand working the lavender oil onto my now very hard erection. Vicki's hands were now too covered in oil and were massaging the oil onto Pippa's perk firm breasts. Pippa was rubbing the oil hard onto and into Vicki's body, Pippa was massaging Vicki so hard I could see the indentation of her fingers in Vicki's body. Rosa and Vicki had turned their heads and were now facing each other as Pippa and I massaged the girls beneath us. The two girls began a strong and passionate kiss. As they did this, Pippa looked across at me. Smiling, she licked her lips. She looked so inviting I lent across and was also now in a very passionate kiss with Pippa. The girls that lay under Pippa and I were now wriggling to every touch that Pippa and I made to their bodies.

Both Pippa and I, while kissing each other and massaging the girls, were also sliding our pelvis back and forth on the girls below us. As if Pippa and I were back in the tack-room, performing our riding moves. Massaging their bodies, tweaking their nipples, and riding their bodies as if we were both in a horse race. The pace that Pippa and I were riding our respective partners was as intense as possible, their bodies both wriggling below us.

Both Pippa and I were pulling on Rosa's and Vicki's nipples as though they were the horse's reins. I heard Vicki say to Rosa, "oh God I have missed this?" On hearing this Pippa was like a woman possessed and ridden Vicki harder and harder the more Vicki wriggled the harder Pippa thrust her pelvis down onto her. Both girls were enjoying what the other was doing for each other. Pippa now lent forward and lowered her body to Vicki's, Pippa was now licking and sucking on Vicki's very dark erect nipples, Vicki's hand holding Pippa's head in place so tightly so Pippa did not or could not lose grip of her erect nipples.

Rosa in the meantime knew exactly what she wanted. She asked me to rise slightly from her body. As I did so, she took my hard erection in her hand and pushed back on it slightly. She asked me to lean forward. As I did so, she moved her pelvis up and pushed down onto my hard erection. She knew exactly where she wanted it and before I knew too much of what was happening; I found myself deep inside this lady's beautiful, warm vagina with her vagina and her labia.

Holding me firmly inside the walls of her vagina, holding and grabbing my penis as if in like a soft vice. I could feel every muscle inside the warmth of her vagina. Needless to say, it was not long before I felt my penis begin to throb and I knew I was at bursting point. One of her hands pulled my face close to hers and she whispered, "it's OK Adam I want you, to give it to me". With these words that was it, I felt a few hard pulses and my penis was climaxing inside this wonderful woman as I climaxed she was bucking and grinding her pelvis and trying to wriggle. So my penis was even deeper inside of her she pulled my head to the side and whispered again, stay inside me, Adam please do not withdraw.

I did as Rosa requested how the hell she was doing what she was doing I will never know. She was applying her vaginal muscles tight around my now decreasing erection. She would increase her grip, then release and repeat the process. It was less than 10 minutes and I felt myself becoming aroused yet again. She had taken total control over my adulthood. Rosa continued to work on my adulthood for a while like this. Vicki and Pippa had now swapped positions and Vicki was now on top of Pippa. Vicki was now doing exactly what Pippa had been doing to her: there was a slight difference while she was rubbing the oil on Pippa's body. One of her hands had stretched across and had a firm but gentle grip on my testicles she was pulling gently back and forth.

She was using my testicles as though they were a grip on a vibrator, my penis being the vibrator. She was so fully in control of what my adulthood was allowed to do, pulling and pushing my penis in and out of Rosa. Still, Rosa at the same time was working her vaginal muscles on my now semi-erect penis.

Pippa and Rosa both now had their mouths locked in a very strong kiss. This went on for what seemed ages. Then there was a bit of movement from everyone on the bed, and Pippa and I found ourselves lying flat on the bed. Rosa was now taking full control of Pippa's satisfaction and to my disbelief I now had Vicki. Both Rosa and Vicki started their moves simultaneously, as if following a script. Rosa started at Pippa's feet and Vicki at mine, both girls now kissing each of

Pippa's and my feet. Rosa was massaging Pippa's legs, Rosa's body was moving forward all the time up over Pippa's legs. Vicki was doing the same, massaging my legs, her nimble fingers teasing the inner thigh near my testicles.

Rosa was first to get halfway up the body and her head now level with Pippa's vagina. Vicky was not far behind and her face now level with my penis. Rosa and Vicki looked across at each other and drew their heads closer and gave each other a strong, passionate kiss. When Vicki and Rosa separated, Rosa quickly moved her head back to Pippa's vagina area. Rosa must have been doing everything that Pippa wanted as lying next to her. All I could hear and see was Pippa groaning with pleasure and her biting her bottom lip. Her breathing became deeper and deeper.

Vicki was amazing all three girls seemed to have a different but equally satisfying technique. Vicki was amazing it was as if her tongue had doubled in size it felt as though her tongue was wrapping itself around the complete diameter of my now very erect penis. Thanks to Rosa, and her magical muscles. God knows how I was keeping my erection as Vicki moved her head back and forth into my adulthood.

Her tongue truly felt like a tiny, wet hand that had clasped my penis. It was all I could do to stop myself from climaxing yet again. I did not want Vicki to stop, but at the same time wished she would. I did not want this fantastic feeling to end, even though in my head I thought I had actually done well. I did not want to let the girls down but wondered how I was going to manage much longer even though I think the three of them could off carried on very well without my input. The smell was so hypnotic, the three different perfumes from each of the ladies mixed with the lavender oil, and I liked to think my aftershave and that individual smell that everyone has their own personal aroma.

I truly thought I was going to lose control of myself, as I was at the exploding point. Eventually, Vicki moved further up my body. The thoughts that were running through my head were hypnotic and sensual pleasurable ones that I did not want to end. Vicki's tongue was now working on my slightly sweaty abdominal muscles, her tongue now circling each and every individual muscle. How was this happening to me?, Rosa was still firmly in place on Pippa where I had last seen her. Pippa's eyes were slowly rolling in her eye sockets, and her head was also rolling in ecstasy, still biting her bottom lip. Vicki keeping in line with Rosa now broke formation and was heading to my nipples, her tongue now working away at my tender nipples. Vicki had a very different way of playing with my nipples, with her tongue very different from either Rosa or Pippa.

Vicki put her entire mouth over my nipple area and sucked so so hard. So hard I thought she was trying to detach them from my chest. But again I wanted her to stop, but also really wanting her to carry on. She would suck really hard then release the whole area and just as you thought your nipples were free, she buried her head and sucked even harder every time she went back down on my chest. She would also put my nipple between her teeth and give quite a hard nip. Yes, it hurt but at the same time was so pleasurable; It was really hard to explain the feelings that were going through my head and my body. Pleasure and pain mixed with each other is something that I had not experienced. I even heard myself holding her head to my chest. Yes, go on harder. I was a man, was I meant to be having these feelings. Was it right for a man to want and like to have his own nipples licked, sucked, and even bitten? The answer was simple: a simple yes; it was my body and if that's what I enjoyed, then why not.

All I knew was I was receiving so much pleasure from what Vicki was doing to me. I thought this could not get any better. Once again, there was a movement on the bed from everyone and a massive shuffle of bodies. I now had Pippa sitting on top of me, her hand was covered in a fresh supply of oil and was now massaging my very tender nipples which I think Vicki was trying to detach. Vicki took no prisoners when she worked on someone and was a real hard lover. With every pass and slide of Pippa's hands across my chest and nipples, I wanted to scream gently, please. But at the same time, wanted Pippa to repeat what Vicki had just been doing to me? I could still feel the power of her sucking and biting, as though she were still there. I had actually enjoyed being pleasured and hurt at the same time. But thankfully, Pippa just continued to gently massage my chest. One of her hands had stretched back and was starting to masturbate my shrinking manhood.

My adulthood also felt confused: it did not know whether to be erect or soft, but as Pippa started her touch, it soon became hard. Yet again she very carefully positioned herself and with a very clever twist of her pelvis. I found my adulthood deep inside Pippa's moistness. I was only inside Pippa for about two minutes I could help it no more and I climaxed again as I climaxed I pulled her body close to mine I held her body tight to my own, kissing her passionately and with a final thrust of my hips I found myself climaxing deep inside of her. As this happened, Pippa was rocking back and forth, grinding her pelvis on to me by this time. Rosa and Vicki were just lying with each other, kissing. Not even noticing or caring what Pippa had been doing right in front of their eyes. It was very late that night and slowly, each of us drifted off to sleep.

Chapter Twenty One

When I woke in the morning, I was the only one in the bedroom. There was not a thing out of place. The aromas from the previous night had also vanished. It was as though nothing had happened. I laid there thinking, had I dreamt all of this. I showered then went downstairs still no one seemed to be about. It all seemed so surreal. I really did not know what to think. I took myself off to the outhouse as there was always stuff for me to work on there.

I spent all day in the outhouse and most of my thoughts were of the previous evening and had it really happened. I knew it had as my nipples still felt tender as my shirt rubbed across them, but the more I tried to remember, the vaguer my memories were becoming. My working day had ended. I packed my tools away and tidied up, as that was one of my pet hates an untidy working area. I went to the house and there was Rosa, preparing our evening meal with Pippa's help. Vicki was nowhere to be seen or heard. Neither of the two girls mentioned Vicki that evening, so I thought it best I did not mention the previous night either.

Rosa just gave me a welcoming kiss, as did Pippa, as they always did. We spent the whole evening talking about our day's activities and just normal, everyday stuff. Pippa was going through her driving lesson schedule and Rosa looking at the paperwork for the farmhouse in France.

The next two or three weeks were what we liked to call normal. Just working and having our evening meals and our evening chats. I never saw Vicki again until one night she popped over to pay me the balance for the work which I carried out on her house. She also gave me a list of phone numbers she had been very busy recommending me to her friends who were looking to have some work carried out. I thanked her and gave her a kiss on the cheek. She said the pleasure was all hers. We spent the rest of the evening just chatting about general stuff. I could not help myself and found myself looking no staring at her tongue as she spoke. I could not get the mental picture out of my head the way that she had wrapped her tongue around my adulthood that night, a few weeks ago.

All I could keep thinking was her tongue looked of normal size and not abnormally big. How had she managed to do what she did that night did I just imagine the whole thing as no one had spoken of that night since? I knew I had not imagined this as four days after-wards my nipples were as tender as hell but still remained to feel very sensual.

The next day I set about phoning the numbers on Vicki's list and over the next couple more days had managed to secure a lot of work. Every number I phoned the people just kept saying yes. No matter what the price was, it was as if I had the Midas touch regarding work.

Chapter Twenty Two

Another couple of weeks passed and everything was going along so perfectly. Obviously, there were sexual encounters between Rosa Pippa and myself but this was our normal life. I just imagined this is how everyone lived OK maybe not as a trio as we were but happy and content with each other's lives. One evening we were all sitting down in the living room and Rosa got up, went to her desk, and pulled out some papers. She turned and said to Pippa and me, it's done, and smiled. The tickets for the ferry have been booked, and we were very soon going to be setting off to France.

Rosa said we can all go in the truck, Adam, if that's OK with you as I would like you to do a few jobs while out there my reply was great yes no problem Rosa. In the next two weeks, we all set about re-arranging our work schedules, as this trip meant taking a fair bit of time away from our regular work as Rosa needed a fair bit done out there but we were also going to make a holiday of it. It was not long before it was time to set off the two weeks prior to departure for France flew by. We all packed my truck up it felt like we had taken everything but the kitchen sink.

Pippa did the first shift of driving as we thought it would be easier on all of us if we split the driving. It was as far south as we could go in France I took us up to the ferry terminal and boarded. The ferry crossing was a little rough and I could see Pippa was not enjoying the trip. When we reached the coast of France Pippa took over driving and as if by magic, as soon as we were off the ferry, she felt fine. Both Rosa and I laughed as Pippa had been struck down with seasickness.

I had done my shift of driving so climbed in the back of the truck, and Rosa and Pippa were sitting upfront. As I was drifting off to sleep, I heard Rosa chatting to Pippa and how excited she was about to be back in France. She said to Pippa that Adam and her would love the old farmhouse and especially Pippa as there were horse riding stables attached to it.

Rosa gave directions to Pippa for nearly 3 hours then Rosa said OK, if you jump in the back with Adam I will take over from here. Pippa pulled over Rosa was now taking control of the driving. Pippa jumped in the back with me and we pulled a big blanket over us and cuddled up and went to sleep. Rosa seemed to be at home driving here and must have driven for hours. Both Pippa and I were stirring from our sleep, and we noticed we had left the main roads behind us and were driving through this forest area. A few sharp turns here and there down some very small country roads and we arrived at a set of massive iron gates. As we approached, the gates opened automatically we still drove for about a mile or so and we approached this massive, and I mean massive, house.

Rosa piped up from the driving seat OK, my darlings, here we are, this is it. This was not a farmhouse, it was a mansion more like a stately home, something royalty should be living in. When we got to the entrance to the house we were greeted by Phillip, the man who looked after this grand old building. Pippa said to Rosa, "Oh Rosa it has not changed at all looks exactly like the pictures you have shown me".

We were shown into the house by Phillip. It was grand. There were massive oak beams that stretched the length of the grand hallway.

Phillip was right in his letters to Rosa: the house needed some tender loving care and it certainly needed a lick of paint. We were all led upstairs by Phillip to the bedrooms, all three of them. Rosa said to Pippa and I not to worry as there would be no change to our sleeping arrangements and it would be as it was at home just to let Phillip do his duty.

It was getting very late and Phillip had left the main house and went to his tied cottage within the grounds. Once he left, Pippa and I made our way to Rosa's bedroom. I had never seen a bedroom this big. The bed was as equally as impressive. A massive four-poster made from solid wood, each post of the bed resembling a tree trunk in itself. There seemed to be hundreds of pillows and the most delicate silk sheets you ever saw.

There was this massive open fireplace on one of the outside walls, which was burning some huge logs. In the other corner of the room, there was a huge cast iron bath which shone as if it were made from pearls. We were all feeling very tired from our road trip to this grand house. We all stripped naked, as we had done a thousand times before, and climbed onto this enormous bed. The three of us lay together as we had always done. The bed felt so big that even though we were in the same bed; it felt as though we were sleeping separately.

It was not long before both Rosa and Pippa were moving closer to me and cuddling right up to each side of me. It was not as warm as Rosa's bedroom or her bed, but I could not help feel there was still something missing, something that did not seem quite right. Did I have any need to complain really I had the most important thing, and that was my two girls on either side of me. We lay there not really speaking very much and very soon we were all sound asleep.

Chapter Twenty Three

The sound of a cockerel woke us up in the morning, crowing as hard as it could it was so loud I thought the animal was on the end of the bed.

The sun was beaming through the windows of the bedroom. As we opened our eyes, our only diffusion from the sunlight was a lace that had draped the whole way around the edge of the bed. A beautiful lavender color that was it, that's what was missing, the smell of lavender which I had become so used to in Rosa's bedroom.

Rosa was the first to rise from the bed. Both Pippa and I were still just lying there, taking in the splendor of this grand old room. Rosa was out of the room for 10 minutes or so and as she walked back in the sunlight hit her body and we saw the steam rising from her shining skin. There was only a towel wrapped loosely around her waist Rosa looked at Pippa and I and said, do not worry, the cast iron bath is just ornamental, there is a shower room through that door, and smiled at us both.

Rosa said it's OK it not as prehistoric as it looks here and laughed. Pippa laughed and was next up and in the shower she did not bother with a towel and just ran naked from the bed to the shower room. As Rosa pulled back the lace that surrounded the bed she sat on the edge of the bed she said you're going to love it here Adam. As she lent towards me her towel, just dropped to the floor and this perfectly formed lady was lying stretched out across the bed before me, the sun kissing every contour of this lady's body. Two minutes later, in walked Pippa. She was still not bothered. With a towel, she stood in the sunlight for a few minutes, letting the heat from the sun kiss and dried her body.

I got up and also went to the shower room it was tiled from floor to ceiling. The shower was the most powerful I had ever experienced. When I came out of the shower and back into the bedroom, the two girls were getting themselves dressed. I walked over to the girls, gave them both a morning kiss, and I too was unpacking and getting dressed.

Rosa asked me to put something smart on, as she had said she wanted me to go with her somewhere today. Pippa said to Rosa, is it "OK if I do not come with you today as she had seen some stables at the other end of the courtyard". Rosa smiled at Pippa and said no problem. Just be careful, those horses have not been ridden for a long time. Pippa was gazing out of the window at the stables and felt sure she had not even heard Rosa's warning, or maybe she had, and it just excited her all the more than Pippa loved a challenge regarding horses.

We all made our way down this enormous staircase and into the breakfast room. They're waiting for us on the table was this freshly baked bread, the steam still rising from the bread as it lay on a plate in the center of the table. The sight and aroma of the fresh bread just added to the whole farmhouse experience.

Suddenly, this young French girl walked into the room. Morning Rosa, Morning Pippa, and to my morning Sir. I laughed and said no need to call me Sir my name is Adam she looked at me timidly and smiled and said, morning Adam. Rosa introduced Pippa and me to this fresh-faced girl, Rosa said, this is Sofia. She was stunning with her jet black hair tied back really tightly in a very long ponytail, her hair stretched halfway down her back. She was very, very petite, probably about a size 6 if that no taller than 5ft 2 inches. A very tiny framed person, she stood there very smartly in her white blouse and black skirt.

Rosa asked if I wanted to go and explore for a while, as she needed to sort some things out before we left on our day together. I said yes I would love too I could not wait to walk around this grand house and explore the place. I left the three girls in the kitchen and set about my mini adventure in this grand house.

There were several staircases in this building, some went up, others went down to the basement area. As I was walking around this house, I seemed to notice that there was something very similar in every wall it was a picture of this beautiful young lady dressed in the grandest of dresses but old-fashioned. As I stood there staring at these pictures, it suddenly struck me it was Rosa when she was younger, it was Rosa in many burlesque outfits.

The old man Marcus had filled the walls of his house with hundreds of pictures of Rosa when she was a dancer. They were amazing pictures and for that time a little daring but not rude, definitely not rude. There were loads of pictures as I continued to walk around, not one of them repeating itself.

I heard Rosa calling up the stairs to me are you ready she shouted out where ever you are. To be honest, I was probably a little lost as I had taken corridor after corridor and was only paying attention to the pictures on the walls. I eventually found my way downstairs and there was Rosa waiting for me, smiling.

Pippa was long gone the thought of all those horses. I asked Rosa, "So where are we going then?" She just smiled, grabbed my hand, and took me to the truck, and we were off.

As we set off, I asked again where were we going Rosa said I thought I would take you into Paris. Personally, I thought this was a great idea, as I had never been to Paris before. We drove for nearly two hours and eventually got to the outskirts of this amazing city. Rosa was giving me a blow-by-blow account of where we were she seemed so relaxed in France it was like this is where she belonged.

We stopped off at this little cafe bar-type thing. As we sat there a few of the older folk, well the men kept staring at us or Rosa so I thought but decided to ignore this. As she was a very attractive woman and even in the UK I had noticed people looking at her, but this somehow felt different. It was not the normal sort of stare.

As we sat there, Rosa said, "Adam, do you remember when I told you when I was younger I started burlesque dancing?" She was keeping her voice very low. I replied, yes I remember, and I had seen her on the walls of the farmhouse. And very stunning you looked I said she smiled and said, yes Marcus did love to have a picture or two of me up in the house. It was so everywhere he walked he could remind himself how lucky he was to have me living in the house with him.

Rosa said she would like me to meet someone who was very important to her. We finished up our drinks and snacks and were back in the car. We went a little further into Paris and pulled up in this slightly run-down part of Paris where the buildings had not been modernized for a long time. But in a special sort of way, looked right just the way they were. The tiny houses were an array of different colors as we parked the truck as the street became too narrow and walked to the end of this minor road. There was this quaint little house, and it was a very light lavender color as we approached the door there was the sound of an old lay singing coming from inside. I could not understand a word of it as it was in French, but all the same, sounded nice.

Rosa pulled on the old cord hanging down just outside the front door, and a bell rang. The singing ad stopped, and a few moments later, the door slowly opened. There stood this little old lady very well dressed and even though she was getting on in her years, her makeup was immaculate, very long dark hair not one bit of Grey, as she opened the door she saw Rosa and just froze like she was looking at a ghost. Her eyes welled up and fill with tears. I looked at Rosa, her eyes too filling with tears. Not a word had been spoken. The old lady in the house took a deep breath and murmured to Rosa, "Is this my dear Rosa?" With this, Rosa stretched out her arms and said yes. The two ladies burst into tears and just held each other so nicely.

Yes, yes, it's me, Elisa. They hugged for ages, the old lady running her hands up and down Rosa's back, occasionally stroking her face in disbelief. Then her story that she had told Pippa and me. I remembered this was Elisa, the lady who taught Rosa to dance. Elisa invited us both to her house was amazing, it looked like a giant doll's house on the inside. There was memorabilia from the old days dotted around everywhere. Elisa also had many pictures of Rosa when she was younger as a dancer and some in just normal, everyday clothes. This was like meeting Rosa's mother, and Rosa spoke and treated Elisa as though she were her mother.

Once inside, I was introduced to Elisa properly, and she welcomed me to her home with open arms and made me feel very welcome. After 30 minutes of the two ladies catching up on old times, it was my turn. Rosa had brought me up in the conversation and who I was, Elisa seemed to live back in the old days. On the way, she spoke and was more than willing to tell me stories of Rosa when she was a young girl. All the time Elisa rubbing Rosa's leg as if she really still could not believe she was there with her. A couple of hours passed and Rosa was telling Elisa how she was staying at the farmhouse for a while and would be lovely if she could spend some days with her there. Elisa agreed and was very excited about spending some time with Rosa.

We set off and said our goodbyes we were back on the road for only 30 minutes or so and Rosa said stop outside that little shop. I did as Rosa requested and she pointed out this old-looking pub-style building she said that was the first burlesque club that I danced in. This must have been a little upsetting for her as this was no longer a club of any sort and had actually been turned into a restaurant that must have gone bankrupt, as the doors and windows were boarded up and were in a state of disrepair. We left the truck where it was as Rosa assured me it would be safe where we had left it and continued our journey on Paris's metro service, which was a little like London's underground system. We went further into Paris we were heading to one of the more upmarket clubs that Rosa used to dance in and she felt sure that would still be there. When we got off the metro service and came above ground we were walking for about 5 minutes and much to her pleasure, the club was still open and in existence.

We went in for a look around. Again this was another massive building, again more like a mansion but in a town. It looked very expensive all around the walls of this building were pictures on the walls, just as in Marcus's house. There were some of the ladies who danced years ago and some of those who danced there now. We entered the main hall and at the far end of the hall was a stage not dissimilar to the one Rosa had me build in the outhouse back in the UK.

As we got closer, my eyes were drawn to the backdrop of the stage. There were three massive murals of burlesque dancers and to my shock, even after all these years had passed the massive picture. In the middle of the three was of Rosa as a young dancer we did not stay long as we only went there for a quick look around. It thrilled Rosa that seeing the picture of her was still the backdrop of the stage as we quietly left the building and saw some of the other sights in Paris and did a little shopping.

Rosa was the happiest I had ever seen her as she was showing me around her old haunts we spent the rest of the day traveling around

Paris. It was about 8 pm and we decided it was time to leave the center of Paris and make our way back to the truck. I was so glad that I had Rosa with me, as I felt sure I would never find my way back to the truck without her. The streets all looked very much alike, and it was a very busy place and if you were not sure of where you were going, I should think it would be a peaceful place to get lost. Some of the areas not looking so friendly and inviting as others, some I would not venture down alone. Rosa seemed to know exactly where she was at all times and where I noticed a difference in areas. She took it in her stride.

It took us about two hours to get back and approaching the farmhouse in the dark actually looked like a scene from a horror movie. When we got there Pippa was waiting for us in the lounge, a massive fire burning in the open fireplace. Even though the room was of enormous size, the entire room was as warm as toast. It was nice to be back to sit down and relax and just watch the flames flickering away that in itself made you feel warm. We told Pippa of our day in Paris and how I had been introduced to Elisa. Pippa told Rosa and I of her day in the stables, she said "oh you were wrong Pippa, the horses had been taken care of and very well. Sofia had also tended to them and their needs". When there was no one else here, she took it in turn and had ridden every horse. Ah, I thought to myself, so she had listened to Rosa earlier on then. Rosa said her trip into her old haunts had brought back loads of memories. With this, she disappeared, and that left Pippa and me alone, just cuddling on the sofa. She felt so soft and warm sitting there in her dressing gown as we both lay there, just watching the flames flicker away in the fireplace. About 10 minutes later, the door opened, and in walked Rosa. She, too, had her dressing gown on. She went over to the old Hi-Fi system on the sideboard and played some soft French songs. I could not understand the words, but the music was very nice.

Rosa walked from the music system and stood in the center of the room in front of the fire. She stood there them looked at us both and smiled, put her fingers to her lips as if to say shush. Rosa peeled off her silk dressing gown as she peeled her dressing gown she said, well you know I said it brought back memories of my old dancing days well do I have a treat for you.

And I would like to know for myself if I can still do the dance. She was holding her dressing gown together with her hands and as the music started to play, she seductively let it fall to the floor. Rosa looked amazing now the dressing gown was on the floor we could see Rosa in a very thin and tiny raincoat. She danced to the music and, as she did so, she would unbutton her thin raincoat. Pippa and I now sitting on the edge of the sofa, looking at Rosa in amazement. First one button, then the other, until all the buttons were unfastened. As she danced, she turned her back to us. And first, the coat came off one shoulder, then the other. She looked over her shoulders at Pippa and me. Then she let the coat slip just a little and exposed half of her naked back.

The flames from the roaring fire still flicking away and partially made Rosa's body a silhouette, her long dark hair hanging down her back. Rosa then allowed her coat to fall slowly from her body, still with her back to us. As the coat hit the floor, we could see she was wearing a black bask, which she had pulled in at the waist and made her body look like an hourglass. She also had a black suspender belt on which connected her black silk stockings, she had a pair of black shoes on and she looked stunning.

Rosa was dancing very provocatively to us she paid special attention to her facial expressions as she looked over her shoulder at us. Her eyes looked amazing never before had she worn her make up this way, her lips shone like stars with her bright red high glossed lipstick Rosa then sat in a chair which was to the side of the fireplace she slowly unbuckled her shoes and removed them and kicked them toward Pippa and me.

Rosa was also wearing a long pair of lace gloves. Rosa stood up, walked towards us, and put one of her legs between my legs. Never losing eye contact with me. She unfastened the clips on her suspender belt attached to her stockings. When the stocking was free from the clasps, she very slowly unrolled the stocking down the full length of her leg. As she did this, she pouted her lips as if to invite me to kiss them as I leaned forward to take her up on her offer. Her hand reached for my forehead and gently pushed me away. She raised her hand to her lips as if to shush me, and with the other hand wiggled her finger at me as if to say no, no.

When the stocking was nearly free from her leg, she lay on the floor, still not losing eye contact. Rosa lay on her back on the floor in front of me. She offered her leg to me to take the stocking from her foot that was now pointing right at my face. Rosa was amazing, and her dancing turned me on so much in every way possible. The eye contact was amazing, the choice of outfit I could not fault this lady. Pippa and I still sitting on the edge of our seats, were both aroused by what she was doing. I was sitting there with one of her stockings in my hand I was never going to give this back as I wanted this as a keepsake and a memory of this night.

Rosa had not finished. She slowly rolled over onto her front seductively and raised herself to her hands and knees. Her back was now facing Pippa, and I Rosa arched her back so she was still facing away from us, as she did this she very slowly untied the lace at the front of her bask. When the bask was half untied, she rose to her knees then to her feet, still slowly undoing the bask. All we could now see was Rosa's back. She then invited Pippa to unfasten the clips on the suspender on the other leg.

Pippa was so excited at seeing Rosa perform for us like this. Pippa wasted no time and unfastened the clips on the remaining stocking.

As Pippa did this, Rosa bent over in front of us, pushing her beautifully shaped buttocks towards our faces. As she was doing this she gracefully unrolled the other stocking, when the stocking was at her ankle she again in a sexy dance move lowered herself to the floor. This time with her leg as straight as it could be, she pulled at the stocking, stretching it to the point of ripping. Suddenly, like a cork from a bottle, the stocking became free from her leg.

Rosa again rose to her knees, then to her feet, still with her back to us. I was at a bursting point with excitement I wanted this lady so much. Rosa continued to dance for Pippa and me in a very provocative manner. She occasionally turned the back of her head to glance at Pippa and me. Whilst doing all of this, Rosa was still unlacing the bask. From the position Pippa and I were in, all we could see was her arm movements and the length of the lace that was being untied from the figure-hugging bask. With only a few lace strands to unbuckle, Rosa slowly turned to face us, the bask now nearly totally undone.

Rosa removed her long black lace gloves slowly from each hand and, pulling the last of them from her hand, using her teeth. It was so erotic to see Rosa to do what she was doing. With the bask not quite removed, you could see the enhanced shape of her ample bosom. When Rosa had removed the gloves, in turn, Pippa and I had a glove thrown in our direction.

At this stage, Pippa had removed her dressing gown and wanted this lady. Pippa clutching at the garments of clothing that Rosa had thrown our way. Rosa was now lying on the floor with her head towards us both and her feet now in the fire's direction. Rosa tilted her neck and was looking towards us and was provocatively sucking on one of her fingers in a very suggestive way.

While Rosa was giving us this amazing show of what she used to do, Pippa had now readjusted herself on the sofa. She was now lying there as Rosa touched herself. Whilst she danced, Pippa would imitate

Rosa's movement with her own hands on her body. Then Rosa raised herself to on all fours in front of us again while the entire time Rosa was being very provocative. Two or three of Rosa's fingers were now in her warm, moist mouth.

Pippa was gyrating her pelvis as if she were being slowly taken from behind. Rosa then rose to her knees and was now facing Pippa and me, who so wanted this lady. She would lick her lips, throw her head back from side to side so her hair was wildly flicking about. Rosa untied the rest of the bask. She rose to her feet. Rosa was very good at what she did, and it was an immense turn-on for both Pippa and me.

Rosa then became very suggestive with one of her hands, the bask now free from this lady's desirable body. We now thought that Pippa and I were about to see and sample this lady's body. Yes, we saw Rosa's body in all its glory, apart from her nipples as they were covered. The whole area was hidden from us by her nipples and her aureola's.

Her nipples were covered by this black stick-on plate. There was nothing to be seen apart from the beautiful shape of her breasts. The black plates had long black tassels hanging from the center of them where the nipples should have been. Rosa continued to dance for us and it was so erotic neither Pippa nor I could resist any longer. Then we beckoned her over to join us on the sofa.

Rosa slowly moved in our direction, when at the sofa Rosa squeezed herself between us and said OK my darling what did you think. There were no words mentioned by me or Pippa. We were both very excited and took a hand. Each led her to just in front of the fire, which was still roaring away as if that too had been excited by Rosa's dance moves. The red glow from the fireplace illuminated Rosa's desirable body. Pippa had laid Rosa down on this huge sheepskin rug and slowly positioned herself next to Rosa on this.

Pippa was complementing Rosa on her dance moves as she did so her hands would tremble over Rosa's body. This time Pippa could not play with Rosa's nipples, so her fingers were entwined within the tassels of the nipple covers. I lowered myself and laid the other side of Rosa. I was feeling the warmth that was being generated by Rosa's body, my fingers now caressing each and every one of her perfectly formed ribs in her body.

Pippa was now in a full-blown passionate kiss with Rosa full-on, but still soft and gentle to watch. Rosa was now running one of her hands through Pip pa's hair, I worked for my hands up and down the full length of Rosa's legs, my mouth now trembling and kissing every one of the ribs in her torso. Pippa had moved herself down and as she passed my lips, Pippa also gave me an equally nice kiss as she had given Rosa. Pippa had continued in a downward motion until she had her face level with Rosa's warm, moist vagina. I, in turn, had moved my body up and was now kissing the sides and the back of Rosa's neck.

Pippa wasted no time at all and soon had her mouth covering Rosa's moist vagina. As I kissed Rosa's neck, I glanced down to see what Pippa was now doing to Rosa. Pippa was kissing, licking, and she would occasionally nibble at the labia of Rosa's vagina, her tongue flicking and playing with her warm, delicate folds of skin. Rosa had now re-positioned herself and was lying on her side I was now lying behind her. Pippa had not moved an inch from Rosa's moistness. As we lay together, I moved one of my hands round to the font of Rosa's neck. As I moved my mouth to her spine, my mouth was now tracing and circling every one of this lady's vertebra. Pippa in the meantime had her mouth fully emerged on Rosa's moistness. Rosa took my hand from the front of her neck gently in her own hand and had placed my fingers to the lips of her mouth.

The more Pippa worked away at Rosa's wanting vagina, the more Rosa's breathing became deeper and heavier. I could feel Rosa's lips of her mouth tremble with what Pippa and I were doing to her. Her breathing became heavier. She started to suck gently on my fingers.

As I lay next to Rosa's back, I could feel my erection press against her firm buttocks.

I felt one of Pippa's hands come through between Rosa's legs. Pippa was now massaging my testicles very tenderly, Rosa was now bucking and grinding her pelvis area to what Pippa and I were doing to her. With each lick or flick of Pippa's tongue, Rosa would push and grind her buttock onto my erection. Pippa was now massaging my erection very slowly, very gently. I had no control over what was or was about to happen.

Rosa was still sucking harder and harder on my fingers that she had not released from her mouth. Pippa was now using my testicles as a handle as she had done before. Pippa adjusted my penis. So it was in the perfect position to enter Rosa's rear. Rosa was now bucking frantically Pippa had now stopped her tongue action Pippa was still massaging my manhood had pushed her head between Rosa's legs still with one hand on my testicles. Her head then found its way through to my throbbing adulthood. Pippa was very quick to react. She knew exactly what she wanted to happen.

I felt Pippa slide her mouth over the full length of my throbbing penis: she was not sucking as she had been before. She would just let her mouth slowly slide up and down the full length of my adulthood, and I could feel myself becoming wetter and wetter with each stroke of her warm, wet mouth. Pippa, after doing this for a while, removed her glorious mouth from my adulthood and slowly withdrew her head back between Rosa's open legs. Pippa went straight back to what she was doing before to Rosa. Rosa was bucking and grinding her pelvis even harder and faster than she was before, and still sucking on my fingers.

Pippa then re-positioned my adulthood, using her grip on my testicles. Rosa was now bucking hard to the rhythm and movement of Pippa's tongue. Rosa turned her head towards me and released my fingers from her mouth and just simply said gently, darling gently. Her head turned back to where it previously was and continued to suck and lick my fingers the truth was I had no control over this situation in any way. And with a short, gentle pull of my testicles from Pippa and a couple of grinds and bucks from Rosa, I felt my throbbing penis slide between Rosa's buttocks. Rosa was very tight, and I had never done this before I really did not know what to do, or what to expect. All I remember was Pippa manhandled my penis, feeling every part of Rosa as I entered her from behind. I did not resist Pippa's wishes, and even though I was being guided by Pippa's hand on my testicle, I wanted to go deeper inside Rosa. She felt so warm and such a snug fit it felt as though there was no room for error. The harder Pippa pushed on my testicles, the deeper I penetrated Rosa as I penetrated a little further each time Rosa would sort of stiffen tense herself and then relax again. I heard Rosa gasp a couple of times and my concern was that I was hurting her but at the same time receiving so much pleasure from this. I knew Rosa was also enjoying this as she never pushed me away, she only dug her fingernails into my leg as if to pull me in a little further. Every time Rosa relaxed she would grind and push a little harder into me, and as if Pippa was feeling this reciprocated by moving my penis, still using my testicles as a handle. This is why Pippa had not sucked as before when her mouth covered my penis. She was using her own saliva as a lubricant.

This was a feeling that I had never felt before yes I was now fully erect and in Rosa's back passage. I could feel the muscles in her back passage gripping my manhood even stronger than when I was in her moist, warm vagina. Her muscles in her back passage were so much stronger, and each time she tensed her muscles, I thought I was going to be pushed out. While I was deep inside Rosa, Pippa was paying very special care to Rosa's clitoris with her tongue. Still managing to have a finger inside Rosa's vagina, it was amazing every time Pippa moved her finger inside Rosa's vagina. I felt her finger on my throbbing penis. It was like I was being massaged on the penis by Pippa's finger, even though we were in separate areas. Rosa by now was groaning and bucking, gyrating her pelvis furiously, her groans of pleasure becoming louder and louder even to the point of echoing in this large room until the heat from the fire felt intense.

I held Rosa's shoulder then I whispered in her ear I'm sorry and with one final push my body tensed and I climaxed inside this wonderful lady. I climaxed and just lay there inside her, still being held in place only by the strength of her muscles and Pippa's grip. Rosa stopped bucking and gyrating. And lay there with me. Rosa moved to her back as I eventually slowly removed my penis from her.

Rosa's eyes were rolling about slowly in her eye sockets, in a state of pure pleasure. Rosa's breathing was slow and deep, every breath she took as if it were her last gasp of air. Pippa now re-positioned herself in front of Rosa, her face still buried into Rosa's moist vagina. This time Pippa was on her knees with her head buried in Rosa's channel of love, her own buttocks standing proud and exposed. Pippa never looked so good, her slender body sloping towards Rosa and her perfect buttocks in plain sight. I moved behind Pippa, my penis now becoming very interested in Pippa. I moved around behind Pippa and started to massage her back. I could now see what she was doing to Rosa, her head moving frantically from side to side and the occasional back-and-forth movement.

As I massaged Pippa's long, slender back, she began to slowly gyrate her pelvis into my growing adulthood. I held Pippa's waist firmly, and it was as if my penis had a homing beacon set inside it. It only took a few minutes of massaging her back, and I found I was fully erect again. I could feel the end of my penis sliding across the entrance to her vagina. The end of my penis finding the moist damp folds of her vagina, she continued to buck and grind her pelvis but slowed as if to allow my penis to find the entrance of her moistness. It was not long before my adulthood was ready and able to enter Pippa's moist vagina.

I slightly readjusted myself, and I was there. I felt the opening to her vagina so moist and damp that the first couple of attempts to enter her I slowly slid across the whole area. I attempted again and as I slowly pushed it was as if she had relaxed her muscles. My very erect penis just slowly slid inside this beautiful lady. As I entered her, I heard her groan "oh yes", and she continued to bury her own head in Rosa's moistness. Still holding Pippa's waist, she lifted her head from Rosa's moistness and slowly started to kiss her way up Rosa's body.

Pippa stopped moving when she had found Rosa's ample breasts and her hard but tender erect nipples. As Pippa settled onto Rosa's breasts, I began to slowly push back and forth. Rosa in the meantime had her hands running the length of Pippa's back, occasionally mixing her finger with my own. The harder I pushed, the faster Pippa bucked into my adulthood. I had not seen Pippa act this way before. She was like she was possessed. She was in a really sexually hypnotic state. Her hair sticking to her sweat-covered body the harder she bucked and gyrated into me. I released the grip of her waist and was to now massaging Pippa's back, Rosa and I, our hands intermingling with each other. Both Rosa and I felt Pippa do a massive shudder and her body stilled for a while, her back arched and then slowly laid to rest on Rosa's body. As she did this, I too felt my own body stiffen I had climaxed again and gently withdrew and laid by the side of the two girls. Eventually, I and the two girls just lay on the sheepskin in a pure heap of sexual satisfaction and that's where we fell to sleep that night.

Chapter Twenty Four

The next morning when we woke we were still in front of the fire, which had decreased in size but was still throwing out loads of heat. We were all still naked, but someone had covered us with a massive warm blanket. I thought maybe Rosa or Pippa had done this in the night. When fully awake, we kissed each other good morning under this blanket and gathered our clothes together. We made our way upstairs to Rosa's room. As we walked the hallways of this grand house and out of the room with the fire, we all felt the chill of this old house. When in the room we all in turn took a shower, got changed, and went down to the kitchen for breakfast. As we entered the kitchen, there was that smell of freshly cooked bread again Sofia, had been busy preparing us another substantial breakfast.

As we sat at the table, Sofia hoped we were all OK and all warm enough. She said I saw you as I stoked the fire I put another log on there for you all and had a cheeky little smile on her face. So it was not one of the girls.s it was Sofia who placed the blanket over us which also meant she had seen us all naked and probably worked out for herself what had happened the previous night between us.

Rosa and Pippa did not bat an eyelid and just thanked her for looking after us. All I could keep thinking was this young girl had seen us all naked and maybe I felt a little embarrassed. Over breakfast, Pippa asked if I would like to come horse riding that day. I said yes I would like to go but reminded her I was only a novice rider so asked her to take it slowly if I came to, to which she agreed.

Sofia had been listening to our conversation over breakfast. I could see she wanted to say something. I too was feeling a little shy after all. She had just seen us naked. Pippa also noticed that Sofia wanted to say something, as did Rosa. Rosa and Pippa were very extroverted, holding nothing back as if there was something that needed to be said they just asked or came out with whatever was on their minds. Sofia had heard what Pippa had said about horse riding. Pippa and I left the kitchen and left Rosa and Sofia alone. Pippa and I went back to the room and got ourselves ready for horse riding as we were leaving the house we popped our heads into the kitchen to say goodbye to Rosa but there was no one to be seen.

Both Pippa and I gave it no more thought and went out to the stables. When we got there, Pippa took charge of the situation and picked out two horses for us to ride. Much to my horror, my one looked like a racehorse and if the truth be known, I was scared out of my hiss at the thought of getting on this thing. But not wanting to sound like a wimp, we got our horses ready just as we were about to set off on our hack. Rosa and Sofia came into the yard of the stables. Rosa said great I hoped we had caught you would you mind hanging on Sofia and I will join you both if that's OK…

As Rosa and Pippa were preparing their horses, I could not help myself and allowed my eyes to wander over Sofia. What was I thinking after all the girls had taught and shown me why would I be attracted to Sofia? Where my two girls had everything and fantastic figures, this girl never really even had any breasts it was like she had a totally flat chest. There was definitely something about her that really attracted me to her. Maybe it was her very long black hair that hung from her head like smooth strands of silk.

Soon Rosa and Sofia were ready we were hacking through the grounds of this farmhouse, as Rosa called it, and came across a woodland area. We walked our horses nice and slowly, which I was so grateful for. As we were going along this narrow bridleway, Sofia piped up and in a gentle voice said, "I know of somewhere we could go?" We all decided to let Sofia lead the way first Sofia then Pippa then Rosa and at the rear was I. I could feel my horse pulling at the reins as he wanted to charge off, I shouted up to Sofia "hey remember just walk the horses" I shouted. Everyone just giggled at me but the reply I got was the one I wanted to hear "yes no problem" came back from the front.

We all wondered where Sofia was leading us to it was becoming it was as if we were in the tropics. Our clothes were sticking to us as we carried on, following Sofia for another 30 minutes or so. The bridleway that we were once on had long seemed to have vanished and we were on a small dusty pathway.

We eventually came to a clearing in the woods that we had hacked through we all rode side by side across this huge grass field towards what looked like a small mountain when we got to the rock face. We had to get off and lead our horses through this very narrow gap in the rock face. The narrow gap lasted for twenty or so feet. When through to the other side we were greeted by this wonderful sight there were a few groups of trees and in the middle of this area was a natural lake of totally crystal clear water. On the far side of this little lake, there was a waterfall. The entire area seemed to be surrounded by this rock face it was as if it had not been seen before. It was totally beautiful, an area unspoiled by humans or anything, a real perfect natural beauty spot. Sofia said it's nice yes we all said yes in amazement that something like this could still exist in today's world.

Sofia said it's safe to swim her no one comes here. With this, Sofia tied her horse's reins loosely to a tree, and before we knew what was happening, Sofia was sitting on this rock beside the lake. Sofia had taken her blouse off and lay it neatly beside her. I was right. She never used a bra of any kind. She was too small-breasted. Her jodhpurs soon followed and to were laid out neatly beside her with her blouse. Sofia climbed onto this fairly high rock about twenty feet above the level of the lake. Sofia did the most perfect dive as she entered the water. Her body hardly broke the surface. She had obviously perfected this over a period of time.

I could not wait to see this girl cooling off and swimming around I had my horse tied to a branch, and I attempted to also do a great dive. As I was about to dive, I felt my feet slip on the rocks so my dive was not as perfect as it could have been in actual fact. I think I looked a fool, but no one mentioned it. Rosa and Pippa, in the meantime, had also stripped off and had entered the water. We were all having such a great relaxing time just swimming around and playing with each other. After about an hour of swimming Sofia, said to us all come and see the waterfall. We all followed Sofia. This was her place, her secret getaway. We all followed her as though she were our leader on a great expedition.

We went behind the waterfall now looking out through the cascading water it looked fantastic to see all this water crashing down in front of our eyes. We followed Sofia even further as we went into some small caves, the rocks on our feet feeling very warm. As we came through one of the tunnels we came to a fair-sized covered area, and there were pools of bubbling Grey/ Blue mud.

Sofia reassured us all it was safe and with this, she slipped her tiny naked body into a pool of bubbling mud which was only about waist deep so you could stand if you felt unsure. When Sofia was in the pool of mud she reached up and tied her hair up into a ball on top of her head, crouching down, and covered her body in this mud. Rosa and Pippa did not need a second invite and entered into a pool just big enough for the two of them. I could hear them giggling as they covered each other's bodies in mud.

Sofia looked at me and said it is OK, it's safe and good for the skin. I got it in the tiny pool with Sofia, and she asked if I would like any help. She was totally covered and looked like an aboriginal lady, not recognizable from the kitchen in the morning. As I lay there covering myself, she came towards me, putting her hands on my shoulders, and turned my body. My back was now facing her, her hands were covered in this warm mud, and she began by massaging it into the back of my neck and my shoulders.

I could see through a gap in the rocks that Rosa and Pippa were having a great time covering each other in the mud. It felt so nice what Sofia was doing to my shoulders as Sofia asked me to lay the front of my body on some rocks. As I did this she massaged the mud hard into my back as she kept saying in broken English it's good, yes. As I stood up, Sofia was still massaging this mud into me as her hands slipped round to the front of my body. Once I stood up, her muddy fingers were now massaging my pectoral muscles after 30 minutes of enjoying this mud Sofia asked us to follow her. Again, we were like sheep being led by a shepherd. Not a word was said, and we all followed her through another tunnel. The tunnel seemed to twist and turn, sometimes walking downhill, other times we had to climb a little to go where Sofia wanted us to follow. Eventually, we came out by the side of the waterfall ten feet above the water level. We all just laid on this rock, the sun beating down on us hard and drying this mud onto us all. As the mud dried it cracked and as this happened you felt a tugging sensation on your skin.

As I lay there on my back pretending to have my eyes shut, I was watching these three beautiful ladies as the mud dried and cracked on their skin. Pippa had put an enormous amount of mud on Rosa as the mud dried on Rosa's breasts. You could see her roc- hard nipples escaping from the mud like a chick hatching from its egg.

Pippa, with her body so trim, just lied there, the sun drying the mud on her body, and she looked like a sculptured statue that had cracked over a period of time. I looked over at Sofia: she had not moved from where she first lay down, her mud had not really even cracked very much. Her stomach was like a way board very flat, her breast did not rise from her chest but I had noticed that. She had a large hard nipple's her aureola was even hardened, and this looked as though this was part of her erect nipples and that was the only part of her that had a crack, otherwise she just looked like a mud statue. A few minutes later, Sofia stood up, and as she moved, you could hear the mud on her body crack. She stood tall, well as tall as she could, and stretched the mud just cracked and fell to the floor. Rosa and Pippa followed suit as Pippa's body acted pretty much the same as Sofia's. Rosa's mud just seemed to cling to her. Sofia then turned and faced the lake and again performed another perfect dive, followed very quickly by Pippa and Rosa.

With all the girls in the water swimming around, washing the mud from their bodies, I followed and done an average dive into the water below. We all swam to the far bank where we originally got into the water and all started washing the mud from each other. Sofia was right the mud had really baked and hardened onto our bodies. As before, Rosa and Pippa were sorting each other, out washing the mud from every crevice of their bodies. Sofia and I washed our bodies the best we could, but did need to help each other in hard-to-reach areas. I was unsure if this was allowed and I looked across at Rosa and she was looking at me and with a reassuring nod of her head, sort of gave me permission. I started by washing the mud from Sofia's shoulders and again looked across at Rosa as she smiled and quietly voiced with her lips, "yes go on.".

Rosa in the meantime had laid Pippa down on a flat rock and was rubbing her hands all over Pippa. I then washed Sofia's back and my hands got to her small but very firm buttocks. Did I dare, I thought to myself. Oh hell yeah, I thought I had a sort of been given the go-ahead by Rosa and her reassuring nods.

I moved Sofia into the edge of the water, her head looking back at me smiling there was a language problem between us but sometimes words not need to be spoken. As I washed her back, my hands would touch and wash her buttocks too. When I was washing them, I could not help myself but give a gentle squeeze. I could tell Sofia liked this, as when I squeezed, she would move her body closer to mine. Sofia's tiny body felt amazing to touch, and I enjoyed every part of washing her buttocks free from the mud. The more I squeezed her buttocks, the harder she pushed into my hand, her eyes now not leaving my face. As I looked at her, I could feel myself becoming aroused. My penis was starting to rise. My thoughts were "oh God I cannot let this happen". I quickly said OK Sofia, your turn thinking that would be the end to that. I asked if she could wash my back yes she replied I was standing there with my back to her facing Rosa and Pippa. Not that they really knew that was happening as they seemed so engrossed in each other I don't think they would have f heard a bomb go off.

Sofia was washing my back so gently I thought she would never get the mud off. Her touch was so soft, so gentle. It was like a butterfly landing on you as she touched. Her nimble little fingers now tracing the line of my spine and her other hand on my waist. She led forward, looked around at Rosa and Pippa to see what they were doing. As she did this her hand had now slipped to my buttocks, she kissed the back of my neck and the hand that was on my waist was now slowly moving around to my penis with her own head still in the back of my own neck.

Sofia then said in her broken English/French accent, "so you like Adam? Yes, you like it's erotic", yes as if to look for reassurance. As she spoke to me, her tiny little hand had now gently clasped my penis and was slowly masturbating my adulthood. I said yes very quietly, as I did not really want anyone else to know what she was doing to me, but at the same time did not want her to stop. I said yes it's nice yes it's erotic Sofia. She pulled her body even closer to mine. Her tiny hands and nimble fingers felt amazing on my now throbbing penis. I allowed my eyes to shut in a moment of ecstasy as I did this: Rosa had come from behind and was pressing her body against Sofia's back, Rosa was now kissing Sofia's neck as Sofia was mine.

Pippa had moved to the front of me and was on her knees, and she watched Sofia's hand as she masturbated my adulthood. Pippa smiled at Sofia and said, good girl, good girl. Pippa liked what Sofia was doing. She was not the only one I thought. Sofia's touch was amazing and now felt I could enjoy what she was doing as both my girls were also now involved with this activity.

It was not long before Pippa's hand had joined with Sofia's and both girls were simultaneously masturbating to my penis. Pippa's other hand had now slipped through Sofia's legs and was massaging Rosa's calf muscles. This went on for some time, and suddenly Pippa's mouth went over the end of my penis. She did not engulf my penis as she had done on previous occasions, she gingerly licked the end of it and Sofia was still slowly masturbating my penis as she had been doing.

Sofia's breathing became very deep as all of this was going on Rosa was still kissing and nibbling at Sofia's neck. But now Rosa's hands were manipulating Sofia's tiny breasts, she was definitely getting a reaction from Sofia's nipples. They looked like two small hard stones upon her chest.

We carried on like this for a while, all four of us now entwined somehow on or in each other's bodies. Eventually, we slowed what we were doing and slowed to just gentle kisses. Then we got our stuff together and dressed ourselves and very slowly made our way back to the farmhouse. The sun was setting and the heat of the sun had now lost its power. As we rode back to the farmhouse, we laughed and joked mainly about the dive that I first attempted when we arrived at the lake. It was all done in good humor and not meant to offend anyone. I had a fantastic day and wow was our little Sofia full of surprise. Sofia joined us at the dinner table that night and every night after our day out together.

The conversation around the table that evening was of the fun we all had that day there was no jealousy. That was one thing. Rosa and Pippa detested there was no need for that to come into our relationship. What we had was very private but at the same time open we could speak about anything and neither of us owned the other.

Rosa's outlook on the situation was no matter who we decided to sleep with or have intercourse with, it was not cheating. We were all involved in the situation.it only became that if there were secrets, which is another thing that Rosa and Pippa requested. There were never to be any secrets between us and she believed that if all involved in the scenario were kept informed or involved, no one needed to be hurt.

There was a lot of truth in Rosa's word as always when Rosa spoke. It seemed to make perfect sense and make everything seem so right. As the evening went on, Rosa said that she needed to speak to me about some work that needed doing in the farmhouse. Rosa said, yes I know there is a lot that needs to be done, but we are here on holiday as well. So for this visit, she said that we could just get away with giving the house or parts of it a good paint job and asked what my thoughts were. I agreed that there was a fair bit of work to do, but for now, a paint job would restore this place to its former glory. I said I would have a look around in the morning to let her know how much paint she would need to get.

Pippa and Sofia had taken themselves off somewhere while Rosa and I were chatting. Rosa and I said ourselves off to bed. There was no sign of Pippa or Sofia as Rosa and I lay in bed, cuddling. Rosa said Adam can I ask you something? I said, "Rosa, the same applies to you if there is anything that you needed to know from me, just ask."

Rosa said did I like what Sofia was doing to me today? My reply was yes, I thought she was very nice and a really friendly girl. Rosa asked if I thought she was as good as Sofia, as there was a huge age gap. My reply could only be this. I said, "Rosa, there is not anyone who will or could match you. Your touch, your tenderness will never be beaten but you know this surely, don't you?"

Rosa just smiled and said it was not a problem. She just wanted to know, as Sofia reminded her of herself when she was younger. Again I just reinforced what I had just said. I said: "Rosa the way about you, your mannerisms what you teach me will never be beaten". I said to Rosa as I lay there with her. She and Pippa were my world. She smiled, gave me a huge cuddle, and kissed me.

Just as this happened, Pippa walked through the door. She was excited and could not wait to see Rosa and me. She explained, "Wow, Sofia has so many pictures of you on the walls in her room, so many articles about you when you were younger and danced". Pippa took a deep breath and said, "Rosa, the girl is infatuated with you it's like you are her mentor". She said, "the girl worships the ground you walk upon" Pippa was saying all this as she stripped and climbed in bed beside us. She gave both of us a kiss and carried on chatting about Sofia for a while, and in mid-conversation we all seemed to drift off to sleep.

Chapter Twenty Five

W hen we woke the next morning, we got up, had our showers, and went downstairs. We all were chatting, including Sofia, about how relaxed we felt after our mud experience the previous day. Sofia had been up early as she always was, baking the fresh bread for our breakfasts. As we were eating Rosa asked Sofia to come and sit beside her Sofia could not be there fast enough as Sofia sat down Rosa gave her a kiss on the cheek saying "so my darling what's with all the pictures you have and the articles in your room?" Rosa smiled at Sofia to reassure her that there was not a problem.

Sofia explained to Rosa that she had always admired burlesque dancers from a young age. When she was a young girl, she went to one of these clubs to have a sneaky look at the ladies dressed in their wonderful dresses. Both Pippa and I looked at each other in amazement as Rosa's eyes shone like stars as she sat there, listening to Sofia. It was as if what Sofia did was a carbon copy of what Rosa did when she was younger. The story was nearly word for word what Rosa had told us she did.

Sofia said after I watched that day I was hooked on burlesque dancing but unfortunately I never had the figure for it well before the bust. Rosa interrupted her story and said she knew of loads of dancers that had tiny breasts and they were very successful at what they did. Sofia explained while doing her research Rosa's name had come to her attention and Sofia said I could not believe how beautiful you were and still are. It was just by pure luck that this job came up when she had finished catering college and did not know you were the owner. But when I found out and saw the pictures on the wall I had to take the job hoping one day, I would meet you.

Rosa was so overwhelmed by Sofia's story, she just wrapped her arms around her and gave her a loving kiss. Rosa then said one day I will teach you and you will be a talented dancer as you thought I was. Sofia's eyes filled with tears of happiness. She said thank you, but I will never be as good as you.

We all finished our breakfasts, and Rosa gave me her credit card and loads of French money. She said, "there you go Adam; you take yourself off into town and get what you need to do the jobs if you don't mind"; I said, "yes, no problem!" Pippa gulped down the last of her tea and said, well if no one minds, I'm going to the stables for the day. We all laughed at Pippa. She could not be closer to horses enough and we thought that her ideal job would be to run a riding stable.

Rosa said she had some stuff to sort out, but it was on the other side of town and asked if I would give her a lift. Sofia piped up Rosa, I have finished my duties here would it be OK if I accompanied you. As would love to get to know you better, Rosa was in a seventh heaven, of course, you can Sofia was her reply. So the three of us set off to town I dropped the girls first they did not stop chatting the entire journey to each other. I went off to the other side of town and went to some suppliers for my materials for the farmhouse.

It is actually quite scary being there on my own, not really understanding the language. The girls said they would not need a lift back, so as soon as I had my stuff, I went back to the farmhouse on my own. Being in the house when I was on my own felt very strange. In each room I went into, I had that feeling I was being watched and got the feeling of the hairs standing on the back of my neck. Each room had more pictures of Rosa and not one of them repeated. Every room was totally clean I had not actually seen a lot of the house, just the bedroom we slept in and the kitchen and lounge.

The house looked immaculate I spent most of that day exploring this old house on my own in my own time. The evening was soon upon us we sat there just relaxing and watching some films. This evening was different, as Sofia joined us in the lounge. Rosa started to speak she said Sofia, and I were talking today and she has been doing burlesque dancing in front of a mirror in her room but had never danced for anyone or in front of another person in her life. Rosa looked across at Sofia and Sofia nodded her head and smiled Rosa asked if we would like to see Sofia dance.

Pippa and I both said yes at the exact same time. Sofia smiled at us and said she would be back in a moment. Sofia ran from the room to get ready. As she left to get ready, Rosa said she had never danced for anyone before in her life, so this was going to be her first time. Shortly after telling us this, Rosa also left the room. About five minutes later, Rosa and Sofia returned together. Both the girls looked amazing. Rosa said she was going to dance with Sofia. Sofia looked great she had a white lace kimono on with white stockings, suspender belt, and the most delicate lace lingerie set. Rosa was dressed equally as well, but her choice of color was a deep red as before, when Rosa had danced for Pippa and me. She went to her music system and started to play some soft music. Sofia had a massive set of white feathered fans, and the two girls started to dance for Pippa and me. We were excited as the previous dance was so great. What did this one have in store?

This was different rather than dancing separately they danced together. Pippa and I felt so privileged to see this. As they danced, Sofia slowly closed the distance between Rosa and herself and started to stroke Rosa's slender shoulders. They danced with the back of her hand as they danced, Rosa caressing Sofia's arms.

When both girls had connected with each other their hands eventually became locked in each other, they turned and their backs were now back to back as they danced like this each of the girl's hands were caressing each other body's running their hands up and down each other. They stayed like this for a short while, then slowly turned to face each other, their hands still entwined with each other. Rosa slowly lowered herself to her knees. Sofia raised one of her legs and gently placed it on Rosa's shoulder. As Sofia did this, Rosa's hands, now free from Sofia's, started to gently unclasp the suspender belt, clasps that held her stockings in place. Sofia was looking down at Rosa and sucking seductively on one of her own fingers. Rosa was slowly unrolling the stocking that she had released, unrolling it so softly and so gently when the stocking was free from Sofia's leg, Sofia turned her back to Rosa.

Rosa now set to work on the other leg and as she was unclasping the straps from this leg, Rosa was gently, barely touching, and kissing the inside of the top of her thigh. Sofia was standing upright, her legs slightly apart, and looking back and down at what Rosa was doing to her. She tilted her head to look at Rosa Sofia's long black hair draped down her slender back like a set of silk curtains. The length of her hair was now clear to see as she tilted her head back. The hair just touched her lace suspender belt.

Every so often Sofia would look across at Pippa and me flicking her hair, and it was as if it floated around her head. Sofia looked at us with such a sexy, sultry look it gave you goosebumps. When Rosa had released both Sofia's legs from those stockings, Rosa gently lead her partner towards the floor. Sofia lied on her back on the floor, with Sofia towards us, Rosa then worked her magic on Sofia. Rosa stretched out Sofia's arms as if they were tied and as Rosa straddled

Sofia, she undid her bask. Rosa did this with her teeth and as this was happening, both girls had their eyes firmly fixed on Pippa and me.

Sofia's bask was now completely untied, the lace ties that held the bask in place now loosely hung to the side of the bask. With Rosa's legs both still astride, Sofia stood over her and slowly stripped. As she slowly untied her own bask and removed her own bask, she revealed the shape of her perfect breasts. As she did this, Rosa danced seductively, and Sofia was caressing Rosa's legs.

Pippa and I thought we were going to see these beautiful breasts in their entirety, but Rosa had those nipple plates on again, which covered her nipples and areolas. These ones were red with long red tassels hanging from them. She moved forward and bent forward, which showed off the contours of Rosa's great-shaped body. As she lent forward, the tassels from her nipple plates hung toward Sofia's mouth. Sofia tried her hardest to reach out with her tongue to catch the tassels as they slowly swung about over her mouth. As Rosa did this and began to stand straight, Sofia followed and soon was on her feet. The two girls then turned to face Pippa and me. As the girls walked toward Pippa and me, they had that come to bed look in their eyes and as they approach us they licked their lips and bit gently on their bottom lips.

As they were about two feet away from us, they both simultaneously slowly let their basks now fall slowly to the floor. Sofia also had those nipple plates on so nothing could be seen, but they masked the size of her breasts and it was hard to tell if she had an ample bosom or not if you did not know. Both girls could see how excited Pippa and I were. Just as Pippa and I thought we were going to get our hands on these two beautiful ladies, they stood still. Looking at us very provocatively, they turned to face each other, bending slightly forward, giving each other a gentle kiss. Their eyes still looking at us as they separated from their embrace, turned their backs to us, looked over their shoulders, and both left the room. Pippa and I were just left sitting there on the sofa, thinking they would come back.

Shortly afterward Pippa and I were thinking this was going to turn into more. Rosa and Sofia returned to the room, but both were fully dressed. Pippa and I were confused but Rosa then said, "so OK, did we like Sofia's first dance?". We looked at each other, smiled, and said yes very good. Rosa explained that was real burlesque dancing, as you were never meant to touch. She then laughed and said not as we had done the previous night, that only happened as she wanted Pippa and me as much as we both wanted her.

Rosa said the true art of burlesque dancing is to let the audience think they are going to get more but do not give it to them. We both smiled at Rosa and Sofia and said, well that definitely happened you both left us both wanting more. Rosa said I think Sofia would have been great at dancing and would love to give her a helping hand and teach her Sofia jumped at the chance at being taught by the person she had so much admiration for.

It was then that Rosa said that Pippa and herself would be away from the whole of the next day, as they were hoping to sort the yacht out so we could all have a little boating weekend away. Rosa knew I would be interested in this but to my surprise asked Sofia if she would also be interested in coming on this trip Sofia answered straight away "oh yes please she replied".

We eventually all went about our day's activities and never really saw a lot of each other for the rest of the day. I was busy preparing some rooms for decorating, Pippa at the stables, Rosa doing paperwork and talking to Phillip, and Sofia going about her duties around the house. We all went to bed that night, Rosa, Pippa, and I in our room, Sofia in her own room.

As we were all laying there going to sleep. Rosa was talking and remarking on how much Sofia had reminded her of herself when she was young. Rosa had said she had not invited me along on the trip the next day, as she knew I had a lot to do. Before too long, we were all asleep that night.

Chapter Twenty Six

When I woke up the next morning, there was no one about I got up, showered, and dressed then went down to the kitchen. Sofia was nowhere to be seen. There was fresh bread on the table, as always. As I was having a cup of tea, I noticed an envelope on the table which was addressed to me. I sat there and opened it this is how it read...

To our dearest Adam,

We will be gone most of the day. We thought we would let you have a lay-in.
I think you should start in the basement area if that's OK with you.
We have had a word with Sofia and told her to look after you (as we would).
Hope you both have a great day. See you soon.

Rosa xxx

As I worked away in the basement area, I thought, *"well Sofia is not doing an excellent job looking after me"* she was nowhere to be seen. And what did Rosa mean by "looking after me" I was now a grown man and probably a little older the Sofia. All the rooms that I entered seemed as though they were going to be so easy, just plain walls with no papering to be done, unlike the rest of the house, which was grand.

I thought I would start by getting several rooms done at once. I heard some music coming from a room at the end of the corridor. As I approached the room, I could see the door was slightly ajar. I could see Sofia lying on her bed. She was wearing a white blouse and a black skirt, which was unzipped at the side. As she lay on her bed listening to some music, she was looking at some photos. I saw one of her hands slowly creep inside her unbuttoned blouse. Her hand was gently playing with her tiny breast. Every so often she would push her head back into her pillow I could see her nimble fingers pulling at tweaking her tiny nipples. This reminded me of the time that I peaked at Rosa through her bedroom door when I was dating Donna I stood there for a while, just thinking back to the past.

Sofia must have heard me. As I was not quiet at all, I thought no one was there. Her hand still inside her crisp white blouse, she turned her head towards the door in a soft gentle French accent she said Adam is that you. Rather than just slip away and not let on what I had just seen, I said yes, Sofia, it's only me as though I had not seen a thing. I am working down here today Sofia said please come in. I said OK and pushed the door open she did not bat an eyelid was still lying there on her bed. Her hand still inside her blouse, Sofia said please Adam, sit with me and patted the edge of her bed.

I sat as requested she did not attempt to hide what she was doing I could not help myself but look at her tiny hands inside her blouse. I could see she was not wearing a bra and that both her hard tiny nipples were darkened and showing through her blouse. When Sofia's nipple became erect, it looked like the whole of her tiny breasts were erected on her chest. Sofia said in her broken French accent, "Adam be honest" I replied, "yes of course" she asked if I liked the dance that she and

Rosa had done. I said yes, it was great, and she was fantastic: Sofia then said yes, but not as good as the dance that Rosa had done for you and Pippa a few nights ago.

Before I could say another word, she explained she had been watching that night through the door at the end of the room. I interrupted and said how much did you see. Sofia said she saw everything and was hypnotized by Rosa's performance Sofia also said she liked very much watching what the three of us had done and experienced together. Her soft, broken French/ English accent made her voice sound so sexual. Sofia added she wished she had the nerve or was brave enough to come into the room and join us.

I said maybe you should have come in and joined us seeing as how well we all get on together. We all seemed to get on the day we all went on that horse ride, Sofia said so you liked that, then yes. I replied yes, of course, I enjoyed that day what man would not enjoy being surrounded by three beautiful naked ladies yes Sofia it was a truly amazing day. Sofia agreed and smiled at me she said if I could have changed one thing that day it would have been she paused and said, no I must not say.

I said please Sofia tell me what you would have changed Sofia smiled and said as much as I enjoyed Rosa kissing the back of my neck she would have liked to have changed places with Pippa. I had sort of forgotten most of the details of that day, as I did everything that seemed to happen between us. As always, the harder I tried to remember, the harder it was for me to remember every detail. I asked Sofia to remind me of the day and the details she would have liked to change.

Sofia said she loved washing the mud from my body and was really aroused that day. The whole thing had made her so excited she said how she loved seeing Rosa, Pippa and I naked, but really enjoyed watching Rosa and Pippa enjoying each other as she washed me. The touching and caressing that they were doing to each other looked so sensual. Sofia then said but Adam I wanted to exchange places with Pippa I was so excited and aroused by what Pippa was doing to you and to feel how excited you were and responsive to her every touch. She said please forgive me but I wanted to feel your penis in my mouth "sorry" Sofia said quickly.

I said no please do not be sorry and listening to her speak I could feel myself becoming aroused by the sound of her voice. I then said look Sofia now sitting close beside her on the bed. Rosa, Pippa, and I have this special relationship, and yes it is truly fantastic. There are never any secrets between us and we are very open and honest with each other. Sofia then said yes. She knew what sort of relationship I had with Rosa and Pippa and that she thought it was great and was jealous if the truth is known.

Sofia then said that Rosa and Pippa were at the breakfast table this morning and Rosa took me to one side and asked me to look after you while they were gone in every way. As Sofia spoke, her hand had not left her blouse and I could see when she was speaking to me she was pulling, twisting, and tweaking her nipple quite hard. Her other hand was now on my leg as we spoke I did not say a thing but inside I was so turned on by this girl I wanted to rip her clothes off and I know what Rosa and Pippa had been teaching me but just wanted to fuck her. The hand that was on my leg was just barely touching me, but I could feel a tremendous heat from her hand as it slowly glided over my leg.

Sofia then said, "so Adam, if I am meant to look after you in every way", and smiled with such a cheeky smile. "Is there anything you would like me to do for you?" again smiled at me. I thought there was plenty that she could do for me, but was I thinking along the same lines as her. As she said this to me she removed her hand from her blouse and turned and lied on her side. Her hand was now slowly moving up and down the length of my back no we were not thinking differently we were both very much thinking the same thing. Her other hand was now supporting her head as she lay there, looking at me. Her long black hair was covering the hand supporting her head. Sofia's thin white blouse was unbuttoned and her tiny pert breast were both on show.

Sofia smelt lovely, a perfume that I had not smelt before was looking at me. Sofia said "Adam can I ask you something?" "Yes," I replied, "anything you want to know just asks". Sofia asked me "Adam do you like me?" and was her body making me excited. She smiled at me as she rolled onto her back. I said, yes of course I like you, Sofia what's not to like. And yes, you have a fantastic petite body and yes, her body also excited me. Sofia then said, "Adam, please touch me, touch me the way you touch Rosa, please." Sofia now lying flat on her back, her crisp white blouse falling to each side of her, her tiny but hard breasts fully exposed. Is this what Rosa meant by what they had said to Sofia.

I wanted to touch her so much. In my head, I kept playing this over and over. Was this wrong if I did as my urges wanted me to, would this be cheating on my two girls? With this, Sofia started to stroke my arm. "What's the matter, Adam? Do you not like it? Do you not want to touch me?" If only she knew how I felt and what I wanted to do to her. I said yes I liked it, and I really wanted to touch her with this Sofia slowly sat up on her bed and removed her blouse. She slowly reached for one of my hands and firstly guided my hand to her flat, very firm stomach. I felt every firm and toned muscle this lady had in her tiny framed body.

Her hand was still on mine, guiding me now to her small but pert breasts, my hands not resisting the guidance I was getting from her hand. My hand now feeling the hardness of her darkened nipples, I removed my T-shirt, Sofia now releasing the gentle clasp she had on my hand. I was now touching this lady of my own accord as Sofia readjusted herself and now lay her head in my lap. Her tiny nimble finger was now dancing, trembling over my abdominal muscles. Sofia turned her head and began kissing each and every individual abdominal muscle I had.

I found this very exciting, and my penis was now becoming harder beneath where her head lay. Moving her head and slowly lying on her back on her bed, I was now kneeling at the side of her bed. Sofia was just lying there looking at me so seductively as if to say please just come take me, make love to me, fuck me. These are the signals I was getting from her eyes as she looks at me.

I moved my mouth to her flat stomach, smelling the perfume that she wore. My tongue was now circling her navel and one hand gently caressing and feeling the hardness of her nipple. Her nipple and aureole were as if it were just one huge nipple. I could hear Sofia muttering something softly in French. I could also feel my penis throbbing in my trousers as if trying to escape and get at this young lady.

Her breathing getting deeper and deeper with every move either of us made, I moved my mouth to her nipples and sucked and caressed them. In turn, I licked and sucked around the outer edge of her breasts, one of her hands now running through my hair. I placed my mouth fully over one of her nipples and slowly took the whole of her nipple, if not the whole of her breast, into my mouth. Whilst my mouth had fully engulfed one of her breasts, my tongue was circling and sucking on her hard little rocket.

While I was doing this to her one of her hands had found the buttons on my trousers and slowly she unopened each one until my penis was free from its restraint. Sofia knew exactly what to do, and as soon as my penis was free from any clothing, she very slowly masturbated my adulthood. It was so soft, the softest masturbation you could think of. Her tiny nimble fingers trembling up and down the full length of my now throbbing penis. We carried on like this for a while I was again in a hypnotic-like state of pleasure.

I soon readjusted myself and was again now kissing Sofia's navel, my tongue darting back and forth in her tiny belly button. As I lay there doing this, I unbuttoned her skirt and pulled the final few inches on her zip and her skirt became free from her body and just lay beneath her. I moved my mouth a little further down so my mouth was just above her pubic area. I would have sworn that I could smell the sweetness of this lady's vagina as I lie there.

Sofia still letting her fingers tremble and dance the full length of my now aching penis, I wanted her so much her hand had a gentle grip on my hair and was pushing my face very delicately to her vagina. Doing this, my tongue flicked and licked its way through her short pubic hair. As she was directing my head, one of my hands had found the outer lips of her vagina and my hand was tumbling with her labia lips. Sofia continued to moan and groan with pleasure in French as I did this: her vagina matched the rest of her body. Her vaginal lips were so neat her pubic hair looked as if it had had a makeover. My head still being pushed slowly down. It was not long before my tongue had found her hard clitoris. My tongue flicked and licked at this until I could feel Sofia grind beneath me and give the occasional thrust of her hips towards me every now and again I would hear "yes yes yes".

After only a little while, I felt this warm sensation on my tongue. Sofia tasted so sweet. As she climaxed, her hand pushed my head harder into her. One of my fingers covered in her own climax was now on her septum, slowly doing the figure of 8 sequences. As I did this, she would grind her pelvis hard towards me until my finger continued in a downward movement. My finger left her septum and was now circling the entrance to her rear my finger would feel the tightness of her rear and every so often just push a little inside her. Every time I did this she would stiffen and freeze, then relax again, her grip on my hair becoming tighter and tighter. Sofia obviously liked what I was doing, and this is how I carried on for several minutes, moving from her back passage to her septum and onto her vagina for some lubrication and repeat the complete process.

As I was doing this Sofia said, "Adam, please, please just take me, make love to me, fuck me, do whatever you want." Her breathing becoming so deep beads of sweat becoming visible on her body, her hair now sticking to her face. I climbed onto her single bed with her, the beads of sweat now appearing on both our faces. The situation was so intense. As I positioned my body on top of her, she looked at me and just slowly opened her legs. I lowered my pelvis area between her legs and we both felt secure. We lay there for a short while just kissing and caressing there did not need to be any words spoken I pulled her long dark hair free from her face so we could kiss with more ease.

I slightly rose to my knees and was now kissing and tracing the line of her spine with my tongue as I did this. I could still feel my penis throb as it now lay between her legs. Sofia said in her soft voice, "please Adam, take me with this" I put my hands around her waist and helped her onto all fours. The hair on her head was flicking wildly apart from the stands that were now stuck firmly in place on her sweat-covered back. I positioned myself so my eagerly throbbing penis would slide slowly inside this lady's warm, moist vagina. I took a firm grip of her waist and as I slowly pushed and entered her moistness, she would buck and grind herself into me. Harder and harder with every push I gave, it only took a few gentle pushes from Sofia's pelvis, and I was deep inside her. We made love like this slowly for a while, enjoying each other's bodies fully. As we were making love in the doggy style, one of her hands came from underneath and was massaging my testicles.

It felt as if I could not hold on for much longer my penis was so deep inside this petite lady, her vaginal muscles caressing every part of my throbbing penis. I slowly ran my hands down the length of her back and as I did this, I slowly removed my penis from her moistness.

I moved back slightly but still massaging her back with my hands; I kissed and nibbled at her perfect buttocks until my tongue soon found the craves between her two buttocks.

My tongue was tracing the line of her craves until my tongue found the entrance to her rear, my tongue felt electrically charged, and was feeling every little bump around the entrance to her rear. Sofia seemed to like what I was doing very much as I let my tongue dart in and out of her tight little hole. Every so often she would buck and grind her rear onto my tongue. As I was doing this my penis had stopped throbbing so felt I could carry on so decided to re-enter Sofia. Her hand that had previously been massaging my testicles had now found its way to my penis, and Sofia guided my penis to the entrance of her rear.

Sofia said in a soft voice, "please Adam, take me anally" she was in total control and placed my penis at the entrance of her bum. She wet her fingers with her other hand and lubricated her rear with her own saliva. With this Sofia slowly guided and pushed onto my penis she felt so tight I did not think I would be able to enter her, but she knew exactly what she was doing as very slowly I entered her all I could hear was Sofia muttering oh yes every so often.

Sofia had her head buried into the sheets of the bed. It felt totally amazing to be inside her. Feeling every twist and movement she made, Sofia increased the speed of bucking and grinding: there was no time to warn her of my climax. I felt I was about to explode at any moment suddenly she slowed down to a near stop with me still deep inside her this sort of gave me time to regain some control over myself. Just as I thought I had regained control. She moved again, slowly at first, and gradually she was working back up to her previous speed. Amazing as it felt I knew I could hold out no more and held her waist and said Sofia I am going to cum. She lifted her head from the sheets, turned, looked at me, and smiled one of her hands stretched back grabbed my leg. She let her head slowly fall back to the sheets this time she watched me rather than bury her head in the sheets.

As I pushed into her, I felt myself climax, and it truly felt as though I was climaxing over and over. Never before had I climaxed this way. As Sofia pulled away from my penis, she asked me to lie on my back as I did as she requested Sofia straddled my body and lowered her face to my chest. She moved her head down my body very slowly I felt one of her hands still on my nipple tweaking, pulling, and twisting sometimes quite hard. As her head moved down my body, I felt her tongue trace every one muscle in my abdominal area. Sofia eventually reached my now-going limp penis Sofia went straight to my penis, picked it from my body with her mouth, and took my limp penis into her mouth.

Sofia's mouth was so warm and soft, and I could feel every movement of her tongue. I could feel the limpness of my adulthood slide down her throat as she sucked on me as she continued to work her mouth on my penis to my disbelief I could feel myself slowly becoming hard once again. Sofia carried on just caressing my limp penis for about twenty minutes or so, until I was somehow fully erect again. Once I was fully erect, Sofia moved her face further up my body. Kissing and licking as she moved up her lips, not leaving my body, for an instance.

When her face was level with mine, she kissed me on the lips, her own lips feeling so soft and warm and even slightly puffed up. It felt great as she kissed me passionately on the lips, her long black hair covering my face in places. One of her hands had moved back down to my penis, and she was massaging it to maintain the hardness that she had worked so hard on. She rose to her knees and positioned herself above my body so my penis was now at the entrance to her very warm, moist vagina.

She held my penis in place as she slowly lowered her warm, moist vagina onto my penis. She shuffled her legs on the bed and had brought both her legs forward, making sure I stayed fully inside her. Her hands stretched back and both hands holding both my legs firmly to the bed. Sofia said you like Adam "yes" I said oh god yes Sofia I like. Sofia said, "we called this *cowgirl position. Do* you like it, Adam?", "yes, yes, yes!" I replied.

Sofia, slowly at the first, rose and down on the full length of my penis. I could feel her becoming wetter and wetter with every bounce she took. Her bouncing was becoming more and more frantic when she rose while on my penis. I felt as though I were going to pop out of her moistness. Sofia seemed to have superb control over what she was doing, and I remained inside this lady. It was my turn to utter some words it felt so good I asked her not to stop as she rode me like a horse, feeling every part of her moistness rubbing gently against my penis.

Sofia slowed to a near stop again. As she did so she lent forward and kissed me. As she sat back up with me firmly still inside her, Sofia turned her whole body around. Now she had her hands placed differently, one hand on one of my ankles, the other stretched back and pulling hard on my nipple until she now had her back facing me, my hands trying to massage her back. Sofia started again to rise and sink into my penis, Sofia becoming even wetter than before. Sofia's moans and groans of pleasure were now becoming uncontrollable and turning to screams of ecstasy. In between her groans of pleasure, she would shout out, Adam, fuck me, fuck me, yes. Sofia was riding me so hard and fast I thought she was going to break me every time she sank her moistness hard into my penis. Every time she sank back down onto me, it was as if I was being spanked by the cheeks of her bum.

Sofia had total control over what was happening. Well, from her side, her vaginal muscles held my penis so firmly in place. I could take no more and barely had time to warn her of my climax as my body stiffened and, with a large shudder of my body, I exploded inside this lady. As I did this, I felt an amazing warm gush surround my penis until she too had climaxed she released the grip of my ankle and nipple and lay her body onto mine. We lay there like this for a while, just relaxing, enjoying what we had just experienced together, both totally and fully sexually satisfied.

I had really enjoyed what Sofia, and I had done together, and it was so different from what I had experienced with Rosa and Pippa. A tremendous amount of guilt came over me as Sofia and I lay together. It was a feeling of guilt that had reached the bottom of my stomach. This must-have shown on my face as Sofia turned to kiss me and said what is a matter Adam did you not like. You did not enjoy what we did. I could see the look of confusion on her face as she said this to me. I quickly reassured her, giving her a kiss and told her she was fantastic and that yes, I enjoyed what we did very much. I tried to explain that I felt I had been unfaithful to Rosa and Pippa.

She sighed and said, "no you have not. Adam, Rosa wanted me to look after you." By what she had said to her that morning, Sofia said I am sure she meant in every way, including this way. True, the note that Pippa and Rosa had left me had been leading maybe this is what both Rosa and Pippa wanted to happen. Sofia reassured me that everything would be OK, gave me a kiss, and left the room to sort herself out and got dressed. She just carried on with her duties as though nothing out of the ordinary had happened.

I carried on with my work in the basement area the best I could. Despite that, the feeling of guilt was eating away at me inside. Whilst working, I had decided that the only option for me was to tell Rosa and Pippa what had happened. I would have to take my chances and hope that both Sofia and I had not read their messages to us wrong.

The day wore on; the morning disappeared in the activities that Sofia and I got up to. The afternoon was full of work and my feelings of guilt that evening came and the girls had returned. Rosa and Pippa were in the kitchen with Sofia. I had never felt so scared or nervous in my life until this point of what was going to be said.

I listened to the other side of the kitchen door just to see what the atmosphere was like. There was lots of talking going on, but the atmosphere seemed to be OK. I stood there a little longer, listening. I heard Rosa speak. So Sofia, how did your day go with Adam and heard both girls giggle a little. My thoughts were this is where I get asked to leave I stood there waiting for an eruption of voices.

Sofia full of the joys of life said, oh Rosa, I had such a lovely day. Adam is such a lovely man and promptly reeled off everything that we did. I just did not know what to do should I just go pack my stuff and leave. Sofia went into great detail with her story. There was no eruption of voices. In fact, Rosa and Pippa seemed very interested in what Sofia was telling them. The door at the other end of the kitchen was also open and as I could not see their faces I went all the way around and was listening to the other door and could see the reaction on their faces too.

Rosa and Pippa were far from being angry with Sofia and me. As I watched from the safety of the door, I could see that Rosa and Pippa were sitting on either side of Sofia as she told of our sexual adventure that morning. As they sat next to her, they both encouraged her to tell the story in great detail and not to leave a thing out. Rosa and Pippa actually looked as if they were getting excited, or even aroused, by the story from Sofia.

It felt safe to walk in, but I was still riddled with guilt. As I walked into the kitchen, the girls stopped talking and Rosa stood from the stool she was sitting on. Was I now going to get a frying pan wrapped around my head, no Rosa stretched out her arms "hello darling, she said come here". As I walked towards her, she cuddled me and gave me a kiss. Pippa also stood and was all smiles, and she too gave me a kiss. Sofia just sat there smiling like the cat who had got the cream and was very pleased with herself. Rosa then spoke she said she was glad that I had had a nice day and was pleased that Sofia looked after me in the way she hoped she would.

Rosa turned back to Sofia, holding her by her shoulders, gently pulling Sofia to her and held her head upwards, and gave Sofia a loving kiss right on the lips. She smiled at Sofia and said thanks for looking after our Adam while we were away. The rest of the evening was just spent talking about Rosa and Pippa's day out together and how they had arranged the boating weekend. What Sofia and I got up to that day was not mentioned any further the whole evening.

Rosa and Pippa were very pleased with themselves and said the boat was in tip-top condition and ready for us to use whenever we were ready. They, too, seemed to have had a great day together. At the end of the night, Sofia said good night and gave each of us a kiss in turn, and took herself off to bed. Shortly afterward, I went off to bed with Rosa and Pippa. As we lay in bed, we just had some general conversations, and what Sofia and I got up to was not mentioned by either of the girls.

I asked Rosa if she was annoyed with me for what I had done with Sofia. Rosa replied, "no Adam, not at all, and said do not be silly". She then said if I did not read the note, she had left me. I said, "yes Rosa, I had read it but was concerned that I may have overstepped the mark." Rosa then said, "look, Adam, there are no secrets between the three of us and you are not our sexual slave to do with as we wish. But if you do ever have a sexual encounter with anyone else and come back to Pippa and me, then we know we must do something right" and smiled at me. Then said both Pippa and I are older than yourself and it would be wrong of us to keep you to ourselves if that is not what you wanted so a little bit of experiment is good for you at your age. And after all, both Pippa and I encouraged this to happen a little. We just lay there chatting and cuddling and all fell asleep together as we normally did, with just the odd kiss here and there.

Chapter Twenty Seven

We all woke about the same time the following morning: Pippa was first out of bed and into the shower. As she was in the shower Rosa and I just laid there together, our arms wrapped around each other, Pippa came out of the shower, the steam rising from her body. She sat at the dressing table drying herself off properly, blow-drying her hair. She looked stunning this morning as she dressed she applied her perfume, which filled the room with a soft gentle fragrance. Pippa put her riding clothes on so there was no need to ask what she had planned for the day she looked across at Rosa and me and said, "come on you two, are you getting up?"

Rosa and I looked at each other, then back at Pippa. Rosa spoke and said we will in a little while. I just want to lie with Adam a little longer. And smiled at Pippa.

Pippa said no problem, looked at us both, smiled, and headed off for the kitchen. As she closed the door to the bedroom, she looked back and said see you both later, and blew us a kiss.

It felt so nice just to lay there with Rosa in each other's arms it actually felt as though we had not done this for a long time just Rosa and I. We turned and faced each other and our arms wrapped around each other's body we lay there so peaceful and as our eyes locked onto each other, we slowly kissed. What Rosa and I were doing was so soft and felt so right. It had so much feeling behind it. As we kissed our hands touched and stroke each other's body's not an intrusive bit in a gentle caring way. Rosa's hands felt like they were covered by silk gloves. Her touch was so soft, warm, and gentle.

Neither of us said a word as we did not need to, as our action spoke volumes. Neither of us wanted this feeling of pure satisfaction to end, whilst neither of us wanting to make the first move. Still kissing, Rosa dragged back the sheets that covered us she slowly pulled away and get out of bed. Rosa, now totally out of the bed, stood there, the sun shining through the window, highlighting every contour of her body, and stretched out her arms. She lent forward taking my hand and slowly pulled I followed with no hesitation at all.

Still kissing, she led us both to the shower room, still holding my hand as she set the temperature of the shower. The shower room filled with steam as we climbed into the shower together. Rosa closed the screen behind us and there we were in this steam-filled cocoon. Rosa turned her back to me and asked me to wash and massage her back. This I did also, with no hesitation. Rosa's own hands were holding her hair up and clear of her back. I could wash and massage the full length of her perfect back with one hand while the other was massaging her shoulder.

Rosa shortly after-wards took my hand from her shoulder and was sucking on my fingers. I washed her back as she pushed her against me, my back against the cold tiled wall of the shower. She sucked on my fingers, gyrating her pelvis and pushing her buttocks into me. I very slowly turned Rosa around to face me. Doing this, I transferred our positions. So she had her back against the tiled wall. I removed my fingers from her mouth and soaped both of my hands. I washed and massage the front of her perfectly formed body as we had our shower together that morning. Our eyes never separated.

We eventually left the shower and stood together in a powerful embrace, and dried each other down very gently with our towels. We returned to the bedroom and got ourselves dressed and walked down to the kitchen together, by the time we were in the kitchen there was not a soul to been seen. Rosa and I spent most of the day together just walking the grounds of the old farmhouse across large grass-covered fields. Stopping for the occasional kiss. But it truly felt as though we were on a different planet than everyone else.

The whole time we were on the country walk we never saw another person it was as if we were in our own tiny little bubble and there was not a soul around to pop it. As the afternoon drew on, we made our way back to the farmhouse after the sun had settled on the horizon of the fields. As we approached the farmhouse, we had to walk past the stables. There we saw Pippa and Sofia: they had both been out on a hack on their horses.

We stopped briefly with them and had a chat Rosa asked how their day had gone. Pippa just smiled at us both, licking her lips, and said, oh it was a great day. Sofia looked hot and ruffled up a little, so I guessed that Pippa and Sofia had spent some quality time together getting to know each other on an intimate level as Sofia and I had done the previous day. Rosa and I made our way back to the house, soon followed by Pippa and Sofia.

We all chipped in together, preparing the evening meal. When the meal was ready, we all sat around the table together, talking about our day's activity. Rosa spoke of me fondly, but soon got on to the subject of the work that needed to be done in the farmhouse. It was agreed that night that I would go and get the remaining materials from the town in the morning. At the end of the evening, Sofia made her way down to her room after saying her good nights. Rosa, Pippa, and I made our way to our room there was no sexual activity that night we just lay together, cuddling as we fell to sleep.

Chapter Twenty Eight

The next morning came, and I was first to wake up, so I quietly got out of bed and got showered. When I had finished my shower, I came back into the bedroom and the two girls were still fast asleep. I sat in a chair in the room's corner just watching them sleep with their arms wrapped around each other it was nice just to watch them sleep so I left them alone.

I went down to the kitchen and got to the kitchen about the same time as Sofia. I asked Sofia if she would like a coffee she looked in surprise as she was the one who normally waited on people but replied "yes please Adam". As I was making the drinks, Sofia went about her daily ritual of baking bread for breakfast. She looked so fresh and lovely in her back skirt and a white blouse, her long black hair tied back in a ponytail.

I finished my drink and said my goodbyes to Sofia, yet there was still no sign of the girls. I said that I was going to get an early start and go off to the suppliers to get the rest of the paint that I needed. Leaving the kitchen, I looked back at her and Sofia was just standing there and gave me a gracious smile. I drove for about 90 minutes. It was going to be another boiling day so after I got the paints; I was close to this small fishing village, which had a nice harbor area.

Parking up the truck in a side street, I went for a walk along the harbor front, the front of the harbor was lined with restaurants and coffee shop-type cafes. I sat on some chairs that were placed outside one of these cafes about midway through the harbor. Doing nothing really apart from people watching as this is what I loved doing, just watching other people go about their business, to see the way they spoke to each other and the way some people dressed themselves.

As I was sitting there doing this, minding my own business, mainly thinking how lucky I was to have had Rosa take me under her wing and the way she and Pippa looked after me. I saw this girl walking along the quayside and would stop nearly at every table that was occupied she was begging for money. Most of the people just shunned her away as the servers would come from the restaurants and move her on so she would not disturb their customers.

I could not help but think how lucky I was compared to this starving girl. As she approached my table her head was down facing the floor without even looking she said in an English accent which surprised me "have you any change sir" She looked so thin and worn out and as if she was on her way out.

As she asked me for some money she lifted her head slightly and when she looked she sort of double looked and quickly lowered her head again. She was about to leave, thinking I would not help my life was good. As I said so, I found some change in my pocket. As I stretched out my hand to give her some money, our hands bumped into each other and the money I was about to give this girl was knocked from my hand and fell to the floor.

I know she was begging for money but did not mean for that to happen I did not want her to be on her hands and knees picking up a small amount of change. As she picked the money up, I lowered to the floor and helped her gather the change together. Without her even lifting her head towards me she said "Thank you, Adam". I was shocked and very surprised as I was not known in this area in any way.

Saying said this she lifted her head and looked at me who was she I could not place her at all.

She then said, "you do not remember me do you?" Looking at her I thought I knew her but could not place where I knew her from. She said I am Rebecca do you remember me now my mother is Victoria. I could not believe what I was seeing and hearing I asked her to sit with me at the table I was sitting at. She did just that and no sooner we were sitting at the table a server came rushing out of the restaurant to move her on. She assumed she was begging from me. The server tried to move her on from my table and I told him to leave her alone the server said she is a beggar sir and does this every day.

In a sharp voice, I said this is an old friend of mine and she was my guest and asked him to go away. The server reluctantly went back inside, and I saw him speaking to what must have been the manager and the manager was standing there shaking his head. I held one of Rebecca's hands and put the other on her shoulder. "Is that really you Rebecca?" I said. Lowering her head again in embarrassment and said yes, and cried. I asked if she was hungry and she just nodded, not saying a word.

I beckoned the server to come to my table, who was still standing there with the manager. It was the manager who came to the table I said "I would like to order a large breakfast please" the manager said, "is it for you, sir?" I said, "not for my friend". He stood there and shook his head and said, no sir, you cannot feed beggars like this. I jumped up from the table and in no uncertain terms put this man in his place. I said this was an excellent friend of mine and if I wanted to buy her a breakfast, then that's what I would do. The manager was embarrassed that I had spoken to him this way.

Rebecca said "Sorry Adam" and went to get up and leave. I said and where are you going? She said she was sorry and did not mean to cause me any trouble. I told her to sit back down. Telling the manager to go and get what I had ordered, which he did, the meal eventually arrived at our table and Rebecca sat there eating as though she had not eaten for a week.

As Rebecca was eating the meal, I told her she could not carry on like this and she was to come with me. As she was eating, tears were rolling down her face. I said I was in France with Rosa and Pippa and she should come back with me to the farmhouse.

Rebecca agreed. While she was finishing her meal, I tried to phone Rosa from my cell phone. The first time it went through to answer the phone I did not leave a message as the information I had was far too important for a voice mail message. I tried again and Rosa answered my battery was now running low on the phone so I explained as fast as I could I have found someone who I was bringing back to the house with me. The line was breaking up I said Rosa, please just get a room ready. Through the crackling on the phone I could hear her ask who have you found and just as my battery died I said Rebecca, Victoria's Rebecca.

Driving back to the farmhouse, Rebecca had fallen asleep on the back seat of the truck. She looked so worn out and so very different from the time I had seen her at her mother's house. Walking full of confidence from her bedroom to the bathroom with her fire-engine red hair, her hair was now a dirty blonde. Her body was nothing like the picture I had in my head. It was as though she was a different person.

I drove as fast as I could back to Rosa's at the old farmhouse. As I drove down the driveway to the old farmhouse, Rebecca was still asleep. Rosa and Pippa were waiting by the front door. As soon as my truck was stopped, the two girls came running over. I got out just before they got to my truck and went to them I Said Rosa, how much of my conversation did you hear.

198

Rosa said I heard you say that you were bringing someone back. Then heard you say Rebecca, Vicki's daughter, and that was it "where is she"? I said she was asleep on the back seat but before you look or wake her up prepare yourself for a shock. She is nothing like how I remembered her.

Rosa and Pippa approached my truck very quietly and slowly, so as not to wake Rebecca. When Rosa looked through the window, she saw this girl and could not believe her eyes and cried, turned and held Pippa. She was sobbing on her shoulder when Rosa had contained herself and regained her composure as she very gently woke Rebecca from her deep sleep. Rosa and Pippa ushered Rebecca into the house and straight up to a room that Sofia had prepared for the new guest.

Rosa remained with Rebecca for the rest of the day. Pippa came down to the kitchen and sat with Sofia and me. They had wanted to hear my story of how I had found her repeatedly. Pippa stood up and threw herself at me, giving me the biggest kiss ever, and just kept saying thank you as if it were her daughter I had found.

Needless to say, there was no work done by me that day. The day seemed to vanish so quickly after that Rosa was nowhere to be seen that day, as she did not leave Rebecca's side. She sat in a chair by the side of her bed as if to watch over her like a mother hen. That evening it was Sofia, Pippa, and I at the dining table. Sofia would flit back and forth to Rosa and Rebecca, taking whatever Rosa requested. When it finally came to bedtime, which had seemed like such a long day, it was just Pippa and me in the bed. Before going into the bedroom, we both quickly looked in on Rosa and Rebecca to make sure they were both OK.

Rebecca was still fast asleep, and Rosa just sat there, looking at her. Rosa said that she was going to spend the night in Rebecca's room because if she wakes up she will not know where she is and panic. Rosa said that terrible things must have happened to her, as every so often she would shout out in her sleep and even scream. She also noticed that she was sweating so much as if she had a tropical fever and was not really sure what to do.

You two run along and get some sleep, Rosa said Pippa said did she want her to stay with her. Rosa said, no it will be fine and she would see us both in the morning. We both left Rosa to Rebecca, as Rosa was doing what she thought was necessary. Pippa and I went to bed, and all she kept saying was thank you, Adam, as we lay there. That night the bed felt empty without Rosa, and I don't think either of us had a splendid night's sleep.

The morning was soon upon us, and we were awake very early. We went down to the kitchen Rosa and Rebecca were both sitting there talking. Rebecca saw me and smiled at me, got off of her stool and came over, held me tight, and said thank you Adam thank you so much. She had a little cry on my shoulder as Rebecca pulled herself together and explained what had happened and told her story.

She started her story by saying that she was very lucky to be here with us, as the man who owned the cafe was basically telling her to go away. If it were not for Adam, she said I would still walk the streets now. She then started her story at the beginning she explained that while at university in the UK she had met this older man and got intimately involved with him his name was Neil. She said he seemed so perfect Neil treated her so well he treated her too many things and looked after her really well.

But in the circle of friends they had, well, Neil had she soon was taking drugs not realizing how serious this was. Neil did not help when it came to Rebecca taking drugs in actual fact, he encouraged it. In the end, he was supplying her with whatever drugs she wanted. She said I dropped out of university as I found I could not concentrate on my coursework. By now my life was consumed by drugs and the need to be with Neil. That is when she said that is when I met you Adam at my mother's house she started to cry and Rosa and Pippa soothed her by cuddling her.

Rebecca said it was shortly after that Neil said out of the blue he was going to Europe. She said the thought of losing Neil was so unbearable so without so much as a goodbye packed some things and she left with Neil. This is when you were renovating my mother's house. I thought I should just keep quiet and let her tell her story, not interrupt or tell her how upset Vicki was. Rebecca then cried again and said how is her mother? Rosa reassured her she was fine but missed her so, so much.

Rosa said it was her not knowing where you were or why you had gone in such a hurry and not even said goodbye. Adding that your mother loves you, Rebecca, you know that, don't you? Rebecca cried again Rosa gave her time to calm down and collect her thoughts together. Rebecca continued with her story. She said first we went to Spain and everything was great we were there for about 10 days and we headed to France. Spain was great it was just like a holiday relaxing in the day, drugs and partying every night. But my drug addiction was getting worse and I not even realizing it.

When we got to France, we were living a high life. Neil had gone to meetings with this new bunch of people. He said they were business meetings, and I did not like to interfere, as Neil did not like me asking too many questions about his work. But by this time I was fully addicted to drugs and was taking so many I did not even know what drugs I was taking and was totally out of control of what I took by Neil.

Rebecca said I would off done anything Neil asked her if not for no other reason but just for the next fix of drugs. After a while, I said I was lonely when he went to his business meetings so he used to take me along with him. Every time I went with him, I was as high as you can imagine. At first, he used to say could I befriend his business associates my drug-taking was getting worse and worse and there was nothing

I would not do for Neil. Often I did not even know where I was or what I was doing. Neil's business partners would also encourage my drug-taking, and once I started the injection, I could not get enough. I also felt I was invincible.

One evening Neil had spoken to her, she said, and he said he was meeting a new bunch of people. Asked me to befriend them when we went to meetings. It was not long before I found myself to be Neil's own prostitute. He was using me as a softener when we went to these drug meetings. I still thought Neil loved me, so I went along with whatever was suggested because this is what Neil wanted and I needed the drugs.

In the end, I was just being taken along to these dug meetings as a sexual plaything, a softener for the other men. I knew this was happening but wanted my Neil to be safe and, of course, my intake of free drugs. I was and am so dependent on drugs I would have done anything. Plus, I did not dare to argue with Neil as he did not like me answering back. At the last drugs meeting, we went on it. All went horribly wrong for Neil and me.

I was taken into this room where there were 5 men, all of them treating me as though I were their own sexual toy, being passed from one to the other. Neil had gone into another room with this other man, and I was left alone with these five men. After they shut the door, those five men set about me and I was being repeatedly raped by them. Thankfully, I was so high on drugs; I did not hurt as they passed me around between themselves. If I objected to something they were doing, I found I would get a slap or a punch from one of them.

Suddenly there was the sound of gunshots that come from the other room where Neil was. The five men discarded me like I was nothing and went running to the room where the gunshots had come from. I heard a lot of shouting coming from the room and somehow found the strength to pull myself together and went into the room. There laid the body of Neil who had been shot several times. All the other people had fled the building. I feared getting arrested for this shooting or for drug-taking, so fled using a fire escape. I could not return to the hotel where we were staying as the police were constantly keeping a watch on the place. I could not return home as my passport was in the hotel room, as Neil kept hold of that for some reason. As a few weeks passed, I had to live on the streets and beg for money for food, but mainly for more drugs. Even though I have lost Neil, I still can't get rid of the need for some drugs. That's what I was doing when I bumped into Adam, trying to get money for my next fix.

I looked across at Rosa and Pippa, both girls sitting next to Rebecca with their arms around her. They were both in floods of tears at Rebecca's story. Rosa then said see Adam the way some men treat women it's not nice as she dried her eyes. I said not all men are the same though, Rosa.

Rosa said I have seen my fair share of the behavior of men towards women, and especially when they have had a drink. This is why I want you to be so different the day just seemed to unfold in front of us. That day I think Rebecca's story shocked the hell out of everyone no one was expecting any of that.

The day was spent all about making Rebecca feel comfortable and secure. Rosa had phoned Vicki that morning and gave her the news that Rebecca was safe and well and with us. Vicki was so happy and was on her way over to collect her daughter on the first available ferry crossing. I pulled myself away from what was happening and got on with some painting. The house felt very strange for the rest of the day, as if maybe I should not have been working, maybe it made me seem a little callous.

A few hours passed, and there was a bang at the door. As I opened it, it was Vicki. She came straight in and spoke to Rosa and Pippa for less than half an hour. She was off again saying she wanted to get out of

France and her daughter back home safe. And she was gone as she left I heard her say to Rosa please give this to Adam. I said nothing much more that day. Everyone was just pleased that Vicky and Rebecca were reunited and on their way home safely.

The rest of the day just seemed to vanish there were some heavy conversations about what Rebecca had told everyone about what had happened. Suddenly Rosa said "oh Adam I nearly forgot, Vicki, has asked me to give you something". Leaving the room, Rosa returned with an envelope. "There you go, Vicki, asked me to give you this" I sat there, in front of everyone. I opened the envelope, there was a brief note the note read:

Dear Adam.

I can never thank you enough for what you have done in finding my daughter.
I am so happy and so sorry I could not stay in person to thank you. But when you return to the UK, I would love to take you out for dinner and show you my appreciation

all my love,
Vicki xxx
P.S please find enclosed a cheque

Inside the envelope was a cheque for £2,000! I looked at Pippa and Rosa and said, "there is no way I can accept this. It was more luck than anything in finding Rebecca, and I had not even set out on a search for her." So I ripped the cheque up in front of Rosa and Pippa. Rosa said, "that was a nice thing to do, Adam."

It was pretty late that evening by the time we all got to bed. I went up before the girls and was fast asleep by the time they came to bed.

CHAPTER TWENTY EIGHT

But it was nice to wake with them on either side of me in the morning.

Chapter Twenty Nine

We all woke about the same time the following morning. Rosa was full of life, she said with all the excitement with Rebecca I forget to tell you it's this weekend that we go on our sailing trip. I got up and showered and got straight on with some painting. That day was full of the girls sorting things out to prepare for the trip the following day I was excited as I had never done sailing before. Wondering what it would be like that day flew past. That evening we were all in bed very early as we had to have an early start the next day.

When we woke the next morning, we all headed down to the kitchen about the same time. Sofia must have been up most of the night, as she had cooked a really hearty breakfast and a few loaves of bread for the weekend away. Sofia had packed a small bag and placed it by the door, ready to go. So that is where Rosa and Pippa placed our bags, too. We sat around the breakfast table and Rosa was trying to plan where we would go on our sailing adventure she never let on where we were actually going she said she liked to keep things like this a surprise.

We eventually got to my truck, we drove for about two hours and we came to this tiny marina. We unpacked my ruck and took our gear onto the jetty. Rosa had had some people prepare the boat for us. This was the first time I had seen her boat I was expecting a little day yacht or something similar.

As we walked down the jetty to our boat, it amazed me: the boat was huge, about 42 feet long. The white hull shone on the sparkling water beneath it. We all climbed aboard the boat and went to the cockpit area. When there, we were greeted by the two men who had been preparing the boat for us. One man said to Rosa where are you heading and she showed him on this map, he looked at her and said do you want me to skipper the boat for you. Rosa said, no we will be fine, and that Marcus had taught her everything she needed to know. The man huffed and said "OK please just be careful, although the weather looks fine now the long-range weather forecast has predicted some high winds. So stick to the coastline as much as possible there are plenty of little coves you can shelter in if you need to," he said. With this, the man and his partner left the boat.

Rosa sat there looking at her map, Pippa, and I looked at each other. Pippa then said to Rosa, "are you sure we will be OK? If there are some high winds coming would you rather re-book for another time?" Rosa said, "no we will be fine". Sofia was nowhere to be seen as she went straight down to the kitchen area. As we went below, I could not believe my eyes it was like a five-star hotel inside this boat. The first area we came to was the galley (kitchen). Sofia was in her element everything had its own space and was so clean, the mahogany wood shone as if the boat had just been built and was brand new and not 30 years old.

The whole interior of the boat was mahogany and had a soft red glow about it. The next compartment was the lounge the seating area was done in white leather with a really deep piled white carpet which really matched the wood. Here was this really shiny chrome pole in the middle of the lounge area a little further down were some doors. The next room we looked into was the shower room. This had gold taps on the sink, a real flushing toilet, and not a port a loo as Rosa had jokingly said. The actual shower was fantastic it had mirrored walls. A little further down there were 3 doors, and they were the sleeping compartments, and beyond this was another toilet.

Bedroom one was a fair size and Sofia pipped up from behind us "shall I take this one? It's nearest to the kitchen and I will not wake the rest of you when I get up in the morning". Rosa smiled at her and said, "yes darling, you can have that one if you wish." The middle cabin was a bit smaller, and it had two bunks in it. Rosa suggested we all use this room to stow our belongings in.

The last room was a little bigger than the one Sofia chose for Rosa, and Pippa flopped onto the bed. Pippa giggled as she lay there and said how sexy a water bed on a boat. I pushed the mattress off the bed with my hands firmly, and both Rosa and Pippa were being rippled about slowly. I slowly got onto the bed with the two girls I had never seen or been on a water bed before. It felt very strange but in a nice way, it also felt very erotic if that's the right way of describing it.

We all changed out of the clothes we traveled in, the girls all put bikinis on, and I put a pair of shorts on. Once dressed in our new gear, we made our way back to the cockpit area of this fantastic vessel. Rosa said that we were going to have to get a move on as we had to leave with the high tide. Rosa then came into her own and had total control over what was happening she said, "OK Adam, please go and untie us from the jetty." As I did this, she fired up the engine: Pippa was pulling the rope that I had unfastened from the jetty. Sofia was sticking to Rosa like glue once, all back on board, before we started off.

The heat from the sun was boiling Rosa at the helm of the boat shouted out I know of a little Island and we headed off in that direction. Sofia, now feeling a little safer, had taken herself off to the galley area and prepared some lunch for us all. Pippa had cracked open a couple of bottles of wine. The sea was very calm as a millpond. Surely the man we spoke to when we had got there was wrong about the weather.

It looked so peaceful and picturesque.

After I had stowed the ropes that were holding us previously to the jetty, I joined Rosa and Pippa in the cockpit. Just chilling out and relaxing, drinking our wine, Sofia came up and joined us. There could not be a more perfect picture of these three beautiful women in bikinis and myself. Rosa kept the engine on for about an hour and a half and we could see in the distance a small island. She had totally ignored the advice from the man who handed the boat to us, as we were far out to sea. Looking around, there was nothing else to see apart from this small island in the distance. As we approached the island I could see it looked deserted, quite a lot of rocks around the Island which Rosa navigated very well. We were about 200 feet from the shore, and · Rosa instructed me to throw the anchor overboard. The boat came to a slow halt, and we were about 150 feet from the island. Sofia and Pippa had taken themselves on the top deck of the boat and removed their tops and were sunbathing, catching the last of the afternoon sun.

I stayed with Rosa, Sofia, and Pippa, who had both fallen asleep lying on the deck. Rosa lent across and whispered in my ear, come with me. The boat was now secure, and the engine was off all you could hear was the water gently slapping the side of the boat. Rosa and I went into the lounge area of the boat, Rosa held out her arm and as I held her hand, she slowly sat beside me on the sofa. She pulled my hand as if to direct me from the sofa, and I was on my knees in front of her. We kissed for a while and then Rosa asked me to massage some sun cream into her shoulders.

She had been at the helm all afternoon. Her shoulders were a little sunburnt as I was massaging her shoulders. She removed her top. You could see the line of her bikini top that the sun had made on her breasts. The part that had been covered up looked so pale against the rest of her. Rosa then laid on her back on the leather sofa as she did this she arched her back as the leather had not heated and had a chill about it. My hands were now both covered in this sun cream so I massaged her complete top half, paying special attention to her warm breasts. I then went to her feet and applied yet more sun cream and was massaging her feet and ankles.

Rosa kept saying "Oh Adam that feels lovely" there was so much cream on my hands they were now sliding down the length of her perfectly toned legs. Her sunburnt legs felt boiling to the touch, and she said the sun cream felt freezing. One of my hands was now massaging her warm, flat stomach. As I did this, Rosa was massaging the top of my head, her fingers running through my hair. I loved the feel, the touch from Rosa, she always seemed to make me feel so relaxed. Both Rosa's legs were amply covered in her sun cream. My hands were now working this cream into her stomach and her waist, then up the sides of her body to her armpits, feeling the soft folds of skin softly under my hands.

Rosa just lay there with her eyes shut, letting my hands explore her warm sunburnt body. I lent forward and the lips of my mouth would only just barely touch her. I could see the erection of both her darkened nipples, I would let my mouth cover her nipples and very gently lick and suck on them. Alternately the more I did this the more erect the nipples seem to come, every so often I would catch her nipple between my teeth and give the gentlest of nibbles not to cause loads of pain but just a little pain just to keep her reflexes going.

Rosa obviously liked what I was doing to her, as when I had her nipple in my mouth, her hand would push my head harder into it. I moved my mouth to the side of her neck as I did this. She tilted her head back to expose more of her neck to me. I was now kissing and licking the side of her neck and her earlobe. As I did this, Rosa held my head tighter and tighter to her neck. I knew I was only meant to be rubbing sun cream onto her, but Rosa made me so excited and she was not putting up a fight against what I was doing.

I had totally forgotten about the cream, as I think Rosa had too. Rosa whispered in my ear. Take me to bed, Adam. I did not need telling twice and as I was kissing her got her off the sofa and while kissing we stumbled into the bedroom. As I laid her on the bed, she delicately removed the bottom half of her bikini. There was my Rosa, totally naked, asking me to join her. I walked towards her and she sat up slightly and stretched out both her arms, got hold of my shorts, and slowly pulled them from my waist.

Rosa could see I was very excited by her actions, as my penis was as erect as it could ever be. She looked at me, then at my penis, smiled, and pulled me to lie on the bed with her I was now laying on this waterbed. As Rosa re-positioned herself, the ripples moved me about in such a gentle, erotic way. Her feet were now near to my head. I could feel the warm dampness of her mouth touching my erection. She would slightly put her mouth over the end of my penis and then remove it without doing anything else. It was such a tease, but at the same time such an immense turn-on. I felt her tongue circling the end of my penis, and every so often her tongue would dart in and out of my penis eye. Grabbing at her hair as she did this and asked her to finish me, her mouth seemed to slip over the end of my penis and sank her mouth fully onto my shaft so much that her lips were resting on my pubic hair.

Somehow she still moved her tongue and give the gentlest of licks. It felt so amazing what Rosa was doing to me, and it was by far the best oral I had ever had in my life. Every time she did this to me, it always seemed better than the last time. Rosa continued to perform this amazing oral on me for a while longer. I could feel my penis twitching in her mouth as I thought, God, I did not want this to stop. Rosa must have sensed or felt the movement in my penis too, as she slowly removed her lips from my now very delicate erection and lay beside me. Her hands gently caressing my chest, she told me to relax and breathe I did this as I always did as Rosa requested I lay Rosa on her back after I controlled myself.

I very slowly parted her legs slowly kissing and nibbling my way up her inner thigh. I pushed her legs further apart. One of my hands was now massaging the inside of her leg. My other hand had found her warm, damp vagina and my fingers were tumbling with the folds of her labia lips. My fingers had exposed her damp clitoris, I moved my mouth to my fingers, my tongue was now licking and playing with the folds of her labia. I had exposed her damp clitoris and my tongue was now sucking on her womanhood.

As I did this, I could hear her muffled groans of pleasure from the waterbed. And the gentle rocking of the boat only made the situation more intense. As I was licking, I felt her legs straighten beneath me and her whole body stiffened she held my head so tightly to her moist vagina as she climaxed. We carried on kissing for a while and just both lay there looking at the low ceiling of the boat; it was even more of a turn on to think while we were doing this Sofia and Pippa were laying just above us, and only an inch or so of wood separated us.

I looked over at Rosa as we lay there together to speak to her, her eyes were shut and she was peacefully asleep. I left Rosa asleep and got off the waterbed, which was a lot harder to get off than it was to get on. When off the bed I went through the boat, I was on my way to see Pippa and Sofia.

I got to the cockpit area and there was not a soul about. I went to where Rosa and I had left the girls laying, their costumes were there and their towels, but no sign of the girls. I looked around in the water, thinking they may have gone for a swim, but still no sign of them. By now I was getting worried so went back down below I was going to see Rosa and tell her of my concerns. But as I walked past Sofia's room I heard the two girls in there and it sounded very personal, whatever they were doing. So I left them alone, knowing they were safe.

I thought I would make a start and prepare our dinner, and even though I was trying to be quiet, I must have made too much noise as Sofia's cabin door opened. Out walked both girls, not even bothering to dress. Sofia said, "no Adam it's OK I want to do the cooking this weekend leave it to me, please." As she was speaking to me, Pippa walked over and passed me. As she passed, she pinched my bum, proceeded on, and re-locked the hatch which I had left open. As Pippa passed me on her way back in, her fingers gently stroked my back as she passed Sofia, still not bothering to dress.

Sofia got on with preparing the evening meal I went to sit on the sofa with Pippa. Just as I sat down, Rosa had come out of the far cabin she too had not bothered to redress herself. I was feeling a little overdressed after our meal. The four of us just sat around with duvets wrapped around us. There was a film to watch, but it really was just background noise. Our conversation was great it never ran dry, nor did it repeat itself. That night Pippa and Sofia both went to Sofia's cabin and Rosa and I went to our cabin until it was quite eerie, really no noise from any cars, bikes, or anything. The only sound I heard as I lay there going to sleep was the wind and the water gently lapping against the side of the boat.

The next morning, we woke up about the same time, apart from Sofia. She was like a robot, her body clock was amazing. She was always there making the breakfast when everyone woke up. I was first to enter the lounge area, but not left on our own for too long. We had time for a kiss and a cuddle, not that we had to hide it, anyway. Pippa was next to join us as she woke and left Sofia's cabin. As Pippa left the comfort of Sofia's cabin, she was yawning and stretching her arms. Just as she was doing this, Rosa came out of our cabin. Rosa walked up behind Pippa and held her waist and kissed the back of her shoulders.

We all sat together, eating a wonderful breakfast. During breakfast, Pippa suggested we all stripped off and went skinny dipping instead of a shower. Everyone laughed but thought this would be fun so as soon as breakfast was complete and out of the way, that's what we all did. Went up on the deck there was not another soul around, not a boat to be seen, just us. It was as if the rest of the world did not exist.

Rosa was first to dive into the clear water that lapped around our boat. The water was so clear you could see the bottom and the small fish that swam around the rock formation below us. As she surfaced, she shouted from the water, come on in it lovely. Sofia was next to the water, which hardly made a splash as her petite body entered it. Pippa and I entered about the same time, just jumping from the side of the boat. We spent about an hour just swimming and playing around in the water. Once back on board, we got some towels and just lay on the deck, letting the early morning sundry our naked bodies.

I must have been the luckiest man alive to have these three beautiful women lying next to me on this sunny morning. After a while, Sofia suggested we go to the little island to explore and see what was there and what it was like. Rosa said that if she did not mind, she would just rather laze about on the boat and do some reading. Pippa said that sounded like a pleasant idea and said she would also like to do that and just relax.

Sofia looked across at me I smiled and said, yes I would love to go and have a look round. I went down below deck and got a pair of shorts from my bag, and Sofia went and put a fresh bikini on. When we came back up on top of the boat, I said to Rosa and Pippa are you sure you don't mind us going to the island. Both girls, by this time engrossed in their books, just nodded and said have a great time. Sofia and I used the small dingy that we towed along behind the boat to go to the island. We set off about mid-morning and the sun was as hot as the previous day, if not hotter, but there was a little more of a breeze in the air today.

As we left the boat, Pippa raised her head from the book and said have a great day. As she said this to us, I saw her lean across to Rosa and put her arm on her shoulder, and then saw Rosa and Pippa have a quick kiss together. Sofia was facing me in the boat and had her back to them, and as I was rowing away from the boat, they had both stood to watch us depart from the boat. As I rowed away, the girls disappeared inside the boat together.

Sofia was full of smiles as I rowed our little boat to the island. As I was nearing the island, Sofia gave me directions and said to go to the left a little. Pointing with her hands, I looked around and there was this large group of rocks. Sofia pointed and said to put the boat in behind that group of rocks, the boat should be safe there. As we got out of our little dingy she grabbed a little bag and said I remembered to bring us some drinks, yes.

I pulled the boat in as far as I could, which was not very far because of the rocks. We went past the rocks and found ourselves on a pure white sand beach which looked as though it had been sieved before putting down it was so fine. I looked back at the main boat and it seemed so far away. Sofia and I walked until we ran out of sand. We went inland a little just to explore. Going through some dense foliage, the island looked uninhabited. We were the only ones on it as we walked further inland until the slow sloping hills took us to quite a fair bit of sea level.

We stood there in a clearing looking back and down at the boat, which in itself looked like a rowing boat. We sat in the long green grass and had our lunch as we did this. Sofia removed her swimsuit. She lay there soaking up the sun, as we lay there Sofia said can I ask you a question Adam "I said yes of course fire away". She said its personal is still OK yes.

I said "no problem just ask" she moved closer to me and said, "that she really liked what we had both done in her room in the farmhouse that morning". I said I liked it too. But I felt a bit guilty that morning.

But she had definitely got rid of the guilt for me by speaking to Rosa and Pippa about it but yes, I really enjoyed it too.

She said that she was glad that Rosa and Pippa had stayed on the boat, as she would like to become closer to me again. Sofia asked if I would rub some sun oil onto her body and passed me the oil. She lay there on her back and I looked at her amazing petite body. I poured the oil into her top half. Giving her a generous covering and as I rubbed the oil into her body, I could see her darkened, swollen nipples becoming erect. Whilst I was rubbing the oil into her skin and my finger tumbling with her nipples, she said that Pippa had told her what Rosa and Pippa were doing with me, or should I say trying to teach me and teaching me to be the perfect lover.

I laughed and said oh, still rubbing oil into her body. I said and how did they say I was getting on really expecting no answer. Sofia then said well, Pippa seems to think you are coming along very nicely and a real agreeable person with it. Sofia then said, "Adam, are you going to spend the rest of your life with them?" I was shocked at this question but I had said it was OK to ask.

I said yes I would like to and what we had was so fantastic, that there could not be a better life. As I was talking to her and oiling her body, I found my fingers were paying a lot of attention to her erect nipples. They were repeatedly slipping through my fingers. Sofia was full of questions that day and with this, she turned on to her front and asked if I would now do her back. I was not going to refuse as petite as her body was. She still had a great proportioned body.

I was massaging the oil onto her back I really liked Sofia's back long and slender with the most perfectly shaped buttocks. As I was massaging her back, she moved her long black hair over her head and I straddled her, sitting on her small but plump buttocks. I was massaging her neck and shoulders and all of her back, right down as far as I was sitting. Sofia said your touch is amazing, Adam. I felt myself becoming very aroused by her naked body beneath me her skin shone as the warm sun hit her oil-covered body.

I leaned forward and could not help myself, and kissed the back of her neck, one of my hands stretching. Both her arms were out in front of her as far as I could stretch them. Sofia's hair was covering her face and from beneath her hair I heard her say "please Adam make love to me". I moved her hair from her face and very slowly turned her over and lay her on her back.

My penis was now throbbing as I lay on top of her and my penis between her legs. Sofia's bum was soaked with sun oil. I think I must off got carried away. She was so slippery to the touch, as if my hands were not really making proper contact with her, as if the oil had formed a barrier.

As I went to position myself to enter her moistness, she slightly raised her pelvis and bum from the towel. Doing this, my now wanting throbbing penis was resting between her two buttocks. Sofia slightly bucked and pushed her bum towards me Sofia spoke again "Adam, she said I want you to make love to me anally". I sort of froze, hoping she had not noticed and did not really know what to say or do, as I was not experienced at this at all. She sensed I was nervous, and I released one of her hands. She very carefully and gently took my penis in her hand and positioned my penis at the entrance of her bum. She flicked her head and cleared the hair from her face. She must have sensed my inexperience, as she said, "please just relax and let me take control" I did as she asked.

She said this has got to be done gently as I don't want either of us to get hurt and smiled and kissed my face. In a very quiet sheepish voice, I said OK; it was like I was a virgin all over again and remembered the nervousness from when I had been a virgin. Sofia tried twice to place my penis inside her, but I could not help myself and tried to help by pushing. Each time I did this, it just went wrong and my penis slid past her entrance or was just too hard and eager. I was feeling like a failure maybe I was not ready for this. Even though I knew in my mind I had done this once or twice before, it differed from vaginal sex.

Sofia said in a reassuring voice, please don't worry, just relax. Sofia moved me onto my back and she straddled me she was now sitting on me as though we were about to do the cowgirl position which Rosa and Pippa had shown me. To start with that's exactly what Sofia did: I was deep inside her moistness and she was riding me in the cowgirl position which I felt comfortable with.

She was slowly riding me like this, covering my erection with her vaginal fluids over the full length of my throbbing adulthood. I closed my eyes for two reasons as I lay there underneath this lady. First, it felt so nice, and Sofia was obviously very experienced in this department. Second, as the sun was full in my face as if I had pulled a strange face, whilst Sofia was doing this to me she may have thought that I was not enjoying what she was doing to me, which I was very much.

She was riding me so carefully she would rise high and nearly come off into my adulthood. She would then sink back down so slowly to the very base of my adulthood. Her moistness was so damp and wet and very warm I just lay there enjoying what she was doing to me. My mind relaxed, and I sort of had forgotten the task ahead of me. Still, with my eyes shut, she rose a little higher and sank back down. Even slower than she had before, she leaned forward and said, "there you go Adam; you are inside me," not thinking too much of what she had said.

I knew I was inside her true it felt a little tighter but I thought that just happened as she sat back up I realized what she meant whilst I had. Having my eyes closed, she was riding me until she somehow had transferred my penis from her warm moist vagina to her back passage. She continued to rise very slowly up and down the length of my adulthood, which felt now as though it were being held in a vice. Feeling more comfortable with what she was now doing to me, I let my hands explore her well-toned body.

As she got used to me being inside her, her movements became faster and harder. My hands were grabbing at her waist as if to steady her, although she did not need that, as she knew exactly what she was doing. Every time she sank her body low and hard into my adulthood, she would grab at my pectoral muscles and squeeze. Her head would flick wildly around her face. I could feel every muscle inside her holding me in place. I felt I could hold on no longer and as I was about to warn her of my climax; she sank hard and low onto me. She stayed there and dug her fingernails into my chest, nearly to the point of penetration. Sofia had climaxed at exactly the same time as me.

Whilst I had had my eyes shut during this fantastic sex, I had not noticed the sun go in and the clouds come over. Sofia obviously had, but this did not bother her as we lay there with her still sitting on top of me. The rain got heavier and heavier; the rain bouncing off my chest and Sofia's hair soaked so much it was flattened to her head. Suddenly there was a massive bang, and the rain got even heavier there was thunder and lightning we both ran for cover under some trees. We looked down out across the bay where the boat was anchored off but could not even see the boat because of the amount of rain lashing down. It seemed within minutes that the tree we were using for shelter was not suitable anymore, the leaves and branches so wet it was as if we were in a shower. We went further back into the wooded area behind us and found a small cave.

Sofia reached for her bag once we were sheltered from the storm and pulled her cell phone from it. She phoned Rosa on the boat it rang and as Rosa answered the phone cut out. This happened several times as Sofia kept trying and eventually Sofia got through to Rosa.

Rosa and Pippa were scared out of their wits, as the stormy winds were lashing the boat. The sea had become very rough since Rosa said that the boat was rocking and rolling about so violently that she feared for Pippa's and her own safety. I took the phone from Sofia and spoke to Rosa. I had never heard so much fear in anyone's voice in my life before. All Rosa kept saying was Adam, "where are you?" I could hear Pippa screaming in the background every time there was a clash of thunder. I told Rosa that there was no way that we could get back to the boat in this storm as we would definitely drown as what once was a millpond now had six to eight-foot waves on it.

The rain somehow came down even harder than before. It was about 8 pm by the time the rain had stopped and the wind ceased to be a storm. Although very windy, Sofia and I made our way to the dinghy there. It was exactly where we left it. It was still in sound condition, just half full of rainwater. Both Sofia and I bailed the dinghy out and carefully made our way back to Rosa and Pippa. Sofia was sitting in the boat shivering so much you could hear her teeth chattering against each other. The boat where Rosa and Pippa were was in total darkness, and there seemed to be no sign of life. I tied the dinghy to the boat, got on board, and then helped a soaked, scared Sofia onto the main boat. The hatch to go down below was firmly locked, and as I banged my hand on top of it, I heard both Rosa and Pippa scream.

Once inside the boat, I had never seen three more terrified people, all three girls now sitting together. Shivering and huddled under a duvet, I locked the hatch back up and asked if they would like a drink. They were even too scared to speak. Although the storm had passed, there was one almighty flash in the sky and the loudest clap of thunder you ever heard. All three girls ran to Rosa's cabin. I followed and the four of us just lay huddled together I don't think the girls stopped shaking all night that night. As we lay there, the boat rolled around on the water quite a lot, but the storm had passed. All the girls fell asleep at some point that night, each of them trying to hold on to me for safety or security, I think.

The next morning there was no movement until about 11 am. As we had all slept in, I was the first up so I went on deck to see what or if there was any damage to the boat. The only thing we lost that night was the dinghy. We either never tied it properly to the boat or the winds came again in the night while we slept. The sea was now like a millpond again how could this be when it was so strong, rough, and unforgiving the previous day. Sofia ventured out of the cabin next, not even having a quick look to see how things were before she just got on with the breakfasts.

Rosa and Pippa were not far behind Sofia in getting up. Rosa put the radio on and the news came on and it also gave the weather forecast and for the next few days, they said there were going to be high winds and rain. So after our breakfast, we had a group discussion, and we made the most of the calm weather while it was on our side and cut short our trip by one day. We headed back to the marina, and everyone agreed. Pippa and Sofia did not even peek at the lookout at the boat the entire journey back. It was left to Rosa and me to navigate our way back to the marina. The trip back was as smooth as silk. There was hardly a ripple on the water apart from what our boat was making. We got back in very good time and tied our boat securely to the jetty before we all took our belongings and headed straight for my truck. We all felt a lot safer in my truck than on the boat. It was a great boat, and it was no one's fault. It had not put me off, and I had some fantastic memories of the short but eventful boating trip, and I was more than willing to try it again. But the look on Pippa and Sofia's faces told a different story.

Chapter Thirty

The journey back to the farmhouse was full of conversation about our short but eventful weekend away. The girls admitted how scared they were and spoke briefly of the sexual encounters that had happened in such a brief space of time. It turned out that the only sexual encounter that did not happen was between Pippa and me. It was great there were no secrets or jealousy between any of us and that we could talk openly about our sexual encounters.

Personally, I could not wait to get back to the farmhouse and have a long, hot shower. We pulled up back at the house and it felt good to be back and have our feet on dry land and by looking at the sky; we had made the right decision to end our trip early. The weather forecast was spot on by the time we had our stuff through the doors of the farmhouse. The sky was as black as black could be and the wind had picked up to storm force yet again. The rain was lashing at the doors so hard you would have thought there was someone there knocking at the door.

Sofia went straight to the kitchen again she was like a magnet to the kitchen area. Wherever we went, the kettle was getting us some hot drinks ready and hot soup. I ran up the stairs and, as I had hoped for, was the first to get a hot shower. I was there for about 10 minutes or so, and both girls came into the shower room. As they came in they laughed and said, come on, move over. I did as I was asked, but quickly finished my shower, dried myself off, and went to get dressed. I went down to the kitchen and left Rosa and Pippa alone in the shower. When I got to the kitchen, Sofia had prepared some bread and hot soup. Waiting there for us. But she too had now slipped off to her shower room.

That evening we all sat together and were listening to music in the lounge, listening to the rain battering against the windows. We were all so glad to be in the farmhouse in front of that massive open fireplace, sitting around just chilling out and feeling safe in our warm woolen jumpers. Feeling the warmth of the fire and thanking the lucky stars we had not carried on with the weekend. The storm we were now listening to was battering on the windows of the house several times worse than the previous night.

Bedtime came, and Sofia said her goodbyes and took herself off to her room. The two girls and I went to our room it felt so nice everything was back to normal. We were in our nice warm bed, both my girls on either side of me. It did not take long to fall asleep that night everyone seemed exhausted it was just a delightful feeling to be home.

Chapter Thirty One

The next morning and as per usual, Sofia was up and preparing the bread and our breakfasts for us all. I was last to arrive in the kitchen that morning. Sofia walked over to me with a tea in her hand for me. She gave me a kiss and said thank you for looking after her while we were on the island and thanks for the other thing that I had done for her. I smiled and kissed her back and gave her a cuddle.

Rosa and Pippa were both looking out of the window, overlooking the large sweeping grass lawn at the wind and the rain. Rosa said it looks like the rain is about to stop. Rosa then announced that she was going into Paris that day to get some more paperwork to sort with her solicitor. Pippa asked if it was OK if she came along for the ride, Rosa said yes no problem. I said I was going to get on with some painting, which was the reason I was actually there. The following few days just seemed to be like this, everyone getting on with their business and my painting. I at long last seemed to be able to get quite a lot done.

It was getting near the end of our stay in France. One evening we were just sitting around talking about going back to the UK. After quite a lot of talking, Rosa asked Sofia what her plans were for the future. She said she really had made none but would have liked to continue to learn burlesque dancing from Rosa. Rosa and Sofia had a conversation in French, as Pippa and I tried to understand what they were saying to each other. Suddenly Rosa turned to us she said I have just had a word with Sofia, and she has agreed that she would like to come back to the UK with us. She was going to live in the house with us, Sofia was full of smiles, as was Rosa as this was being said to Pippa and me.

A few more days passed, and it was our last evening together in France. We were all busy packing our bags, as was Sofia, who seemed so excited. We all went to sleep that night in this grand old house and for the first time in our stay there, the house felt different. It felt cold even though the fires were still burning as normal, but the house really had a chill about it. The next morning, we were all up and out of our beds very early. We had a quick breakfast and loaded the truck with our belongings.

Rosa spent more time at the lodge before we set off speaking to Phillip, just sorting out the bits and bobs for him and paying him a sum of money. We had one last look back at the farmhouse, and we set off for the ferry. The ferry crossing was a very easy crossing, unlike our last venture out on a boat. We crossed the channel in good time and took in turns to do the driving. Sofia was just looking out of her window the whole journey as she had never left France before in her life this was like a new beginning for her.

Once back at Rosa's, I checked my e-mails and there were lots of inquiries of work for me. Pippa went online and was checking her customers and trying to make some order of the number of lessons she had to book. We had spent longer out in France than we had all originally planned for. Sofia was shown her room as she was just so grateful and so pleased. It was our first evening back, and we were sitting there in the lounge and the doorbell went. Sofia said it is OK she would go and answer the door. Two minutes later, Sofia returned to the room with Victoria.

Vicki was talking a lot about Rebecca and what was now happening with her. Victoria explained all that was happening and the whole of what had happened to her daughter. Never interrupting. But we actually knew most of the harrowing story, as Rebecca had told Rosa. Vicki said that she had got her into a rehab clinic, as she could not do what Rebecca needed regarding getting her off the drink and drug addiction. That when Rebecca felt better. She was going to return to university and restart her courses. We were all very pleased to hear the progress Vicki had made with Rebecca, and that they had re-bonded their mother-daughter relationship.

I said, "Vicki, there was no need for the cheque. I would not or could not accept it" and that I had destroyed it and I had burnt it on the fire in France. She said, "well Adam, if you will not accept that, how can I repay you for the kindness you have shown?" I told her she did not need to do or say anything and I was just happy that she and Rebecca were back together and reunited. She smiled at me, walked over to me, and gave me a huge kiss and cuddle.

She said, "OK, if you will not accept what I have offered, will you please allow me to take you for a meal one night?" I said, "OK, I will have a meal with you one night," Vicki said, "well thank you for at least agreeing to that." She turned to Rosa and Pippa and said, "you do not mind if I steal him away from you one night?" I could see Rosa smile and she said no one night should be OK and laughed with Vicki. Vicki asked how the rest of our trip went, and Rosa and Pippa explained about the boat trip and how scared they were. Vicki laughed and said how exciting.

The evening was getting late, so she said her goodbyes and left. Just as she was leaving she turned to me and said "Oh Adam expect your phone to ring like crazy I have recommended you to everyone I know". I smiled and said, "maybe it's you who I should thank then and taking you for a meal." She smiled at me again and said, "remember you said yes", winked at me, turned, and left the house. We went to bed that night and it was as normal with Rosa and Pippa on either side of me. This time the girls could not get close enough if they cuddled me any harder. I would have popped out from between them.

Chapter Thirty Two

The next morning came and Vicki was so right my cell phone did not stop ringing. There was the offer of the job after job via Vicki's recommendations. As Pippa left for work, she gave me a kiss on the cheek and returned to her driving instructor's job. Rosa was busy in town, seeing her solicitors as she always seemed to do. I was going from job to job, pricing every call I had received. Sofia had taken on the role of a housemaid and looking after the house even though she was not asked to. It seemed to fit in nicely with what everyone else was doing.

One evening we were sitting around and everyone had finished what they were doing, and Rosa said to me "well Adam you seem to do very well in the work situation". That reminds me the solicitors would also like you to price their offices up if you have time. She continued to speak, "hope you are not getting too busy for what I have in store for you". I replied quickly, "Rosa I will always make time for you, and I would never be too busy to miss out on a chance of being with you and Pippa". I said that my girls would always be the first place in everything I did, and would never come second best in my life always would be my major priority and that I promised her.

Rosa smiled at me as did Pippa and Rosa then said I will hold you to that darling. That night we went to bed and Sofia was asked to join us in our bed. We stoked the fire up in the bedroom as if to remind us of our stay in France and to keep warm. Rosa and Pippa proudly stripped each other, slowly kissing as they did so. I was also stripping and getting ready to hop into bed with these beautiful creatures.

Rosa said to Sofia, "come on, don't be shy" she was slightly red in the face. Rosa and Pippa slowly walked over to her and led her to the edge of the bed. By this time I was in bed, just watching what was happening. Both Rosa and Pippa were trying to put Sofia at ease, and both were kissing and caressing her shoulders as they slowly removed her clothes. Sofia was now smiling and in turn would alternately kiss Rosa and Pippa.

As they removed her clothing, Rosa was talking softly to Sofia as she stripped her. She said that Pippa had told her how good and loving you were. Rosa said I would like to sample this for myself. As the girls were stripping Sofia, I found that my hand was now slowly rubbing my penis and that the sight of these girls stripping and getting ready to get into bed with me had aroused me somewhat. Pippa was the first to notice what I was doing and sat on top of the bedsheets next to me. As my hand was under the sheets on my penis, hers was above the sheets on my hand and penis.

Slowly rubbing the same as I was, Sofia was eager to please Rosa, and it was as if this is what Sofia had wanted all along. Rosa removed the last of her clothing, Sofia turned her head to Rosa and their lips met. They were locked in a sensual kiss, just standing there by the side of the bed. While this happened, Pippa's hand had moved under the sheet to join my hand on my now very firm penis.

Sofia would disappoint no one. She was so pleased to be in the UK with us. I think she would have done anything at this point in her life. Rosa had stripped Sofia totally naked and had placed her on the edge of the bed sitting next to Pippa and me I. Rosa walked over to a chair in the bedroom's corner and from beneath the chair brought a box over and placed it at the end of the bed. Pippa bent down, opened the box, and pulled a set of handcuffs from it before she then walked around to the left-hand side of the bed. She took my left hand and placed it firmly on the cuff, and locked the other end around the top of the headboard. Rosa at the same time had removed another set of handcuffs and repeated what Pippa had done but to my right-hand side. Sofia just lay across the end of the bed, watching their every move as I was. Sofia was caressing her legs, Rosa asked Sofia to come to her, and Sofia got up from the bed and did what Rosa had asked of her. Sofia was standing there with Rosa and Pippa and they gave her some red rope, which had shackles attached to it.

Sofia lent forward and attached the shackles to my ankles, whilst Rosa and Pippa had tied their ends of the rope to the foot of the bed. I did not resist throughout the complete process, but found that I was securely fastened and held down on the bed. Not even being able to continue touching and pleasuring myself, I had done nothing like this before. I was watching them in anticipation of what was about to happen to me now all three girls approached me from different directions.

Sofia, still at the foot of the bed, caressed kiss and suck on my feet. Sucking each of my toes in turn as she massaged them. It was as though she were performing oral on my toes. Her small petite hand holding my feet in place it truly felt amazing what she was doing. I could not reciprocate and return the sexual pleasure I was getting from what she was doing just as I spoke and tell her how good it felt. Rosa approached me, her hands behind her back, Pippa approaching from the other side. Pippa held my head down on the pillow and kissed me on the forehead as she did this until Rosa produced another item I had not seen before. It was a ball with several straps coming from it Rosa said, it's a ball gag she said to me, remember everything I have said to you from the beginning, and to relax and breathe through my nose. I would be fine.

And she placed the ball firmly into my mouth, and Pippa lifted my head and Rosa fastened the straps behind my head.

Rosa had now climbed onto the bed and straddled me as she held my head in her two hands. I was looking into her eyes and she said it's important you remember to relax and breathe. She moved up my body, and her moistness was only inches from my lips. I so wanted to perform oral on her, but the ball gag had been put in place so correctly I could not move my tongue. All this time, Sofia was still doing what she was doing to my feet, which was already an immense turn-on.

Rosa every now and again would lower her moist, wet vagina to my mouth, the gag stopping me from getting any penetration, and she would gyrate her wetness on the ball. I could not move, but wanted to pull the gag from my mouth and complete what Rosa had started. Rosa would run her hands down the length of my arms as she did this, which just added to the immense turn-on I was receiving.

While Sofia was working her area and Rosa working her magic on me, Pippa was the most devilish. Having positioned herself against my now throbbing, twitching penis, her hands were massaging my testicles with one of her hands. The other was rubbing up and down the length of my about to explode penis, not content with this Pippa would every now and again place my penis inside her mouth and give the gentlest of sucks. My arms were pulling at the restraints but going nowhere as they were tied firm. I tried to move my legs and feet too, but there was also no movement in that area. I could not even speak or ask them to let me free so I could join in this amazing situation. All three girls were now working on my body in individual areas. Sofia would suck hard on my toes, Rosa at the same time would lower her moistness onto the ball and gyrate, and as if that was not enough, as those girls did Pippa would take the full length of my adulthood deep into her throat and suck.

Rosa showed me some mercy and loosened the straps on the gag.

Not full just enough for me to be able to work on my tongue. Sofia was also making a move and was kissing and caressing my legs as she slowly moved up my legs at the pace of a snail. Pippa was now dribbling on the end of my penis and blowing cold air into it. Rosa lowered herself again. This time my tongue could only just move around the ball gag. And then she lowered. I could taste her warm, moist vagina and the juices that she was producing. Just as I thought I could enjoy the dampness of Rosa, she would pull away, out of my reach again. Sofia was now up to my inner thigh and Pippa sinking her mouth deep into my throbbing penis. Suddenly Pippa stopped what she was doing and removed herself from my body as this a break I was about to receive.

No sooner had Pippa removed her body contact from my genitals than Sofia slid in and took over. How could two mouths feel so different and so sexually fulfilling, Sofia was performing oral and even though she too was now sucking on my penis, it felt nice but very different in the way their mouths worked and their tongues?

Pippa had gone to the box of tricks that Rosa had left at the end of the bed and pulled a whip from it. Rosa still gyrating on my now half able to work mouth, and Sofia rising and sinking on the full length of my adulthood. Pippa stroked the whip across my abdominal muscles, each of the leather strands caressing each and every one muscle in my stomach. It was meant to be pleasurable, which is very much was but also felt like the nicest torture you could ever receive all at the same time. Pippa moved the whip across my stomach. Her other hand was now caressing Rosa's breasts as she rose and sank into my mouth. As Pippa was playing with her breasts, Rosa's hand would squeeze and pull and twist my nipples. Sofia had now moved to Rosa's back and was kissing her spine. As she rose up to her back, as she did this, she used one of her hands and placed my very delicate penis at the entrance to her moistness.

With a quick little shuffle of her pelvis, I found my penis to be sinking deep inside her warm, moist vagina. Rosa was now sitting on my chest and moved further back towards Sofia's body. I now had Pippa releasing the straps on the ball gag completely. As she did this, she straddled my face and was lowering her moist vagina onto my eagerly waiting mouth and lips. As she fondled Rosa's breasts with her hands and they kissed. I could take no more and had the most powerful climax I had ever had to that day. Sofia still moving and working her moist vagina on my now going limp penis, she was relentless and did not stop rising and sinking into my adulthood until I actually slipped out.

Eventually, someone released my restraints, and at long last, I could touch and feel these beautiful women. I asked them all to lie on their backs on the bed, which they did with Sofia in the middle of Rosa and Pippa. All three girl's hands were everywhere, touching and caressing each other's bodies. They were kissing what looked wild at first but at a second glance; it was more than that it was so caring and special and each kiss they gave to each other was as if it were their last kiss. I so wanted to join in with the activities they were doing. I could not join in, well, not just yet anyway. As far as I could remember, Sofia had made me climax at least twice while I was inside her.

I looked through Pippa's and Rosa's box at the foot of the bed there was a selection of vibrators among the other sexual aids in that box. There was this purple vibrator about seven inches long, at a guess. It had the girth of about two fingers. I picked this one up, turned the end of it and it had full battery power and buzzed and vibrate in my hand.

All three of the girls were still in a kissing, touching frenzy with each other. Not one of them was being left out, all getting equal pleasure from each other. I knelt on the floor at the foot of the bed in front of Rosa. I held Rosa's knees in my hands and slowly separated her knees until there was no resistance from Rosa. I placed the vibrator between my teeth and lips; it gave a funny tingling sensation as I did this. I slowly moved my mouth to Rosa's moistness. Holding the vibrator between my lips, I slowly entered her and was giving her oral with a twist. Not my tongue, but this buzzing little toy.

I slowly worked on Rosa like this for about 15 minutes till she could take no more. My mouth now pushing, sliding this toy in and out of her moistness, as I would push it in she would buck and gyrate her moistness as if it were a penis that was doing this to her. Rosa seemed to enjoy what I was doing as every time I lowered onto her moistness one of her hands would cup the back of my head and hold if not push my head harder onto her. I very slowly removed my head from between Rosa's legs and placed the hand which had cupped my head on the vibrator which I had left in place. As I withdrew, Rosa's hand was more than ready to take over as I pulled away. I could see she was well using this toy.

Next in line was little Sofia: I don't think the girls really needed me there at all, like the sounds of pleasure coming from themselves were amazing. I was enjoying what I was doing. I could see for the first time what Rosa had meant when she said, "only another woman can know how to touch another woman". Believe me, if any man was involved in that kissing and touching frenzy that they were in, there was without a doubt, would have wanted to penetrate one if not all three of these women. But the girls seemed to have everything under control and enjoying every moment of what they were doing.

But what the girls were doing with each other looked so soft, sensual, and sensitive. I moved to Sofia's legs and slowly separated them as I had Rosa's. Again, there was no resistance from Sofia. I moved my mouth closer to Sofia's moistness, kissing as I approached her vagina. As I got closer, I could see her vagina sparkle with the moistness she was producing from what Rosa and Pippa were doing with her. I lay there just blowing gently from my mouth onto her damp vagina. Her legs were so relaxed as I moved closed, she opened her legs a little further for me.

I started with a gentle flick of my tongue on her clitoris. I then circled her clitoris with my very eager tongue. Sofia never had a free hand, as her hands were busy caressing and fondling both Rosa and Pippa. I let my tongue slowly slide down her moist vagina, my tongue now covered in her juices. I began licking each of her labia lips in turn with my tongue, the folds of her labia lips were gently settling on my tongue as I touched them. All Sofia could do while I did this was to give me the occasional look and such tiny small thrusts of her moistness onto my wanting tongue.

It was Pippa's turn as I approached Pippa. She looked at me and what I had been doing; she smiled at me as I moved closer and I did not have to say or do a thing as I got closer. She slowly lowered and parted her legs. Things were going to be different for her, as she had been watching what I had been doing. As I had managed somehow to regain my erection, I lifted both her limp legs and held each of them in my arms. I moved closer to her, Pippa, who looked at me, surprised but pleased to see I had managed another erection. I braced her legs in my arms and moved closer still to her.

With no hesitation, I inserted my penis fully into her soaked vagina. As I pushed in, Pippa gasped where I was holding her legs. She could not buck and thrust into my adulthood. She decided she would swing side to side the sight of these three girls continuing to do what they had been doing all along was an amazing sight. Pippa was desperate to try to regain some control over what she and I were doing. I climaxed within minutes of being inside Pippa as I felt her vaginal walls clamp around my penis. I felt a bit of a failure as the girls continued to do what they were doing previous to my intervention eventually we all fell asleep that night in a heap of sexual satisfaction.

Chapter Thirty Three

I was the last one downstairs the next morning I went into the kitchen and there was Sofia as normal; she had really taken the role of housemaid as she was in the farmhouse in France. I sorted out my work thanks to Vicki. I now had loads of wok and the phone ceased to stop ringing for further inquirers.

We were all doing our own stuff with Pippa, with her driving lessons. Sofia was pottering around the house doing the maid stuff, and Rosa in her study writing. No one ever disturbed her when she was in there. This was the only private thing about Rosa. As I said, we were all just doing our stuff, and I was thinking about taking someone one. I could not offer a full-time job, so a semi-retired person would have been a great help. The next couple of weeks passed, and things were just very normal. Sofia had taken to sleeping with Rosa, Pippa, and me a few nights a week, but returned to her own room on occasions.

One night we were all lazing around in the lounge and Rosa was talking about Rebecca and how she was now getting on. How she was getting back to her normal self with every day that passed. Then Rosa spoke about Donna and how much she was missing her being around, and at some point must attempt to go out and see her in Australia. To meet her new partner and her grandchild, she said she was pleased that she had made herself a new life out in Australia, but she missed her terribly.

She then directed her conversation to me "Adam!" Rosa said, "do you remember how I did not want you to become a customer at a burlesque club or strip club but made a point of saying customer?". I answered "yes" I remember Rosa why I have not been to any feeling a little confused. She said she was also worried that now my business had taken off very well, that I had not got the time for her anymore. I said yes I remembered that bit too, and my answer to you was I would always make time for you if you remember. I repeated myself and said, Rosa, I will always make time for you, you're my number one.

Rosa said, "there is a reason I bring that up now. I hope I have some good news for you, Pippa and Sofia." "What's that then, Rosa?" I replied. Rosa said, "I have been busy sorting out some licenses for the outhouse that you so lovingly restored." "What licenses did you need to sort out?" I asked. Well, Rosa replied, "I am going to open a burlesque club in the outhouse and have the licenses to sell alcohol, but the club is going to be a strict membership only club. Which members will have to qualify for and it will be quite a strict membership, it is going to be a very up market type of club for high rolling business people who need to entertain their clients." Then Rosa said, "I want you to manage it for me my," first thoughts were "oh God, I don't have the time what with my business." She saved me from looking like a fool. She said the club will only be open from Thursday evening through to Sunday evening. I felt relieved as I could do the evenings and weekends so would not have to go back on my word to her. I said, "great idea!" But when was she going to get this started?

I was very pleased and proud that Rosa thought I could run such a club. Pippa then spoke the wheels have already been put in motion, and we have advertised for dancers. They have to be the best of the cream of the dancers if you like.

The reason the dancers have got to be of such a high caliber is the membership is going to be a thousand pounds a year to be a member. Wow, I said that's a lot for membership. Rosa then spoke, "yes it is a lot of money, but the type of person we want to become members will pay that amount". Knowing the clients they are entertaining are free of any hassle and are safe they will be of character and not the grabbing louts where I first started.

The weekend came and there had been so many calls from dancers they seemed to have blocked the line. Rosa's name, even though she had given up dancing years before, was very respected and very well heard of. When the dancers heard she was opening her own club, it was like every dancer in England wanted to dance there. The club was to be called "ROSA'S".

Rosa, Pippa, and I went to the outhouse to do the interviews there were girls from all walks of life. Wave after wave of stunningly beautiful women came before us. Rosa knew exactly what she was looking for. Pippa had already asked me to get my camera ready for the day of the interviews, as I would take the pictures of the girls who passed the first stage of the interviews. First, the wanna-be dancers would sit in front of Rosa and Pippa and go through some questions. If they passed that stage they were sent backstage to me where I was to do a short portfolio for them.

There were quite a few that did not even make it to the photography section. Some of those girls who did not make it were totally stunned. Most men would have jumped at the chance to see them dance. The ones who got through, I thought, were the most beautiful I had ever seen in my life. I was even a little nervous to photograph some of them as the beauty shone in person, and I was afraid my photography would not be up to standard.

The end of the day came, and I had photographed about forty of the most stunning ladies I had ever seen. We went back up to the house that evening. Our conversation was all about the girls we had seen, and we lay the pictures out on the kitchen table. We looked at the pictures and the application forms. Rosa had the final say, but she welcomed the input from Pippa, Sofia, and me.

Rosa whittled it down to about twenty girls I could not believe some ladies that Rosa had decided against, but she knew what she was doing. We all went to bed totally shattered that night. We woke the next morning and went down to the kitchen for breakfast. As we sat at the table, there was an envelope tucked under Rosa's plate it was another application, or was it one we had missed.

Rosa opened the envelope and burst out laughing, Pippa and I just looking at each other in amazement. We had never heard Rosa laugh like this before. It was Sofia's application. Once Rosa regained control of herself, she asked Sofia to sit with her and put her arm around Sofia. Rosa said that there was no need for her to fill an application form and that Sofia reminded her of herself when she was younger. Rosa said, "you have a guaranteed pass to this" and that she would be a dancer at this club. Rosa said, "also, I am going to teach you everything I know." Sofia smiled and gave Rosa a kiss and said thank you so much.

After breakfast, we called the girls that Rosa had chosen. There were about twenty that made it to this stage. Rosa invited them along to the last stage of the interview, although that is not the words she used. This stage of the interview was to see how well they actually moved. All the girls contacted seemed so happy, and three or four of them actually came on that Sunday.

For their trial dance, I was looking at the outhouse as a club and no longer a shabby outhouse. In my mind it had now come together, looking at it in a different light. Now it really looked the part, a stage, a bar, cleverly placed lighting. It was not until this point that I realized the job I had done and some girls were saying what a lovely club it was.

This time I was doing a full photoshoot for these ladies in all their dancing clothes. The first four that came on that Sunday were chosen to be dancers at the club. If you saw them in the street, you would think they were pretty but would think no more than that. In their normal clothes, but in their dancing outfits, they looked dynamite. The girls were very chatty with me, as Rosa and Pippa had told them I was going to be the manager. I don't know whether they thought if they spoke to me nicely I would help them, but it really was Rosa that called the shots. Some of them were even flirting with me. The rest of the girls chosen came over the following weekend. They did their last shoot with me there were a couple of girls that Rosa had second thoughts on for some reason, which she kept to herself. She recalled the spare girls from the previous interviews.

Rosa sat all the girls together in the club, got on the stage, and stated the club rules. Saying the rules of the club were never to be broken and if at the end of her talk anyone thought they could not abide by them, they were to leave. The rules are simple, she said, no girl working in the club is allowed to date a member, not in or outside the club. If a private dance had been asked for by a member, there was to be no sexual contact or activity at all.

If the girls disagreed with another girl, it was not to be sorted out in public in front of the members or in the dressing room area. If a problem arose, they were to go to me or go directly to Rosa, and it was to be sorted out in private. If the problem persisted, both girls would be asked to leave and their contract ended. Every girl accepted the rules and not one of them left. Shortly after the talk, all the girls said their goodbyes and left with the timetable of when they would dance next.

Pippa, Rosa, and I were talking when everyone had left. Pippa said that the memberships were coming in thick and fast. According to Rosa, we were limited to 200 members because of the size of the club and the number of fire exits. I now realized how clever Rosa was and what a wonderful businesswoman she was. It had cost Rosa next to nothing to get the outhouse renovated.

Even the dancers were expected to pay £25.00 per session when they danced, as they would earn a lot more from Rosa's members in tips. So whichever way you looked at this, Rosa or the club earned every time it opened its doors. Rosa had 200 hundred members paid up, at a thousand pounds per Annam. Having dancers paying £25.00 per shift and the members would pay slightly more for their drinks in the club than they would anywhere else. Rosa could do this, as she had selected the memberships very carefully.

After our long conversation about how the club was going to be run, we all headed up to the house. Sofia, as always, had been busy preparing us for our evening meal. When we sat down at our meal, Sofia said to Rosa that she was getting worried. In a soft voice, she said to Rosa that she was getting butterflies in her stomach and she wondered if she would be good enough. She had come down to the club and had a sneaky look at the girls' dance. Rosa smiled, looked at Pippa and me. She said, just like I was. She smiled at Sofia and said to her please do not worry. She gave her a kiss and said she would be fine. Rosa said, "the members will love you Sofia I promise you that, you have something that other girls do not". What's that then Sofia asked nervously, looking down at her flat chest.

Rosa smiled and said you have innocence, and that is what I had when I first started many years ago. Explaining her story of how she met Elisa and how under similar circumstances Elisa had taken Rosa under her wing as to speak. Which is what Rosa was now also doing for Sofia.

Sofia walked across to Rosa and gave her the biggest cuddle ever, and said thank you to Rosa. The rest of the evening was taken up by going over the ultimate choice of girls who were to dance at the club. Rosa spent a fair bit of time on the phone talking to the new members that she had secured. These people were important people within their community there were business managers or proprietors of some quite large companies.

We stayed awake till the early hours of the morning, just sifting through the hundreds of photos I had taken. Eventually, we went to bed totally shattered. The next morning and it was back to work. Rosa was sitting in her study, looking very sexy without even trying in her dark-rimmed glasses. Pippa was off teaching her students how to drive, and Sofia slipping away to her room to practice at every opportunity she could get. I had secured so much work thanks to Vicki and her referrals so much so that I took this semi-retired man on his name was John.

John was a great asset to me, as what this man did not know about the building industry you could write on the back of a postage stamp. For the next few days, this is how the girls and my days unfolded I was keen to learn from John. Before we knew it, the opening of the club was upon us all the girls scheduled to work had turned up with their outfits and accessories.

Backstage looked like a carnival with all the bright colors. The dancer's ages ranged from 20 to 40 years old, some of the more mature dancers were helping the younger ones get ready and we're giving them some advice. Sofia looked so nervous, but the other dancers tried to make her feel welcome and part of the crew. Rosa had come to the back of the stage area and saw Sofia and gave her a reassuring hug. Rosa said to Sofia please do not worry and trust me you will be fine and they will love you.

Pippa was still out front, greeting the new members and their guests. I was working in the bar area and the music was playing. If I had shut my eyes and did not know better, I really could have thought that I was in that burlesque club in France that Rosa had taken me to.

Vicki had been drafted in to help me in the bar area, and to waitress on the tables. We were expecting to be really busy that night. These really well-to-do businesspeople were coming to the bar and just leaving their credit cards with me, and I was about to attach the card to their table number. The lighting in the club now looked fantastic. The mood was great for both members, and the dancers had all turned up in high spirits and were looking to have a great time.

The evening was going along so well, none of us really having time to talk to each other. I had lost count of the number of wine bottles I had opened, even though the drink was flowing nicely. There was not one bit of trouble. The dancers seemed to go offstage with their fists full of money in tips. I could hear the members talking and they would sit around the table, picking their favorite dancers so far. All the dancers looked amazing to me, so how these people could pick a favorite I did not know. Their make-up was done to the highest standards. The outfits were stunning and the dances they performed were so erotic. When some dancers used the pole, it was a feat in its self how they stayed on it the way they threw themselves around.

Vicki kept looking across at me, hinting that she wanted to speak to me, but every time she got near the bar she would be called away again. Vicki grabbed her moment and said, "Hey you, remember we have still got to do this dinner date" and smiled. I said, "Vicki it is I who should take you for dinner for all the work I have received from your friends."

But before I could finish what I was saying, she was gone again. A table had called her over for yet another order. Just as the last girl was finished all the music stopped, the lights went bright on the stage, and out of the dry ice, smoke appeared Rosa looking totally stunning. The entire hall fell silent, and everyone looked at the stage. Rosa was standing there looking so so good, she grabbed a microphone and spoke.

"Hello, my friends, old and new welcome to my club and I hope you have many enjoyable evenings here". The cheers went up she raised her hand and smiled at everyone as if to hush them. Rosa then said I have a great treat for you all I now have a dancer from Paris, France. This lady's moves will blow your mind away a few tables cheered and clap their hands as the light slowly dimmed, Rosa said to the hall I give you Sofia.

The stage was in near darkness. You could see the other dancers standing to the side of the stage behind the curtains so they could see for themselves what Sofia was about to perform. The lights on the stage slowly got a little brighter. Suddenly there were some sparks from fireworks after the sparks came from red and white rose petals. Out of the mist came Sofia, dragging a small wooden chair behind her. She placed the chair in the center of the stage, looked up to the lights, and the color changed to lavender. The lavender light and the mist in themselves made the place feel warm and erotic.

Sofia slowly danced around the chair until the hall was in total silence. Sofia was wearing a white, coped raincoat as she stood in front of the chair and ran her hands down the raincoat. Her tiny fingers slowly undoing the large buttons and even larger buckle to the coat. The crowd was in awe at Sofia: you could not have heard a pin drop if it were not for the soft French music playing for her to dance to.

Sofia walked around the stage undoing her coat, looking at the customers as if she wanted to take them to bed. She would stand there looking as though she were looking at just one person and would slowly open the large buttons as she licked her lips and not losing eye contact with the customers. As Sofia did this, the cheers went up the crowd got louder and louder. Sofia started with her back to the members she slowly lowered the coat from her shoulders, revealing one petite shoulder at a time. Then both of her naked shoulders. She then slowly lowered the coat halfway down her back. The members were going wild at Sofia's, dancing with this slow erotic tease. As she danced, the stage was being littered with money. Sofia then released the grip on her coat and let it slowly slide down the rest of her body to reveal a tiny framed body.

Sofia was wearing a small lace white bra, white lace knickers, and suspender belt with white fishnet stockings. Sofia continued to dance provocatively around the little wooden chair. As she danced, she dragged the chair closer to the edge of the stage. Sofia would stretch out one of her hands and stroke the side of one member's face if they were close enough for her to reach.

Sofia left the chair briefly and moved to the chrome pole in the center of the stage. I had not seen her work on a pole before. She was as equally as good as the more experienced dancers she danced around the pole very erotically. She would put her face to the pole as if to lick it. As she did this, the men were going crazy and threw even more money at her and onto the stage.

Sofia then lies on her back on the floor tipping her head back, looking at the members. Sofia then raised one of her legs and her tiny hands unfastened the clips on her suspender belt, Sofia slowly unrolled each stocking and pulled them separate from her legs, As she stretched the stocking on her leg the customers would cheer, the cheers were nothing like I had heard before it was like being at a football match. She slowly wriggled to her feet as she went back to the chair and stood with her back to the audience. Again, looking over each shoulder in turn, she looked very provocatively at the members.

Sofia moved her hands behind her back and slowly unfastened her bra, with the bra just now only being held in place by her hands. She turned to face the members and most of the members were chanting more, more, more. Her dance had driven them into a wild frenzy all you could hear was people chanting her name. Sofia moved very slowly to the front of the stage, her hand still clasping the bra in place. As she stood there, she put one of her fingers to her mouth.

She slowly licked and suck on one of her fingers, whilst doing this her eyes would flutter occasionally. People were leaning forward to give her even more money and then she turned again with her back now to the audience. Looking over her shoulder and blew the loud chanting crowd a kiss and slowly walked off the stage, the crowd was going crazy chanting Sofia, Sofia, and clapping.

A short time passed and as Rosa appeared on stage, the lights were fully on and the hall was illuminated. Rosa spoke on the microphone and said, "I hope everyone had had a good time and enjoyed the opening evening". The cheers were so loud it felt as though it could have lifted the roof off, so I guess everyone had enjoyed their selves. The bar had closed during Sofia's performance, and Pippa and I were standing at the exit door. As the members left, all you could hear was talk of the new dancer from France. Sofia's name was on most of the member's lips as they left the building, all the dancers apart from Sofia were leaving by the side door to their own car park. Rosa and Pippa asked Vicki and me if we could finish up and close the building for the night. We said yes, and Rosa and Pippa left, taking Sofia with them.

Vicki and I were now left alone. Before we even tried to make good of the mess, Vicki and I sat and had a drink together. The hall was eerily quiet, as there was only Vicki and me here. We sat at one table and had a relaxed drink together and at last a peaceful chat.

Vicki said, "so Adam, the drink and the meal, I said, oh yes, I am sure I have to treat you". She smiled and said maybe we could treat each other. I asked, "when did you want to do this?" She answers, "how about next Thursday evening?" I agreed to the dinner date, and we cleaned up the hall the best we could and we locked the hall up for the night.

Vicki went home for the night and gave me a quick kiss. And said she enjoyed working with me. I went up to the house Sofia was fast asleep on the sofa when I got there. Pippa had already gone to bed, as she had an early start in the morning. Rosa and I chatted about how well the evening had gone we sat on the other sofa. As we chatted Sofia was out for the count, Rosa and I sat there chatting with our arms around each other. I said to Rosa, "Where did Sofia get the time to practice her dance moves?"

Rosa said that while Pippa and I were at work, she was teaching Sofia a routine: Rosa said "Sofia, had done the exact routine that Elisa had taught her many years ago when she first started", I said Sofia was amazing. All you could hear from the members was Sofia's name they were so pleased with her dance. Rosa then said, yes Sofia is very good and probably does not know how good she actually is, she said again that Sofia reminded her so much of herself when she was younger.

Both Rosa and I went to bed that night, totally exhausted. Sofia was still fast asleep on the sofa, so we just covered her with a blanket and left her there. The three of us, Rosa, Pippa and I slept like logs that night. The next morning came and for the first time since I had met Sofia, she was not in the kitchen, nor had she prepared breakfast. I went to look for her in her room but her bed had not been slept in. I opened the door to the lounge and there was Sofia, still fast asleep on the sofa where Rosa and I had left her. We let her sleep, maybe thinking she was doing too much looking after the house and trying to fit in a dance routine.

Pippa and I took ourselves off to work we left the house with Rosa gently trying to wake Sofia from her sleep. The next couple of days were just normal stuff, working and relaxing in the lounge of an evening in front of the fire.

Chapter Thirty Four

Well before I knew it, it was Thursday; I went to work as normal. While I was at work, I got a text message from Vicki. She was reminding me of our dinner date. I said I would pick her up at about 8 pm. I asked where she would like to go and she suggested a little Chinese that she knew. I worked until about 4 pm that day. My day was full of thoughts about Vicki that day. Some of them were sexual. I knew I should not be having thoughts like this, but it was only thoughts, and that would harm no one.

All-day I could think of nothing else but our encounter that evening and her amazing tongue. I went back to Rosa and Pippa and they said that they had not cooked me anything as I was out with Vicki that evening. I went upstairs and had a long soak in the bath so long that I think I must have fallen asleep for a while. Rosa came into the bathroom and sat on the edge of the bath she said she hoped that I was going to have a nice evening with Vicki.

Rosa asked if I wanted my back washed and, of course, I said yes. I adored Rosa's touch. Rosa lathered my back with so much soap and was washing me so gently. Her touch was amazing and would put anyone in a hypnotic state. As I finished my bath, Rosa was standing there with a warm towel in her hands and dried my back for me. Rosa said have a good time tonight, Adam, as she toweled my back dry and kissed me on the back of the neck.

Rosa then left the bathroom, and I continued to get ready. I put on a nice suit and a white shirt but still could not wear a tie, as I hated them. It felt like a noose around my neck. I slashed on some aftershave and went downstairs. As I walked into the kitchen, there was a note on the table for me. The note read as so.

Dearest Adam,
We hope you have a great evening with Vicki. We have decided to go out for the evening as the club is closed tonight. We have gone for a meal and to the theater, and not to worry if I was back before them, as they may stay in a hotel room for the night.
lots of love,

Rosa Pippa Sofia xxx

Part of me felt very jealous, as I think I would have liked to have gone with them for a meal and especially to the theater as my last memories of the theater were very special to me and very eventful.

Chapter Thirty Five

Shortly afterward, I left to go and pick Vicki up from her home. I knocked at the door and she was ready to go straight away. I thought we were going back to my truck, but she said we should take her car a BMW 3 series. We got into her car and drove for about 40 minutes to this small village, and parked outside a small Chinese restaurant. Before we even got through the doors of this place, the smells coming from it were fantastic. Once inside, we were shown to our table and Vicki removed her coat, which was a black mink coat I thought she looked absolutely stunning. Her hair was in a loose perm, her eyes looked amazing, they were very long dark lashes and on the eyelids an electric blue color, her lips a bright red full gloss lipstick. She wore this amazing pearl necklace which sat across her full bosom she was wearing a body-hugging silk dress which really showed off the contours of her body really well.

We sat there chatting for what seemed like an eternity. We spoke of our trip to France, and how scared the girls were on the boat trip that night. Looking back on it I could see the funny side of it. We also spoke very briefly about Rebecca and how she was now doing. Speaking very little of about what had happened to her, I think Vicki wanted to forget that part well as best as she could.

Vicki had taken her shoes off under the table and was gently running her foot up and down my calf muscles. Vicki then said, so my darling, how am I meant to thank you for what you have done, I said the meal was plenty good enough. There really was no need to thank me at all, and it was I who should be thanking her for all the work she had put my way. "Inside I was yearning to say well I would love to feel that fantastic tongue of yours again".

Instead, I said that to go to dinner with her was a privilege, and then I said that I wanted to pay as it only seemed fair with all the work I had got from her. Friends, Vicki just said we will see. It was nice to have a meal with her, but I found I was getting a little hot under the collar with the way she was playing with my legs. How she was.

Vicki had great for putting people at ease. The meal came to an end, and it was still quite early. I took the bill from the table before she had a chance to take it, and as we left, I paid the bill. She looked at me and said naughty, naughty that was meant to be my treat, then said, I will have to think of something else now. We went to her car and I can remember there was a definite chill in the air that night and it had just drizzled with rain. The rain felt freezing as we walked to her car. As we got in the car Vicki said, "let's not let the evening end just yet, Adam."

I asked her what else she would like to do, and she looked across at me and smiled she said, "you drive my car Adam and I will give you directions." We drove for about 30 minutes right out into the countryside and it was so so dark, no street light, not another house in sight. As I was driving her car she sat very, very close to me and had her hand on my leg. As I drove, you could see the ice forming on the glass of the car. Vicki then asked me to turn left in this little lane. I smiled to myself as this had happened to me before with Pippa, when she took me to her stable. We drove down this little lane, not another car in sight, and it was very dark. Eventually, we came to this small lake surrounded by trees. The rain got a little heavier, and the temperature had dropped a fair bit too. Vicki said to me to park over in the corner under some trees.

I did as she requested and I left the car running for extra warmth, then as we were sitting there Vicki asked what is my sexual fantasy. I was a little shocked, but I had hoped this is how it would go. I had to think hard about what my fantasy was, as Rosa and Pippa had fulfilled most, if not all, of my sexual fantasies. Even Sofia had fulfilled one or two of my fantasy's too.

As hard as I tried, I could not think of a fantasy that I had. The main fantasy that I had was to have two women at the same time, and I had done that. Vicki said, well you're a very lucky man than Adam. All the time she was leaning against me and running her hand up and down my leg. I had to know, so I asked her what her sexual fantasy was, she was very straightforward and said I have two Adam "what are they I asked".

She kissed the side of my face and then Vicki said one of my fantasies is to be stripped naked and to be tied up. While two other women make love to her partner and I not able to join in and then tease me with my lover.

The other fantasy that I have, Adam, she said, was believe it or not to make love in the rain on the bonnet of a car. With this, she unzipped her silk dress and let it fall from her shoulders. She then said, "you could help me with that one, Adam, if you wanted to." One of her hands had now turned my face, and we kissed. Her lush, plump, cold lips felt so nice against mine. One of my hands was now underneath this silk dress. I could feel the smoothness of her legs. The heavy petting became heavier and heavier. Vicki pulled the latch on the passenger door of the car and stepped out of the car. As soon as the door was open, you could feel the coldness from the outside rush in.

She stood just outside the car door and removed her dress and placed it on the passenger seat, looking at me the whole time. She raised her hand and beckoned me to come to her. The raindrops that hit her body were now running down over her naked body and over her ample breasts. The coldness and the rain just seemed to add to the excitement.

Vicki then walked round to the front of the car. As was standing there looking at me through the windscreen, she beckoned me again. All Vicki had on was a pair of red high heels. I got out of the car and as I walked round to the front of the car; she laid *her beckon the rain-soaked bonnet*. I was standing before her and as she lay there; she touched herself intimately. I was standing there in my suit trousers and my white shirt, which was fast sticking to my body because of the rain. Vicki could see my nipples through my soaked shirt and sat up on the bonnet and pulled me close to her. One of her hands had found its way in my shirt and she was playing with my nipple. Her mouth was on my other nipple over my shirt and was sucking on my nipple via my shirt, which was an immense turn on. The hand that was previously inside my shirt was now tumbling around with the buckle on my belt. This she overcame with insignificant problems and was now starting on the buttons on my trouser.

This too was not a problem for her. The rain was now coming down fairly hard, but this did not seem to worry her at all. Her loose permed hair was now soaked and stuck firm to her warm scalp, you could even see steam rise from her scalp. Vicki let my trousers fall to the floor. She then, still looking at me, mounted the bonnet once again. We were both soaked through to the skin, which was easy for Vicki, as that's all she was wearing (skin).

I was standing there, my trousers round my ankles and my shirt now stuck to me like a second skin. She asked me to come closer to her as I did so I lifted her legs and pushed her further onto the bonnet, both her hands were now stretched back and both placed on the windscreen of her car. She was muttering "oh God yes, please let it happen" with her lying on the bonnet as I kissed Vicki slowly, making my way up the length of her legs. My hair was flat to my head, the rain running down my face as I looked up at her I could see the enormity of her erect nipples on her breast, the rain just bouncing off her breasts.

As I kissed my way up her legs, my hands were going on before, as if to clear the way. Sweeping the rain from her legs, my hand had found her perfectly formed vagina, still kissing my way up as one of my fingers found the entrance to her moistness. Even though the rest of her body was now so cold and wet from the rain, the moistness from her vagina was very warm to the touch. The speed of my kissing increased as I was eager for my mouth to join in the fun my fingers were having. As my mouth reached her moistness, I gave a gentle lick and suck off her labia lips. I stood tall in front of her, my fingers now deep inside her warm, moist vagina. I moved my fingers about. Vicki would wriggle about and slide on the bonnet of the car every so often her pelvis would leave the bonnet and buck hard against my fingers.

I could feel that I was very aroused and had a great erection. I moved closer to her, her hands now holding the windscreen wipers, even pulling on them. She asked me to take her; I did not need telling twice. Moving closer still, and pulled her body towards my own. Her hands not letting go of the wipers, I lifted her legs and slowly moved my very willing, eager penis towards the entrance of her now very lubricated, damp vagina. I held her legs and pulled on her body until my penis entered her with no trouble at all and very soon found myself deep inside of Vicki's vagina.

Vicki was sliding on the bonnet of her car with great ease thanks to the rain. Each time I pulled her towards me, I felt myself slide a little deeper inside her moistness. I could hear her saying as she was biting her lip, "oh God, yes this is how I imagined it to be", followed by "oh yes". The rain was now beating down heavier than before. Both of us soaked the rain, made Vicki's body shine in the moonlight. We continued to make love this way for a few minutes more. She was right. It was a great turn on making love in the rain outside. I asked her to move down, and she just released her grip on the wipers. I removed my penis from her moistness and she slid all the way down the bonnet.

She sat on the edge of the bonnet for a while and we kissed. I stepped back, and she moved to a kneeling position in front of me. With her head tilted she looked at me and took my penis in her hands and without a second to think about it, she had covered the whole of my penis with her warm mouth. Her head was moving back and forth. Every so often as she pulled her mouth back I could feel the freezing rain hit my penis, only to be warmed up seconds later by her mouth. I could feel that I was about to climax, and asked her if she wanted to return to the car for some warmth. She removed my penis from her mouth and looked up at me, and smiled.

With this, she stood tall and put her arms around me. As we kissed and cuddled, she had turned my body and was now slowly lowering my body onto the bonnet of the car. The rain-soaked bonnet felt freezing, and just as I lay there, she repeated what she had been doing on the floor. One of my hands was holding the wiper and the other massaging her warm scalp as her head bobbed back and forth on my throbbing adulthood. It was only a few more minutes, and I felt myself climax she carried on sucking and my body thought all the nerves in my body had come to the surface.

We eventually got back into the car, her dress still nice and warm on the seat and everything I had soaked through apart from my suit jacket. As she redressed herself I turned the heating up on the car in a vain attempt to dry my trouser and shirt. Vicki smiled at me and said, thank you Adam that was lovely now let me get you home and dry you off. Vicki drove the car back to hers and when back at her house she invited me in to dry off and the promise of a hot drink. Once inside, she stripped again, took all of my clothes and put them in the tumble dryer. We kissed and caressed each other under a duvet and sat on the sofa in her lounge while my clothes were drying. She asked if I wanted to stay the night with her, but I was unsure as Rosa and Pippa were nothing to do with this. Had I broken the cardinal rule she said that Rosa had texted her, and that they were staying in a hotel that night, so I stayed.

Vicki lead the way to her bedroom, and as we entered, she began stripping. Her body looked so fresh from the natural rain shower we had both had earlier that night. She climbed into her bed as pulled the sheets back for me to climb in next to her. As we lay there together I lent across and gave her a kiss. She was just staring at me. I lay on my back and her hands were running over the top half of my body. Nestling her lips into my neck, and kissed me very gently. The hand that had been caressing the top half of my body was now including my genitals. In her caressing each time her hand got to my adulthood, she would slow her hand movements to a near stop. Her hand would hold my penis, soon she had left my top half alone and her hand was permanently on my penis. Very slowly rubbing back and forth. Her hands felt so warm and soft. I did not want to stop her. As I lay there, I was thinking about what Vicki and I had done with each other that night. Her lips left my neck, and she was now slowly, gently kissing my abdomen, still her hand performing this amazing genital massage. Her head soon joined her hand and before I knew too much of what she was doing, her magical tongue had now joined her hand.

Whereas before I thought Vicki had this amazing tongue tonight, she and her tongue seemed very normal. It did not feel enlarged. Nevertheless, she was very good at what she was doing, so good that it felt like I lasted only minutes before I had climaxed. We lay together cuddling, and that is how we fell asleep together. I woke about 5.30 am and Vicki was still fast asleep. I went to the kitchen and made myself a hot drink after the drink I went back up to see Vicki but she was still sound asleep. So I went back to the kitchen and wrote her a note. I said in the note thank you for an excellent night. I had really enjoyed myself and hoped she had to, but I had to leave early as I had to prepare myself for the day's work ahead and hoped she understood. That's why I was not with her when she woke I signed the note and left to go back to Rosa's.

Chapter Thirty Six

When I got to Rosa's there was no one there, as Vicki had told me they were staying over that night in a hotel. Just as I was about to leave for work, the three girls walked through the door full of the joys of life. I sat and spoke to Rosa for a short while, her first question as well "how did the evening go then, Adam". I explained all that we did and how we started off at a Chinese restaurant. Rosa never batted an eyelid as I explained everything to her only words were, I am so glad you had a nice evening with Vicki.

Sofia was talking to Pippa, and Sofia wanted to drive lessons, and Pippa was trying to work her into her very busy schedule. I went off to work, picked up John on the way, and went to our first job. It was a hard day's work, as I felt I had very little sleep that night, but we got through the day. I dropped John off at his home and continued on my way to Rosa's.

I went to bed that night with the girls and we lay there talking about their trip to the theater and what fun they had had. There was not really even a mention of my night with Vicki, apart from Rosa saying she had received a message from Vicki and to tell me she understood I had to go and sort myself out for work. We all just fell asleep in each other's arms that night, everyone totally exhausted. The next few days were just normal everyday stuff work and obviously, the shifts that we had to do at the burlesque club (outhouse as I always thought of it.)

We had several good evenings in the club, but there was this time that I noticed Rosa looked down in spirits, which were unlike her. As we worked alongside each other in the clubhouse and seeing her in the house, there seemed to be something about her that shifted her personality from a confident, happy-go-get type of person. One night when we had finished in the club, I asked her to stay behind so we could have a chat.

Rosa said, "yes she would like that". I was now thinking it was maybe because of what Vicki and I got up to on the night of the dinner, but said nothing as she was always very OK with every other situation.

I think it was a Sunday night and everyone had left the club quite early that night. Pippa and Sofia had gone up to the house to prepare us all for some late evening snacks, as we had not had time to eat that night. When Rosa and I were alone, we sat at one table in the club's corner. I said were you OK Rosa darling, as you have seemed very quiet and distant from everyone the last couple of days. Rosa sat there, her eyes filled with tears, and she opened her heart to me.

She said that she had not felt right since France and that day that I had come back to the farmhouse with Rebecca. Rosa said that ever since that day, she had been thinking about Donna constantly. She knew in her heart that Donna was OK, she said, and she was happy with her freshman and her new life in Australia and that they were financially OK.

They lived in a new house in a pleasant town, but she could not shake from her head how Victoria must have been feeling, not knowing anything about or the whereabouts of her daughter. She then said as I sit there that night with Rebecca when you found her that's when she got a yearning to see and miss her own daughter. I said the solution was simple, why not take yourself off on a holiday and go and stay with them for a bit, maybe a month or so.

Rosa said well yes, that's what I have been thinking about doing. She said that is the time scale I was thinking of a month. I said well just go darling; you have been working so hard, what with arranging the boat trip, and laughed as she did briefly. I said you have been in your study for what seemed like for eternity and been to your solicitors arranging licenses for the club and all that the club entailed.

I repeated myself and said, go darling, please and enjoy yourself. I said I would have loved to have gone with her, but seeing as the trip in France was actually extended a fair bit I could not as I had work to catch up with, but reassured her that everything would be fine. And that Pippa, Sofia, and I were very capable of looking after the house. The club ran so well that it nearly ran itself, so that was not a problem either.

Rosa gave me a kiss and said I was great and very understanding and again said I was far advanced in my years than my actual age. Every time she said this it made me feel old, but at the same time very proud of myself. I just said, well, the way I am is down to you and Pippa. You have both taken me from being an inquisitive young man and basically turned me into the person I now am. I told her I loved her for what she and Pippa had done for me. She just looked at me and smiled.

Rosa poured us both another two glasses of wine, and she sat close to me. She said I know you can all look after everything very well and that is not a concern of mine but that there is something inside of me telling me not to go. And she said she was unsure why she was getting these feelings. We finished our chat and went up to the house to join Pippa and Sofia. The next couple of weeks were full of our daytime jobs, and in the evening it was working in the club. I noticed Rosa was still not her normal self.

With my work commitments, I had been forced to take someone else on to work behind the bar in the club. Even though I was still a young man, I was doing very well thanks to everyone's help. I now had someone working the day job with me and now employed someone to help with the club's bar. I watched Rosa over the next few days and every day that passed; she looked more worried.

I saw that Rosa still had a worried look on her face, so once again I asked her what was the matter. Rosa said that she really wanted to go but was so worried and the last time she felt this worried was when her mother had died and Marcus had asked her to go and live with him. Something is telling me to stay. I again said is it the house or the club or even us all here without you, Rosa smiled and said no.

I said if it were that her fears were unfounded and everything would be here and in working order for her on her return. Rosa said Adam I have no doubts about any of what you just said and I believe you with all my heart. I said I would take the morning off work and help her with her flight booking. Rosa said yes OK. You could hear the reluctance in her voice. We spoke to Pippa, who was getting herself ready for work, and she thought it a good idea if I helped with the booking. As Pippa left for work, she jokingly said sort her out Adam, her life is in your hands.

I waited for everyone to go and do their stuff. Pippa to go to work and Sofia in the clubhouse practicing her next dance routine. It was about 9 am and I phoned different airlines to see when I could get her a ticket. It just so happened that I could have got her on a flight that night. As I put it to her, she looked at me and shook her head as if to say no. I continued to look for a flight and I had got Rosa on one the following week. Rather than ask her, I just booked it and paid with my credit card, as I had the feeling she would say no to every flight I could find. I came off the phone very pleased with myself and looked at her. I said it's sorted, Rosa you go a week today and the look of sickness came over her face. I had never seen her look so pale.

Seeing as I had booked a flight so quickly I went to work as I was already behind and really could not afford to take the day off, and fall further behind with my work as my reputation would be damaged as I prided myself as always being on time.

The week prior to Rosa's departure absolutely flew by, and before we knew where we were, it was the day of her flight. Both Pippa and I took the day off to take Rosa to the airport. Sofia gave her the longest hug ever. Just before we left the house, Sofia started to cry and Rosa just about smiled. Sofia said that she was going to miss her while she was away. Rosa cuddled her back and said she was going to miss us all, and was already looking forward to coming home before she had even left.

I drove to the airport, and Pippa sat in the back of the truck with Rosa. Rosa seemed very clingy that day this was well out of character for her as she was the one who held everyone together normally. She was the confident one. The one in charge of organizing everything.

We got to the airport with Rosa in good time and sat in a coffee lounge just chatting. Her spirits seemed to lift a little as we sat there together. We made our way to the departure gates. She cuddled Pippa and me in turn and gave us both a pleasant kiss. When I was getting my cuddle Rosa whispered in my ear, "Adam you are so very special to me" and that I had turned out to be a lovely man and she then said, "Adam I love you".

This blew me away she had never used the word I love you before in the relationship's whole. It was a word I thought I would never hear her say, and there were so many times I wanted to hear those words from her. It would have been better if it were said on one of our encounters in the bedroom, as I thought I could not say those words. So I tried so hard in other ways to show her, but I had now heard them. As she walked through the departure gates, she stopped, and the old Rosa had sprung back to life. She stood there, looked at Pippa and me and blew us both a kiss, and laughed as she walked through to the boarding area.

Pippa and I just looked at each other and smiled. I breathed a sigh of relief as it looked like at the last moment our Rosa was back to normal. It was only a holiday; we were going to see her very soon well a month. Both Pippa and I had a tear in our eyes as we walked back to the truck.

The entire journey back to the house felt cold and empty, even though the heater was on in the truck. There was live music playing some opera I think it was Ava Maria, which was one of Rosa's favorites. Pippa and I returned to the house that day and just spent the day chilling out. We went down to the club and as Rosa did as a youngster; we peeped through a window at Sofia and her routine. It was as if she had a new flow, a new grace about her. She looked as though she had been dancing for years the members were going to love this new routine.

Chapter Thirty Seven

We went to bed that night and the bed felt so huge. Pippa and I laid there cuddling, but there was something missing. We both agreed it was Rosa and as we lay there, we both really wished we had gone with her on this trip. In the early hours of the morning, feeling quite bad that we had let her go on her own. The funny thing was when I was booking it the lady on the phone said yes she had tickets but only three did I want them all. And without consulting Pippa, I just took it on myself to book just the one for Rosa.

We woke the next morning. Neither of us had a good sleep, not having our Rosa with us. As we ate breakfast, Pippa and Sofia talked of their night at the opera, the night I was with Vicki at the Chinese and the lake. They spoke of the fun they all had that night and how they had never heard Rosa laugh so much. Even Pippa said I had not heard her laugh like she did that night for a long time.

As they were telling me the story of their night out the news came on the TV in the kitchen's corner it was just background noise, really. Suddenly, we all just stopped what we were doing and focused on the TV.

There was a report of a plane crash and it was as if the universe had just stopped still, no air or smells in the kitchen you could off heard a pin drop to the floor. There was a plane that had gone down in the Philippine Sea, which was near to where Rosa's plane was due to refill on fuel.

The flight number had come up across the bottom of the screen for anyone who was concerned about the news bulletin. I ran up to the bedroom as fast as my legs could carry me. I grabbed the original booking information and ran back to the TV; I checked the flight number against the number on TV and to my shock and horror; it was Rosa's flight number. Another number came up for concerned parties and I immediately phoned it.

We were all in a state of pure panic the news I received was devastating the plane had been hit by a freak storm and the turbulence had brought the plane down into the sea. As we spoke, there was a search going on. The lady on the other end of the phone could only tell us that so far no survivors had been found.

We were asked our address and told to wait in as an airport representative would be in touch shortly. I put the phone down and conveyed the shocking news to Pippa and Sofia: I have never felt so cold and alone as I did at that moment. I had Pippa and Sofia with me, but it was as if I were standing alone in the middle of the North Pole. About 30 minutes later, there was a knock at the door and in the whole previous 30 minutes, not any of us had spoken a word. It was 30 minutes of hell.

I went to answer the door, and there were the police standing with a man in a suit. The police officer asked who we were and if it was OK to come in and talk. I led them both through to the kitchen, the two girls sobbing their hearts out. Once again we were asked who we were and somehow in our grief, answered their questions. The man in the suit was from the airport and he looked through the passenger list after we gave him Rosa's name, and after a couple of minutes which seemed like hours, he lifted his head from the sheet of paper and explained what had happened to the flight. I hoped he was going to tell us she was OK, but that was not the news we got. All he could say was that at first light they were going to resume the search, but as of an hour ago there were no survivors. The pilot had tried his best to crash land the plane into the sea.

The police officer then took charge and asked us if there was anyone he would like us to call or did we need a doctor as the news was affecting us all so badly. We politely declined his offers I took their numbers and showed them to the door. As they left, the feeling of guilt came over me yet again. All I could think was it was my fault, as I was the one who booked the ticket.

I was sitting there looking into space, just shaking as Pippa and Sofia came over to me as they could see I was in a terrible state. They tried to console me, but I was in floods of tears. I just could not get it out of my head that it was my fault. We all cried all day, hoping in vain that the phone would ring, and it would be Rosa telling us she was OK and safe, but we knew that was just wishful thinking. We had lost her, and we had to come to facts with this. The complete day was just a blur. We had all cried so much that we had given ourselves headaches.

The next day came, and it was phone calls all day to everyone we could think of to let them know of the devastating news. As we spoke, we again were trying our best to hold back our tears. The house felt strange, cold, and empty. I would never be able to tell her I love her. But she had told me Pippa just seemed to be in a world of her own. Floods of tears most of the day. Sofia sitting on the sofa with her head in her hands, Rosa had meant so much to so many people. Obviously, work stopped for the entire week, and the club shut. Everyone understood our reasons. We all tried in our own ways to deal with what had happened.

The following week came, and even though there was nobody we were told by officials, it would be OK to make funeral arrangements. This just brought the feeling of guilt back to me. Why did I have to interfere and book that ticket? There were still so many calls to be made, Victoria Had moved in with us that week to help us through our hard time.

Chapter Thirty Eight

The day of Rosa's funeral had come, and the number of people was amazing and overwhelming. There must have been over 400 people at the church. We arranged for the coffin to be taken to the church by a horse-drawn carriage. There were four black horses pulling into a shiny black carriage. When at the church, Donna and I had a quiet talk alone, away from everyone else. Donna said that her mother had spoken very well of me, and she knew that I and her mother were or had been in a relationship. And that she wished things were different, but was happy that we had found each other before her death.

She said that after the funeral I was not about to think badly of her, that the house held so many memories that she did not want to relive, and that she was going home to Australia. Donna gave me a kiss on the cheek and went to mingle with the people who came to pay their respects. It was Rosa's wish to be cremated on her death, so that is what we had arranged. It would have been better if we could bury her coffin. At least we would have somewhere to go and talk to her if needed. There was no point at all in collecting her ashes, as they were not her ashes, as she was not there. We just put a few things in the coffin that we held close to our hearts and meant something to us and Rosa.

As the curtain came round the coffin, we burst into tears but quickly had to regain control of ourselves as the guests were about to leave via the side door. As the guests left the church, it was Rosa's wish that they left for the song (Ava Maria).

After the wake, Pippa, Sofia, and I went back to the house, and as I walked through the door of the house it was as if I had walked straight past Rosa. As I walked into the house, there was this most powerful smell of lavender mixed with her favorite perfume. We had given her a send of that she would have been very proud of as we walked into the house it was as if the coldness that we had previously felt had been lifted. We sat together in the kitchen it was as if there was the warmth that we used to feel when we slept in a bed with Rosa, a comforting warmth that made you feel special and safe.

In a strange sort of way, it felt as though Rosa was back with us, even if that feeling only lasted momentarily. It was maybe her coming to say goodbye to us it felt warm for the rest of the evening and when we went to bed the warmth stayed with us that night. The following two weeks felt so humdrum, we just got on with our work the best we could. As time passed, we came to terms with the fact that we had lost our Rosa and we would not see her again. After about two weeks, we reopened the club, which Rosa had worked so hard to open and set up.

I did something for Rosa or was it for my peace of mind; I had got some pictures of Rosa, some that I had, and some that Sofia had brought over from France with her. I had the pictures put on to the canvas and put them up all around the club, there was a picture of Rosa, Pippa, and me I had put up behind the bar as if she could keep a watchful eye on us and still be very much part of the club.

There was one picture of Rosa that Sofia had that was of her when she was younger and used to burlesque dance. I had this picture made as big as possible and this was to be the new backdrop of the stage where everyone could see her as she was years ago. As I said, life went on for us. We did our day jobs and worked hard in the club as this is what Rosa would off wanted. A couple of days later we received a letter it was from Randell and Co which was Rosa's solicitors.

The letter was read by Pippa but it basically requested the presence of Pippa and I at the office at a time convenient to ourselves. Pippa had made an appointment for the both of us to go there the following day. We both dressed smart and conservative and went to the offices of Rosa's solicitors. We were greeted with drinks and snacks we were asked to go into this office and it was the office of the main man (Mr. Randell).

Mr. Randell said I have asked you here today for the reading of Rosa's final Will and Testament. He then said I have been asked to give you these letters in the event of Rosa's death. He then passed a letter to each of us, he then said I will leave you alone for 10 minutes whilst you read your letters and left the room. Pippa was first to open her letter, her hands trembling. I could not open my letter, as I did not really want to accept that Rosa was dead. In my mind I never saw a body, so she was not dead.

Pippa opened hers and went and sat on a large window seat and read her letter. As she read her letter, she cried and was clutching the letter close to her chest every now and again, looking down at the letter and crying again. I pulled myself together and plucked up the courage to open my letter. As I took the letter from the envelope, there was that smell again of lavender. I looked around the room, half expecting to see Rosa standing there. The fragrance was so strong. My letter read as follows:

To my dearest Adam,
If you are reading this letter, then the worst has happened, and I

have passed away. If I never got the chance to tell you some things, I will tell you now.

Sorry, it has to be this way.

For me, it all started when you were dating my daughter, Donna.

You thought I did not see you looking through my bedroom door at me.

I saw you, and I knew then.

You were the one I had to teach the ways of love. I hope you.

think I have taught you well, that I never used or abused you.

I hope you enjoyed whatever we did and hope you never felt pressured when I introduced Pippa into our relationship.

I was meant to teaching you the ways of love, and Adam,

I have to say it even if like this, it truly was a pleasure,

as you are far better than you know you are.

You are also a lovely man who is mentally far in advance of your years.

I am truly sorry you are hearing from me this way. And although I never said it to your face, Adam, I had truly fallen for you.

I just hope that I told you this in person before my death. If it is just me that has passed away, then I know you are going to be OK.

as Pippa is still around and with you, I hope.

And if that is the case, she will look after you, if that's what you wish. I know she has a huge soft spot on you...

Thank you, Adam, as even though you are still young when We made love; you made me feel so happy.

Very shortly, a man called Mr. Randell will be speaking to you.

Take care, my darling.

Try to remember the things we did and the fun we had together. Oh, and you really are the perfect lover in my heart and I will take that with me.

and yes Adam I really loved you....
Rosa xxx

After reading our letters from Rosa, my heart felt heavy and my eyes full of tears. I looked across at Pippa, and she was clutching her letter and sobbing her heart out. We sat together at Mr. Randell's desk, and in he walked Mr. Randell as he had with him this massive folder. He asked if we were ready for him to continue both Pippa and I wiping the tears from our eyes, said yes.

He spoke. He said well Rosa was a very well individual and these are the last words and wishes of Rosa. First, I leave £250.000 to my daughter Donna and 10% of the net profits from the club per year. Mr. Randell then said I have forwarded Donna's money to Australia.

Second, and this is of the upmost importance, Rosa said that she could not decide between Pippa and me, and what she has now left will be left jointly between the two of them. She left £100.000 for each of us to do with as we wanted. She also left us the farmhouse in France but it was never to be sold or the original furniture removed and was to be used as a second home for us.

She also left us the boat, and all that came with it and, of course, the burlesque club and the house that we were now living in were also left to us. Mr. Randell then asked are you in agreement with Rosa's wishes? Our eyes filled with tears yet again and said yes, she had planned everything down to a (T). Mr. Randell said all would be drafted within a week.

Pippa and I left for home, feeling very dizzy at what had just happened. We got back home and Sofia was waiting there for us. We all sat in the kitchen and explained to her what had happened. We assured Sofia that she never had to worry again and would always have a place to live, and that was with Pippa and me for as long as she wanted.

Over the next few weeks, we tried to carry on the best we could. It was difficult without Rosa, as she was so organized. I returned to my building work and working in the club, Pippa returned to her driving instructor job. Nighttime was the hardest for the first few months, but as time went by, it became a little easier. Sofia was now sleeping with us at nighttime and sometimes just every so often. As I cuddled Sofia with my eyes shut, she felt the same as Rosa. The pictures that I had put all around the club were a blessing for me as I felt she was looking over us and in some way still with us.

Some nights as we lay together in bed we would swear blindly we could smell her wafts of perfume. She was always on our minds and we spoke fondly of Rosa, and sometimes if things got hard we would even talk to her as if she were there with us. If nothing else, it was reassuring for us.

Rosa was always going to be missed.............

Printed in Great Britain
by Amazon